MW01181109

Gracie's Inheritance

With

Part 2

Lydia's Legacy

By Augustine

For my mother for her undying love

This story is a work of fiction. Names of characters, places and events are all fictitious and any similarities to actual persons living or dead are of pure coincidence.

Special thanks to DB Stephens

And Cat Lenderi

Copyright©2013 by Rachel A. Dyson

All rights reserved

3

Chapter One

Gracie stumbled up the front steps in exhaustion. She fumbled in the mail box, grasped the stack of mail and then opened the door. Barely making it to the sofa, she kicked the shoes off of her aching feet and collapsed in the billowy softness. She tossed the mail, along with her keys onto the coffee table, leaned back and closed her eyes.

Silently, she thanked herself once again for having the foresight of purchasing this one prized piece of furniture. She lay back into the softness of the couch, letting her dark hair drape over the arm of the sofa.

This had been her one big splurge. When she had moved in five years ago, she didn't have the money to furnish the apartment. On the advice of her boss and now ex-boyfriend, she bought the couch. He had rightly expressed that it could double as a bed. It was the only decent thing that came from that relationship; she thought and stroked the jade, corduroy upholstery. The room was still bare other than the sofa and a glass-topped coffee table.

She bent down and rubbed her blistered, throbbing feet. What had possessed her to take an evening waitressing job, anyway? Sure, she needed the extra money, but there had to be an easier way. Though the eighty dollars in tips would come in handy, wasn't being secretary to the great Spencer Naughton tiring enough in itself?

Amazing how wrong she had been about him. He was so sweet, handsome, and oh so charming in the beginning. She had been thrilled when he had offered her a position. He was a great psychologist and highly accredited and she had been lucky to get such a position. It sure didn't take him long to change from Prince Charming back into a toad. Four years later, she still hadn't gotten a raise.

Well, tonight, she didn't have the energy to think about it. Thank God it was Friday and she had two whole days not to have to see Spencer's arrogant, ugly face!

Gracie fell asleep, fully clothed on the soft sofa. She didn't awaken until the sunlight streamed in through the window and glared into her face.

Stretching, she got up and then took a quick shower and made a pot of coffee. With a cup in hand, she padded back into the tiny living-room. She pulled her bathrobe close around her to ward off the slight chill in the room and noticed the mail lying on the coffee table. She set her steaming cup down on the glass top.

She picked up the stack and felt a little quiver go through her when she saw that three of the letters were addressed from Maytown, Oklahoma and recognized the handwriting on the first envelope, immediately. Oh, Lord, something had happened. It was from her cousin, Jeanette.

Gracie sat down on the couch with the three letters. Hesitant to open it, she slid Jeanette's to the bottom of the stack. The other two were both from the same lawyer, a Humphrey Lowood III. She opened the first one and scanned it, quickly.

Her grandmother, Lydia Mason, had passed away. The funeral was set for Tuesday of the next week. There would be a private reading of the will that same afternoon.

That was it, then. Gram was gone. So many mixed feelings began to rise up, but Gracie tamped them back down. It had been nearly five years since she had left Oklahoma and hadn't been back even once. Well, the woman had raised her. She would have to go for Jeanette's sake, at least.

Gracie opened the next letter. Strangely, the lawyer was requesting a private conference with her on Wednesday. How odd. Why would the lawyer need to see her again if the reading of the will was on Tuesday? Why wasn't Jeanette included?

Finally, Gracie opened Jeanette's letter. The note was very short. 'Grace, please, please, call me.' And a phone number.

Gracie pulled out her cell phone and dialed her cousin's number. Jeanette answered on the third ring.

"Hello, Jeanette," Gracie said, nervously. They hadn't exactly parted on the best terms five years ago.

"Gracie, is that you? Please tell me you are coming. I'm really not handling all of this well on my own. You can stay at Gram's if you like. No one else is there now," Jeanette said, pleading.

"Of course, I'll come. I'll have to make arrangements before I leave. Hang in there, okay? I'll call you when I get there."

"Thank you, Gracie. The kids are so upset and with Jim still gone, I am really having a hard time."

"It will be okay. I'll be there soon."

"Gracie, I love you," Jeanette said, with a cry in her voice.

"I love you, too," Gracie answered, truly touched. "Goodbye."

Her phone call to Spencer wasn't as congenial.

"I don't know why you want to go. They wrote you off years ago, didn't they? I need you here. I have a full week of appointments, Gracie. You can't just throw your responsibilities out the window." Why did he always have to sound so condescending?

"I have to go, Spencer. Jeanette needs me. Gram and I may not have seen eye to eye, but she was the only parent I've ever known. I haven't taken one day off for four years. You can give me this. It will only be a few days."

"I'll give you until Thursday. You had better be here bright and early or I'll have you replaced." She could see his sneering face in her mind's eye. How he could take that incredibly handsome face and screw it into the ugliest, vicious look was beyond her.

"I'll be back on Thursday. If I'm not, feel free to replace me." She hung the phone up and cursed the day she met that man.

*****

Gracie wasn't able to leave as soon as she had hoped, but she arrived at about 1:00 p.m. on Sunday. She had had to rent a car for the duration. So much for the last few months' savings.

Though Gracie was sad about her grandmother, her eyes were dry and she remained calm through-out the drive. She was looking forward to seeing Jeanette and her children. Too bad it had to be under these circumstances. Gracie had felt bad that they had parted with such hard feelings, but Jeanette just didn't understand.

Their grandmother, Lydia, had been such a hard woman in a lot of ways. Though she had supported Gracie's decision to go to college in Oklahoma City, she had been angry and unreasonable when Gracie wanted to leave the state to work in Little Rock. It wasn't really that far, after all. Lydia wanted Gracie to stay in Maytown, get married, and raise a family. She didn't understand why Gracie would want to actually use

8

her degree, and certainly couldn't fathom why she had to go so far away to do it.

Finally, it all blew up. Gracie told Lydia that she needed to get away from Lydia herself! The woman was stifling. Gracie loved her grandmother, but was tired of being smothered and controlled. She knew that she had pierced the woman's soul, but she couldn't take it back. Gracie needed her own space and her own life. Lydia had been angry beyond words, but managed to tell Gracie not to come back -- ever.

And she hadn't. Jeanette thought it horrendous of her to talk to their grandmother like that and told Gracie so. That was the last contact she had had with her family until today.

Gracie had always thought that somehow she would make amends. Now it was too late. Lydia was gone. It seemed unreal. The strong force that dominated her life for so long was gone. What would it be like to enter that house, suddenly void of Lydia's forceful presence?

Chapter Two

Gracie pulled in the drive of her grandmother's house at 1:30 pm, Sunday afternoon. She tiredly, got out of the car, relieved to finally get here and found the key in the mailbox where Jeanette had left it for her.

The house looked pretty much the same as it always had. What a far cry from her shabby little apartment. Gracie was mildly surprised to see that her pictures were still on the mantle along with Jeanette's smiling visage. *Lydia may have cut her out of her life, but she still cared enough to want to see her*, Gracie thought.

Instinctively, she made her way to her own room. Or what used to be her room. As she turned the light on, she saw that it remained unchanged. Even some of her clothes were still left in the closet and chest of drawers. She pulled out an old nightshirt, yellow with blue rose buds on it. It used to be her favorite. She undressed and put it on feeling comforted and slid under the heavy quilt on her bed. It felt so good, so familiar.

That was when the tears finally came. For the first time she could remember, she cried, loud choking sobs. It went on for several hours. When she finally slid out of the bed in search of some coffee and something to eat, she caught a glimpse of herself in the bureau mirror. Her dark hair was mussed from the bed and hung limply to her shoulders, as if it, too, was in mourning. Her green eyes were bloodshot and her face was red and splotchy, but somehow, she felt a little better.

She padded down the hallway, quietly, though there was no one to disturb. When she got to the kitchen, she found that there was enough in there to make herself a sandwich.

She took her coffee and sandwich into the living-room, looking around guiltily. Gram never allowed them to eat in here and she half expected the woman to come into the room to lecture her.

It seemed to be the longest evening she had ever spent, alone in the empty house. Gracie was glad when she looked up from the television to discover that it was bedtime.

*****

The doorbell woke her the next morning. Gracie knew that it had to be Jeanette. She pulled on a robe and walked to the door.

She was pulled into a bear hug as her cousin enveloped her.

"Oh, Gracie, I'm so glad you are here," she said as she finally let go.

"It's good to see you, too. You wanna put on some coffee? I'll get dressed real quick." Gracie knew she looked horrible. Her eyes were sore from all the crying.

"Sure," Jeanette agreed and left toward the kitchen.

Gracie dressed quickly and did her best to cover her red blotchy face. She pulled her thick, black hair into a ponytail and went to meet Jeanette in the kitchen.

"Where are the kids?" she asked as she entered the room. She saw that the coffee was done and grabbed a cup from the cabinet.

"I left them with the neighbors. They offered to keep them today while we finalize the arrangements. It's all done, really. I just wanted you to go over everything, just to make sure it was all right with you."

11

"I figured Gram had already taken care of everything," Gracie said and sat down at the table across from her cousin.

"She had for the most part. Even down to what she was going to wear. Pastor Rayburn will be giving a eulogy and performing the service, and Marta Grayson and her granddaughter will be singing. Pastor Rayburn asked if either of us wanted to say something. I declined, but didn't know about you. I wasn't even sure then that you would be coming." Jeanette gave her a sad look.

"I wouldn't know what to say. She had cut me out of her life, anyway," Gracie said, looking down into her coffee.

"She loved you, Gracie. She was angry. She ranted and raved for a couple of months, but after that, she seemed depressed. I think she was really sorry about it all."

"Well, she could have called. She could have told me if she was sorry, but she didn't."

"She was so proud, Gracie. You know that. I think she thought that you would call."

"I thought about it a hundred times, Jeanette, but I always chickened out. I just couldn't handle the thought of being rejected again. She was so hateful and mean that day. It was like she hated me. Why couldn't she understand that I just wanted to live my own life? I wanted her to be part of it and be proud of me," Gracie said, feeling the tears coming back.

"Understanding was not one of Gram's virtues, Gracie. She wanted things her way. She could be mean. I never had the guts to stand up to her. It was just easier to do what she wanted. I kind of admired you for it. Yeah, I was mad, but maybe I was mad more at myself for not being like you."

"Well, at least now we can be family again."

Gracie grabbed their cups and headed to the sink with them. Then she remembered the lawyer's letter. She rinsed out the cups and turned to Jeanette.

"Gram's lawyer sent me a letter, Jeanette. I thought it was strange. He wants to see me privately at his office on Wednesday. Do you know what it's about?"

Jeanette looked up surprised. "No," she said, "there will be a reading of the will Tuesday afternoon. I have no idea why he would want to see you after that."

"Well, I guess I'll have to wait to find out," Gracie said.

Chapter Three

Sitting in the front row of the church, Gracie listened quietly as the minister named off the virtues of the deceased. *Apparently, he hadn't known Lydia Lawson*, Gracie thought to herself. She had thought that she had gotten over her resentment, but seeing her grandmother lying motionless in her coffin brought all the hurt back full force. She wanted to yell and scream at the corpse laying there or shake her back to life long enough to give Gracie the closure she deserved. It was a ludicrous thought, anyway. Lydia certainly wouldn't have apologized or admitted to any wrong-doing if she had lived to be a hundred and ten years old.

Tears seeped out of the corner of Gracie's eyes as she held the hand of her cousin, Jeanette, who was a pillar of strength. Gracie knew that she would be until it was all over. Jeanette was like their grandmother that way. The minister quietly announced one of the young church women who sang 'Blessed Assurance' with a low, sweet voice. Suddenly, Gracie felt like she was suffocating and knew she had to get out of there. She squeezed Jeanette's hand and walked quickly down the aisle and out the back double doors.

The bright sunshine was blinding as she stepped out of the gloomy church. Gracie sat down on the concrete steps and took a deep breath of fresh air. She brushed back her dark hair as the light breeze threatened to blow it into her face.

That last scene with Gram, three years ago kept running through her mind. Gram was angry when Gracie wanted to move to Little Rock to work for the Ozark Gazette. It was a great opportunity-her dream job. They had been talking in the dining-room of Gram's house.

"You aren't going anywhere, young lady! There is no reason that you can't get on at the local paper. I simply forbid it." Lydia waved a veiny hand in the air and turned around, in dismissal.

"No, Gram. I am going. I'm leaving Monday. I can come to visit on weekends. It isn't so far," Gracie said, determined. She was totally unprepared for the icy glare she got when Lydia turned back to her.

"If you go, don't bother coming back. It is obvious that family loyalty means nothing to you." Lydia turned and walked into the kitchen. Gracie had felt the grip of panic overtake her, but she knew she couldn't give in if she was ever to have a life of her own. Jeanette was perfectly happy to let Gram control her life for her, but Gracie would never be.

The old-fashioned church bell rang and people began filing out the door. Gracie jumped up and moved out of the way. When Jeanette didn't come out, Gracie went back inside to look for her. She found her cousin bending over the casket in grief.

Gracie put an arm around Jeanette. "Time to go, honey. Everyone will be at the house waiting for us."

"I know." Jeanette stood erect and took a deep breath. She wiped her face with a tissue and gave Gracie a wavering smile. "Let's go."

Gracie let Jeanette go on and she looked down at the shell that had once been her grandmother. She reached down to straighten the string of pearls around Gram's neck. She could feel the hot tears welling up and snuffled as she attempted to control the emotion.

At that moment, Gram's head turned. With eyes closed, the corpse seemed to be glaring into her. Gracie took a step back in shock and almost stumbled. Then a rush of air came off of the body and brushed by Gracie, seeming to touch her to the bone. She glanced down to see goose bumps on her arms.

Looking back to the casket, she saw that Lydia's head was once again in the original position. Terrified, Gracie turned and ran out of the chapel room.

*****

That afternoon, the two of them sat grimly at Gram's dining-room table across from the attorney.

"Ladies, this won't take long. If you are ready, I will read the will," Humphrey Lowood III said, respectfully.

Gracie and Jeanette nodded and he began.

"To my dear, lovely grand-daughters, you have been the real joy of my life. You have both grown into lovely young women - Jeanette, a wonderful mother, and devoted wife, and Gracie, an independent, brilliant young businesswoman. I couldn't be more proud.

At first, this will seem strange and unfair to you both, but, Gracie, you will understand shortly. And darling, please don't ever think that I held our little quarrel against you. I knew from the beginning you were right, it was just my stubborn way of wanting to hold on to you too tightly. I also know that given enough time, we would have made our amends.

Jeanette, I leave my house and the bulk of my money to you, with the understanding that Gracie gets my blue china. She so loved it as a child.

16

Gracie, I leave to you, your own legacy. It is time for you to know the truth. I have written you a letter. You are to read it, and then you will see our little Humphrey to understand its ramifications.

I wish you both a long and happy life. Be safe."

Gracie's mind was whirling, what did she mean 'the truth' and 'your own legacy'?

"Well, that is all. I have the paperwork all ready for you to sign, Jeanette."

Jeanette stood up, shaking. "I'm not signing anything until I know that Gracie is provided for, as well." She looked at Gracie. "Gracie, I'm not taking all this from you. It should be shared equally! If she wasn't still angry, why would she do this to you?"

Gracie grasped the envelope that the lawyer pushed across the table for her. It was obvious that the stress of the day was getting to her cousin.

"Its okay, Jeanette. I didn't expect anything when I came here. Besides, she must have had something else in mind for me." Gracie held up the envelope with her name on it, written in Gram's handwriting.

"Well, I will see you tomorrow, Miss Lawson," he said and stood up to leave.

"I have to go, too, Grace," Jeanette told her. "The sitter will be ready to leave."

"That's okay." Gracie stood and gave Jeanette a hug. "Maybe, we can all do something together tomorrow afternoon. We could take the kids somewhere."

"Bye." Jeanette kissed Gracie's cheek lightly and left the room.

17

Gracie lingered at the dining-room table and heard the front door shut a few moments later. She picked up the unopened envelope.

Chapter Four

Now that everyone had gone and the house was quiet, Gracie made herself another cup of coffee and headed to her own bedroom. She threw the manila envelope onto the bed.

It still surprised her that Gram had kept her room just as it was when she had left. All of the treasures that she had left behind were still on the shelves. Her basketball trophies, her prize awarding photos and her stamp collection.

Though it was only 5:00 in the evening, Gracie undressed and slipped the nightshirt over her head. If she didn't think too hard, she could almost make herself believe that the last five years hadn't happened. That she hadn't yet ventured to Arkansas and virtually ruined her life. That she hadn't met Spencer Naughton and let him rip what was left of her to shreds.

Had Gram been right? Should she have stayed here under the old woman's thumb?

Gracie piled the pillows at the head of the bed and crawled in. The smooth sheets still smelled freshly laundered. It was the first time since she arrived that she actually felt like she was home.

The ominous yellow envelope still lay on the other end of the bed, out of arm's reach. She eyed it as if it were a snake that had climbed into bed with her. It would be the last she would ever hear from Lydia Lawson.

She took another sip of her coffee. What was this all about, anyway? One more way to humiliate her? How can you hate someone so much and still love them? Gracie was unsure whether she was thinking about her feelings toward Gram or Gram's feelings toward her. Perhaps they were the same. The tears that she had resisted all day suddenly came in a rush.

Half an hour later, eyes sore and puffy, Gracie refreshed her coffee and went back to her bed, intent on opening Pandora's envelope.

She picked it up and sat on the side of the bed. Sitting her cup down on the end table, her hands trembled enough to spill hot drops on her hand. Cursing softly, she tore the yellow seal open.

Inside, was a three-page letter and a strange, expensive-looking necklace. She settled back on the pillows and began to read.

>   *My dear Gracie,*
>
>   *I hope you don't hold it against me. I never really intended to hide the truth from you. I was waiting for the right time to tell you. Sometimes, the right time never seems to come. I'm going to tell you a story, a true one.*
>
>   *I grew up in a small town in Georgia. Things were hard back in the fifties and my family had a tough time just putting food on the table. I was thrilled when I got a job at the Mallory plantation. It was only a maid's position, but it would help feed my younger brothers and sister.*
>
>   *The Mallorys had a daughter, Belinda, who ultimately became my best friend. Edgar, Belinda's father, was not only strict, but a*

religious fanatic of the most dangerous kind, as well.

Belinda fell in love with a farm boy and I helped her sneak out of the house at night to meet him. It worked for a while, but Edgar caught on to our game. By that time, Belinda was pregnant. She and Billy planned to run away and get married.

On the night of their departure, Edgar confronted Belinda and fired me for my interference. Billy turned up dead.

Of course, they said that it was a farm accident, but Belinda was sure that her father had killed him. Fearing for the life of her baby, Belinda was set on running away. I decided that there was nothing left in Georgia for me and went with her.

We wound up working in a bed and breakfast in a town in Nebraska. We were starting to do well. The owner was a kind lady. Then, disaster struck. Belinda died in childbirth. I was left with the newborn to care for. I named her Susan and she became the light of my life. I never told anyone that Susan wasn't mine. To me, she was. Susan grew up and Mrs. Foster, left the boarding house to me. We had a comfortable income.

I was too busy running the business to realize that Susan had become a wild teenager. Before I knew it, she became pregnant. The boy in question denied it, of course. The baby came along. Another girl. Susan called her Anne.

My Susan found out after her pregnancy that she had a heart problem. I couldn't believe it. She was only eighteen years old. But I lost Susan when Anne was only three years old.

Losing Susan almost did me in. I went through a breakdown of a sort. There was a man that I had been seeing for a while and married him. Joe was a good man and moderately wealthy. He doted on Anne. We moved to Maytown, Oklahoma, where he had a little family. We were married for five years before he died of a massive heart attack.

You know the story from here. I've told you about your mother, Anne, many times. She was a lovely girl, so young to have her life snatched away, as well. I'm not sure why I was chosen to raise these children, only to have them meet an early death. Sometimes, I think if only I had done something different, they would have lived. I hope you can understand now why I was so strict and held on so tightly. You, my dear, Gracie, are all that is left of Belinda.

I have enclosed Belinda's ruby necklace. She would have wanted you to have it.

Your inheritance is waiting for you and your heritage lies in the deep south of Georgia. I wish you a long, long life and know that you will always be close to my heart.

With deepest affection,

Gram

Gracie read through the letter three times. Her tears from grief had turned into tears of compassion for this poor woman that had lost everyone that she had ever loved. There was a lot of confusion, though. Where did Jeanette fit in to this? If there was an unclaimed inheritance, why didn't Gracie's mother or grandmother claim it? Did Gram never tell them about it?

She refolded the pink stationary and slipped it back into the envelope. Her fingers wrapped around the heavy necklace and she pulled it out. It was a large square pendant, intricately carved with an exotic design. In the center of the silver square was a large red stone. Was it really a ruby? It was kind of creepy. It looked like a red eye.

Gracie put the necklace on, feeling its heaviness on her neck. It wasn't something that normal people wear. She got up and stood in front of the dresser mirror. It was impressive, but definitely looked wrong against her blue and yellow rosebud nightshirt. The red ruby did contrast her dark hair nicely, though.

She took it off and laid it on the dresser top. Well, she and Jeanette had a lot to talk about in the morning.

Chapter Five

After her third cup of coffee, Gracie decided that it was time to call Jeanette.

Her night had been pretty well sleepless. Gram's secrets and then, remembering that moment when she had been alone in the chapel were enough to keep her from sleeping for a long time. Finally, she had convinced herself that the incident in the church had been her own imagination.

Gracie picked up her phone from the kitchen table and dialed Jeanette.

"Hey, I wondered when you were going to call. I didn't want to wake you," Jeanette said, sounding more cheerful than yesterday.

"I've been up for hours," Gracie admitted. "I wondered if you could come over for a while."

"Sure. Just give me time to take the kids over to the neighbors. Are you okay, Grace?"

"I'm okay. Really. I just need to talk."

"Give me half an hour and, Gracie, I am so glad you're home."

"Me, too."

Gracie hung up and went to dress for the day. She took her time, knowing that she would have to see the lawyer that afternoon. She took a hot, cleansing shower and decided on her red skirt and blue top. It was dressy enough without overdoing it. She looked at her reflection in the mirror and might have been happy with it if it weren't for the ever-present black mole on her left ear lobe. She redressed her hair, covering her ears this time and gave herself a semi-approving look.

Jeanette arrived just as she was finishing up. Gracie met her in the living-room with a light hug.

"I have been worried about you all night, Grace," Jeanette said, in her best big sister voice.

"I'm fine. I just wanted you to read this." Gracie handed her Gram's letter. "I'll get some coffee, then we can talk about it."

Jeanette dropped to the couch, her blonde curls bobbing with the motion.

Gracie went to the kitchen to leave her alone. She made a fresh pot of coffee and heated some cinnamon rolls that were brought by one of the church ladies.

She was sitting at the bar, nibbling on a roll when Jeanette walked in. She didn't say anything until she had her coffee and roll in hand.

"So, what do you think the inheritance will consist of?" Jeanette asked, finally, seating herself at the other end of the counter.

"I don't know. Gram didn't say." Gracie took another bite.

"Well, maybe it is some money. I don't know what your living situation is, but money is always good." She reached for the sugar canister.

25

"It's not been too good, lately," Gracie said, keeping her eyes on the roll.

"You aren't the top dog at the Gazette?" Jeanette teased, lightly.

Gracie sighed. "I'm not working at the Gazette. I never did."

"What?" Jeanette looked at her sharply.

"I spent all that money to move there and the position was given to someone else. I-uh didn't get the time right on the job interview," Gracie said, sheepishly.

"Gracie! Have you been out there that whole time with nothing?" Jeanette asked, worriedly, thankfully sparing Gracie another lecture on responsibility.

"No. I went to work for a psychologist. It's a secretarial position. Nothing much, but it has got me by." No way was she going to tell Jeanette about the waitressing.

"Maybe you should just come back home. You can stay here as long as you need to. I'm sure that they would be glad to have you at the local paper," Jeanette said, already making plans.

"You don't know how many times I've almost run home. I wouldn't admit failure when Gram was alive and I won't do it now." Gracie slid off the bar stool and took her plate to the sink. "You should move in here, Jeanette. You would have so much more space."

"I was thinking about that last night. Maybe, I'll talk to Jim about it," she said, then changing the subject, "It is so weird to find out we aren't related at all."

"That is one thing I couldn't figure. Where did you come in to all this?"

"Gram explained that to me a couple of years ago. I am Grams great-niece. You remember the story of how my mother, Sophie, came here with me when I was small, then died of cancer? Sophie was Gram's sister's child."

"Oh." Gracie said, slightly confused, then more brightly, "So what if we aren't cousins? We are sisters by love and circumstance." Gracie gave Jeanette a wink.

"Yes, we are! I hope you stay for a few days, Grace. I was hoping to get to visit." Jeanette gave her a hopeful look, her bright blue eyes, pleading.

"Sure. Though, I need to get back to work soon." Very soon, Gracie thought, or she would really be in the poor house. She really would love to spend some time with Jeanette and her kids. She missed having family around.

*****

That afternoon, Gracie once again sat across from the blond lawyer and his untidy office desk.

"Hello, Miss Lawson. I assume that the contents of that envelope made things a little clearer to you." The small man leant back in his chair and looked at her intently.

"Well, only that there is an inheritance of some kind from my great-grandmother." Gracie absently fiddled with her earring.

"Yes. There is an account already set up at the Maytown Bank of Commerce in your name. Of course, you can transfer the funds anywhere you wish as soon as you go in and sign

27

their paperwork. Also, there is the matter of the plantation. Here is the deed."

"So, I've inherited some money along with the plantation house?" Gracie asked.

"Correct," he said, looking irritated at her interruption, and continued. "It looks like it has been looked after by a grounds keeper. You will have to see him for the key. Now, if you would just sign these documents to show that I have given you all the paperwork, our business is finished."

He was certainly in a hurry, Gracie thought as she signed the papers. Probably late for an afternoon golf game.

"It has been a pleasure, Miss Lawson." He stood and offered her his hand. She shook it, still in a state of bewilderment. He turned away in dismissal.

Gracie left the office not much more enlightened than she had been when she walked in. Well, she would find out at the bank, she supposed.

Chapter Six

Gracie sat trembling in the car in the bank parking lot. She was in no condition to drive as yet and just sat staring out of the window. She had asked the clerk three times if there was some mistake. The woman just chuckled and assured her that there wasn't. The account had been set up ten years ago in the name of Gracie Renee' Lawson. Ten years ago! How? None of it made any sense at all. Gracie knew little of how things were done in the legal process, but something just wasn't right about this.

Finally, recovering, she picked up her cell phone and dialed Jeanette.

"Hi," Jeanette answered cheerfully.

"Twelve million dollars." It was all Gracie could say.

"Twelve million dollars? Oh, my gosh! Gracie, really?"

"And the plantation in Georgia."

"Wow!"

"Something is off about it, Jeanette. The account was opened in my name ten years ago. Why would Gram wait until now to tell me about it?"

"I don't know, Grace. Gram was a secretive person. She told you more in that letter than she had all the years raising us. What are you going to do now?"

"Well, I don't really know."

"Well, I know. I've seen your wardrobe, dear. We should go shopping and have some fun. Spend a few days with us and mull it all over. We both deserve a chance to get to know each other again."

"That sounds like as good a plan as any." Gracie smiled. "Let's go shopping!"

She hung up from Jeanette, grinning from ear to ear.

*****

The next day, the two were sitting at the mall food court having lunch.

"I think I have enough clothes, now," Gracie said, looking at all the bags around them. "I love that pink sweater you bought."

"You've barely bought anything," Jeanette objected. "I'm shopping while you watch."

"Not true. I bought that cream skirt and blue blouse. The pumps, too," she said, and took a bite out of her burger.

"You wouldn't have if I hadn't practically forced you. Anyhow, I think we should buy you a car. You don't want to pay for a rental to drive all the way to Georgia."

"I haven't said I was going to Georgia." Gracie looked up, surprised.

"Of course, you will. You have to, at least, decide what you are going to do with the plantation. Who knows? You might want to stay and play Scarlett O'Hara."

Gracie watched Jeanette dip a french-fry in her cup of cheese. "There is a house. I've always wanted to have a house of my own. I need to go there. Gram left a lot of unanswered questions. After that, I don't know."

"Well, you have a life in Arkansas," Jeanette observed.

"Yeah." A life of drudgery and stress. "Nothing really to hold me there."

"No guy in your life?"

"Nope." Gracie smiled, thinking about how great it would feel to call Spencer and quit her job.

"Awfully happy about that," Jeanette said, curious.

Gracie explained about her relationship with Spencer.

"Well, you are better off without him."

"I'm going to quit. I can surely find something better." She nodded, drinking the last of her soda.

"You don't even have to work at all if you don't want to," Jeanette reminded her. "You are free as a bird. No man to tie you down. Do what you have to for yourself, Gracie."

Gracie took a closer look at Jeanette. *Was there a little jealousy in that statement?* "I thought you were happy, Jeanette," she said, deciding that there was indeed a little bitterness in her cousin's expression.

"Oh, I am, really. I love Jim and the kids. It's just that he is gone so much and I feel alone. Sometimes, I wish that I had been more like you. Silly, really." She gave Gracie a wavering smile.

"Not silly at all, Jeanette. I'm sorry."

*****

31

For the rest of the day, they threw off their troubles. Gracie bought a small used blue Honda hatchback, resisting Jeanette's efforts to steer her toward a brand new cherry red Jaguar.

That week they took the kids bowling, shopping, and a picnic at the park. It was the first time Gracie had got to spend real time with the children. Three-year-old Jasper had his mother's blond curls and sparkling blue eyes. Aubrey, at five, looked more like their father with brown hair and brown eyes. Gracie melted every time they called her 'Aunt Gracie'. It was a new feeling. One she could sure get used to.

*****

By the end of the week, Gracie knew it was time to go. She didn't know what would be waiting for her in Swanson, Georgia, but she couldn't put it off any longer.

That Friday, she packed her things in her new little car and said a tearful goodbye to Jeanette and the kids.

Chapter Seven

As Gracie neared the small town of Swanson Georgia, she felt a new sense of purpose fill her being. No matter what awaited her there, she was leaving her past behind. She was shrugging it off like a shroud.

Feeling carefree and happy for the first time she could even remember, she passed the city limit sign: Swanson, population 2,003. Interesting number, she thought as she came into town. Not exactly a metropolis, but it sure was pretty. Neat little blocks with colorful houses, separated occasionally by a wooden fence. It was very picturesque with lots of pretty green trees and mowed lawns and flowers. May was beautiful in this part of the country.

The road took her to the town square, which was surrounded by brick streets and little shops. She figured that she might as well get to know the town a little. She had thought a lot about it during the trip. If the house looked even a little livable, she was going to stay. Heck, she had enough money to rebuild it if she had to. Swanson was going to be her new home. A fresh start was just what she needed.

Gracie pulled into a parking space near the corner of the square. She had a whole day to waste. She wasn't due to meet the caretaker at the plantation until the next morning.

She enjoyed visiting the shops and milled around until lunch time. Gracie decided to stop at a little cafe on the corner of the square. It was a quaint little place that seemed to suit the small town perfectly. She went in and sat at a table near the front windows. A chubby waitress in a blue gingham dress came over and handed Gracie a menu.

"We don't get many strangers in town," she said, looking at Gracie, enquiringly. "Just passin' through?"

Coming from a small town herself, Gracie knew a town gossip when she saw one. Still, she liked the blonde's bubbly smile and saw no harm in telling the truth.

"Actually, I'm not sure. I've come to look over some property."

"Oh, really? Not many people move in. They tend to move away. But if you're interested, Brett Galeman has some nice houses for sale. Does all the renovations himself. Does a beautiful job, too." The woman gave her a dimpled smile.

"Well," Gracie said, smiling back, "I'm not really in the market to buy. I've inherited a property that I came here to check out."

"Oh, well, too bad for Brett. What property is that, honey? Might be able to tell you some about it." Gracie recognized this as a ploy to get information, but what the heck? They would all know soon enough, anyway.

"The Mallory plantation," she told the woman, matter-of-factly.

The woman lost her smile and looked shocked. "Did you say the Mallory plantation?"

"Yes, I did," Gracie said, amused at the woman's flustered expression.

"You inherited the Mallory plantation," the woman said dumbly.

"Yes. Sounds like you do know a little about it," Gracie prodded this time.

34

"Uh, yeah. There have been books written about that place. You should check out the city museum. Oh, my God! If you inherited the place, then you have to be related to the Mallorys." The woman was practically gleeful.

"Yes, I am a descendent," Gracie said. "May I order now?"

"Oh, of course, dear. I am just beside myself with this news. What'll ya have?" she asked as she fumbled with the order pad in her apron pocket.

"How about the pancake platter? That sounds great," Gracie said. She was sure that she would get it cold while the waitress made fifteen calls from her cell phone to tell the news of her arrival.

The waitress almost snatched the menu out of her hand and ran toward the kitchen. Gracie couldn't help chuckling.

An old man in green overalls walked cautiously toward Gracie's table. He was tall and thin. He gestured with a frail hand "Ma'am, excuse me, but did I hear ya right? You goin' out to the plantation?"

"Well, yes, sir." Gracie thought this a little odd. "Though I don't know the way exactly. I was to meet the caretaker in the morning, but would like to have a look this afternoon."

"I live out that way. I don't mind waitin' if you want to follow me. I pass it on the way home." The old gentleman gave her a concerned look.

"Really, that is very kind. I would appreciate it, Mr..." People were certainly friendly enough here.

"Name's Grandy, Ma'am. Art Grandy. I need to go on over to the feed store. Be back to get ya," he said and walked out the door.

Fifteen minutes later, the waitress was back with Gracie's plate. She set the plate in front of her and then just stood there.

"Umm, do you know Mr. Grandy?" Gracie asked, not knowing what to say.

"Sure, Art is an old sweetie. He lives up the road from the plantation. He and his wife, Meredith. They are good people. I'm Mary Joe Campbell, by the way. I hope you are a return customer." Mary Joe moved away from her table. Her attention was diverted by a couple who needed to be waited on.

*****

Gracie had finished and was ready to leave when Mr. Grandy returned.

"Just follow me and I'll point out the drive for you," he said, getting into his truck.

Gracie got into her car and obediently followed him out of town. About three miles out, Mr. Grandy slowed and pointed out the drive to the plantation. Gracie waved at him and he went on. Gracie followed the drive for some time before she saw the house. She was completely in awe of just the size of it.

The house had a wide front porch with great, round pillars that reached past the second level. It looked like it could fill half a city block. Surely, it wasn't as big as it looked.

When she got closer, she noticed a blue ford pick-up sitting in the circle drive in front of the house. She parked next to it and got out. A man got out of the truck, as well.

Gracie looked at him, curiously as he approached her. He was well over six feet with short blond hair. He wore jeans

36

and boots. Momentarily, she wondered where the cowboy hat was.

"Hello, Ma'am. Hope you don't mind, but Art gave me a call. He was worried about you goin' in there alone. Could be all kinds of structure damage. 'Name's Brett Galeman." The southern drawl was strong.

"That's very nice, Mr. Galeman, for you to take the time out of your day to help a stranger," Gracie observed, suspiciously.

"No, trouble. You see, I'm the caretaker here since Art was getting a little up in years. I'm awful curious about this place. Would sure like to see the inside."

"Oh. Well, I apologize. I know we were supposed to meet in the morning. I just couldn't wait to get a look. You haven't been inside?" Gracie said, thinking it was odd when he had the keys.

"Nope. Art didn't want anyone in there. I do have the keys, though." He held them out to her.

"Well, let's go inside," she said, "I'm Gracie Lawson, by the way." She held out her hand.

"Good to meet you, Miss Lawson." He gave her a grin as he shook her hand and they walked onto the great front porch.

Chapter Eight

Gracie wasn't really sure about trusting a male stranger in such a remote place, but he seemed pleasant enough; quite attractive to be sure.

She put the key into the front door lock, but it didn't want to turn. Mr. Galeman tried as well, but to no avail. Then he sauntered back down the steps to his truck and pulled out a can of oil out of his tool box. It did the trick and the door opened.

They walked through and both stood inside the entrance gawking into the darkness. They had entered a large entryway. On one side of the room was a huge curved staircase but it was too dark inside to see much else. All the windows had been boarded up.

"I'll go uncover a couple of windows so we can see," Brett said and left the room. A few minutes later, sun streamed through the front window, lighting the whole room. The marble floor was covered in dust and the chandeliers, with cobwebs, but nothing could hide the beauty of it. In the alcove under the stairs stood a baby grand piano. The walls were covered in portraits, presumably of long dead Mallorys.

"This is amazing!" Brett said from the door, taking it all in.

"It is, isn't it? It's like the people just stepped out. Nothing was packed away, covered, or anything." Gracie walked further into the room.

"I don't know much about the family, only that there are many stories. This place dates back to the early eighteen hundreds, way before the civil war. It seems in good condition considering."

It certainly did, though all the windows would have to be opened before they could really see the rest of the house.

"Well, I guess, I'll have to get someone in here to help open it all up and inspect for structure damage. Looks like it might take an army to just clean this place," Gracie said, feeling disappointed. This wasn't a home. It was a museum. No way could she live here. It would take forever just to renovate it.

"I could have my crew down here in a week or so," Brett said.

"Oh, I didn't know you were a contractor."

"I'm not so much anymore. I own a construction company in Atlanta," he said.

"Well, I'm not real sure how much to invest just yet. This place is so big! I don't know what I'm going to do with it. But I should at least make sure the structure is safe. I want to be able to see what I can find in here about the family and the history of the place. If you are willing, you could give me an estimate on what it would take to renovate it. Though I'm not sure yet that that is what I want to do. It might be smarter to sell it."

"I guess that I assumed that was why you were coming here. To sell it, I mean."

"That wasn't my original plan. I knew there was a house, but I didn't even think about this. I've seen smaller shopping malls."

"There has to be thousands of dollars' worth of antiques in here." Brett picked up a brass lamp and blew the dust off.

"Yeah. Just what I need. More money." Gracie felt tears welling up. She had really pinned her hopes on making her home here. She turned quickly back to the door so he wouldn't see. "What use is a run-down mansion? It is too far out of town for a museum. Too big to live in."

"You expected to live here?" He turned to watch her go out the door. He followed her onto the porch.

Gracie sat down on the top step. What was she going to do now?

"You know, if it is just a house you want, I've got a dozen for sale." He sat down beside her.

"I'm not looking for just a house, Mr. Galeman. I wanted a home. Somewhere I felt a connection. I'm sorry." Gracie wiped the tears out of her eyes. "You probably think I'm crazy."

"Hey, I don't think you're crazy." He looked over at her and thought for a moment. "Do you have any plans? I've got something I would like to show you. You know, there is no such thing as 'just a house. They are all homes."

She knew he wanted to show her a house. "This is not a home," she argued, looking over her shoulder at the mansion.

"Sure it is. Just a little big for one person. Come on. I have something that I haven't shown anybody just yet. I think it's pretty special." He stood and held out his hand to help her up.

She locked the door and then followed him back to town.

*****

His house was just on the edge of town. Gracie fell in love with it immediately. It was a large cottage house. All the rooms were large, yet not to the point that they were

40

uncomfortable for just one person. There were two large bedrooms downstairs, one that would be perfect for an office. Three more bedrooms upstairs, the master with its own bath. Gracie noticed that Brett had put a lot of detail into the work. The woodwork in the living-room was hand-carved with an intricate design all the way through.

"Did you do the carving yourself?" she asked him, as she ran her fingers over the wood trim.

"Yep. Even the cabinet doors," he said, obviously proud of his work.

"It is beautiful. I really love your house!" she said, and smiled at him. "So what are the people like around here?"

"Oh, same as most small towns, I guess. I like it. As long as you don't mind everyone knowing your business, it's the best place in the world." He grinned back.

She said, "I would like to see the back yard." The back door opened onto a pretty brick patio. There were several shade trees along with a few flower beds. The large yard was fenced in with a charming arched gate entry.

"So, what do you think?" He came up behind her, startling her for a moment. She was entranced with the fresh spring smell of flowers on the light breeze.

"I think it is beautiful. Why do I feel that there is something very personal about this house to you?" She turned to look at him.

"Well, actually, I had planned to keep this one to live in," he admitted.

"So, why are you showing it to me, then?" Gracie asked, confused.

"Why don't we go down to the café? I'll buy you dinner – a business dinner that is." He gave her a wink.

She eyed him suspiciously, but she wanted this house.

Chapter Nine

Gracie felt a little self-conscious sitting across from Mr. Galeman in the café. They had at least a dozen set of eyes on them.

"The chili burger is pretty amazing," he told her.

Gracie wasn't really hungry, but ordered a salad to pacify him.

As soon as they ordered, he started talking. "I have a thought about the plantation. Really, it is more than a thought. I've spent years thinking about it." He hesitated as if he wasn't sure he wanted to share it.

"Go on," Gracie prodded.

"Well, a retirement home. It is the perfect size and not too far from town."

"You mean like a nursing home?"

"No. I'm thinking about the elderly, but those that can pretty well care for themselves, but don't want to live alone. There are people that love the country life. It could be almost like a resort. Put in a swimming pool and hot tubs. There is plenty of garden space." He looked at her excitedly.

"Wouldn't something like that take a lot of money?"

"It would, but I think it would make enough to keep itself going after the initial investment. When it comes to the renovation, I happen to know a guy who knows a guy." He grinned, his blue eyes sparkling.

"So, what exactly are you proposing?" Gracie asked, trying not to let his charming grin over-ride her good sense.

"You are wanting to stay here. We are both attached to that plantation. I'm suggesting a partnership. I would trade my lovely cottage house for my half of the plantation. The contents of the plantation house, excluded, of course."

"Wait, wait, wait." Gracie looked him in the eye. "Your house has to be worth more than that. Honestly, I know nothing about what real estate is worth, but it seems to me that you'd be getting the short end of the stick."

"Oh, not at all. You have to realize the historical value of the plantation house. If you don't believe me, talk to Henry Link. He's the realtor in town."

The waitress brought the food. Gracie saw that it was a brunette this time. She gave Gracie a friendly smile as she sat her salad in front of her.

They ate in silence while Gracie thought about his proposal. What did she have to lose? Nothing, except for the fact that she knew nothing about running such a business. It did sound like a perfect idea for the old place, though. It would be fun, maybe and give her something to do.

"You know, if you decide you want out at any time, I could buy you out, entirely. It would be nice to have a partner, though. I can't do it all by myself and it will need a woman's touch to the interior," Mr. Galeman said and took another bite out of his burger.

"Mr. Galeman, I know absolutely nothing about running such a business," Gracie admitted.

44

"Call me Brett. And that makes two of us, but I happen to know a woman that could run any kind of business. She is utterly remarkable with figures and could be our manager."

"Really?"

"Yep. We could do all the fun stuff and leave the book-keeping to her. If you agree, of course."

"Fun stuff? What is going to be fun?" Gracie asked, amused.

"What isn't going to be fun? We get to design and decorate the place," Brett said.

"What about after that? The running of the business part?"

"We will simply split up the duties and hire people to do what we don't know how to."

"In other words, you have no idea," Gracie smirked.

"Well, we have to take some things on faith, right?"

"Okay," Gracie said, knowing that Jeanette would lecture her later.

"Okay?" Brett said, looking at her in astonishment.

"Okay." Gracie nodded. "We can go get the legal documents drawn up in the morning. Are you sure that I'm not breaking your heart by taking your cottage?"

"Oh, I can pick up another house like that one to redo. I'm not happy unless I'm renovating something." He nodded in assurance.

Gracie decided to have a talk with that realtor. She wanted to be sure that she wasn't cheating Brett in some way.

*****

"Gracie! You don't make life-altering decisions in one day," Jeanette said loud enough that Gracie had to move the phone away from her ear.

"Why not? If it's the right one. You should see my new house. It's gorgeous!" She sat on the edge of the bed in her cheap motel room and took off her shoes. "For the first time, I will have a real home of my very own. I can't wait for you and the kids to visit."

"You should at least have someone check out the electric and the plumbing."

"Why are you always so suspicious? Don't worry. I'll make sure the paperwork is on the up and up." She propped up the pillows and lay back on the head of the bed.

"I just want you to remember Spencer. That was a good deal, too, in the beginning."

"Well, I'm not involved with Brett. Not everyone is like Spencer," Gracie said, bothered by the comparison.

"Just be careful, Grace," Jeanette said. "Gotta go. Love you."

"Love you, too, sis." Gracie hung up and closed her eyes. Life was so much simpler when she didn't have family. And lonely, she reminded herself, chidingly.

Chapter Ten

The next morning, Gracie got up early and dressed quickly. It occurred to her that Brett had had years to study the plantation grounds. She wanted another look on her own. She wasn't due to meet Brett at the lawyer's office until ten. That gave her a few hours.

The sun was barely up as she pulled in the drive at the plantation. It was really lovely even in the state of deterioration. Everything was green. The grass had been recently cut and the scent was on the air as she rolled down the window.

She pulled her car up in front of the house and got out. She walked around the house and found an old brick patio. She could see where there used to be a garden, the old fencing was still there. In her mind's eye, she could imagine a nice pool out here and a few patio tables. A flower garden could be replanted and maybe even a vegetable garden.

The old carriage house caught her eye and she made her way toward it. It was a solid brick structure. The door swung open as she gave it a tug. To her surprise, there were two cars inside. Apparently, it had been used in later years as a garage. Behind the cars, there was an old pick-up truck. It sure was a large building. It somehow hadn't seemed that big from the outside.

Gracie made her way deep into the building and the only light came from the open door. She was intent on inspecting the truck that looked like it might have been from the 1940s when the light suddenly dimmed.

She turned instinctively toward the big door. It was about half closed. The wind must have blown it. She made her way back around the vehicles just in time to see it slam shut, leaving her in almost complete darkness. She felt her way to the door. She could see the light seeping in around the edges as she approached. She put out her hand to push it open, but try as she might, it stayed firmly shut.

Tamping down the panic that was rising inside, Gracie tried to remember if there was a latch on the outside or if the door could simply be stuck. She didn't remember a lock. She had easily pulled the door open, though she might not have noticed since it was unlocked.

That was when the noises began. At first, it seemed like the rustling of small animals. Perhaps mice or squirrels. She turned around, but could barely make out the silhouettes of the cars. As the sounds grew louder, Gracie stood frozen in fear. A loud metal clang made her jump and she started to bang on the wooden door, shouting for help. All bravery had flown. Then it got deathly quiet and Gracie could feel someone behind her. When a cool hand curled itself around her bare arm, she began to scream. As if startled, the hand released her, suddenly, and the door sprung open wide.

Gracie ran across the property to her car and left, frantic to get away.

By the time she had got back to the motel and changed for the meeting, she had decided that she had just been silly. The wind had sucked the door closed and she had let her imagination get the better of her.

*****

Gracie was thrilled to her toes as she got the keys to her new home and the deed in her hand. She had spoken to the realtor that morning and was assured that she had made a good deal. *All I need now is a couch*, she thought amused.

She spent the afternoon shopping for household items. She realized that it was hard to be thrifty when she was starting over with nothing, but, at least, most of this she would only have to buy once.

She was in the house putting things away when the doorbell rang. Wow, she hadn't even known that she had a doorbell. She went to the door and opened it. A little group of old ladies were there bearing casserole dishes.

"We wanted to welcome you to the neighborhood," one portly little woman said, she was obviously the leader of the group.

"Well, please, come in," Gracie told them and held the door for them. "I'm sorry the furniture hasn't been delivered yet."

"Oh, we know, dear. It will be this afternoon," said a tall slender lady.

"Well, why don't we all go in the kitchen so you can at least set those down?" Gracie said, amused that they knew about the furniture.

They all followed her to the kitchen and set their dishes on the counter.

"I'm Gracie Lawson." Grace reached out to shake their hands.

"Very good to meet you, Gracie. Aren't you a pretty young thing! I'm Veronica Brewer. This is Gladys McCarthy, Marilyn Marrs, and Lucy Cowan. We are your neighbors on this block, but don't worry there are young people here in Swanson, too." She laughed.

49

Gracie shook hands with each of them, finding them charming.

"We are also members of the bridge club, the historical society, and St. Lutheran's church," Gladys McCarthy said.

"Well, it is lovely of you ladies to visit. Could I offer you some coffee?" Gracie asked.

"Oh, Rhoda mentioned that you bought one of those new chrome coffee makers!" Gracie assumed that Rhoda must be the orange-haired store clerk she had seen earlier that day. She started some coffee and washed some cups while the four watched her new pot perk in awe. *Well, now I know what to give them all next Christmas*, she thought, smiling. She poured each of them a cup as soon as it was finished.

"Anyone like cream and sugar?" she asked as she pulled the cream out of the fridge. She finished preparing and they all stood around the kitchen island marveling at the wonderful flavor of the coffee.

"Well, as members of the historical society, we are certainly interested in your connection to the plantation," Mrs. Brewer said.

"Well, it seems that Belinda Mallory was my great-grandmother," Gracie told them. "I really don't know much about the history of the family or the plantation. I only recently found out about the inheritance myself."

"So you truly own the plantation?" Gladys asked.

"I do, but now I co-own it. I traded half of the plantation to Brett Galeman for this house," Gracie admitted. "We are thinking to make it into a nice retirement home."

"Well, I don't think there is anyone here that would be brave enough to enter it. It is haunted, you know. There have been fifty-two deaths on that property. A lot of them were reported to be murdered."

"Gladys, let's not scare the girl!" admonished Veronica.

"Well, she will find out soon enough on her own. It's not fair not to warn her," Gladys retorted.

"Well, I want to learn the history," Gracie said.

"Well, you should talk to Maria Scully, down at the library. She runs the museum, as well. She has written several books about the plantation. I hope you don't mind. Everyone had thought that the family had died out. I'm sure she didn't know to get permission," Veronica said.

"Well, I don't really mind. So long as she used facts and not rumors," Gracie said.

"Oh, Maria is a stickler for that! She is very professional."

"Well, after I am settled, perhaps I can make an appointment with Ms. Scully. It is lunch time. Would you ladies share all this lovely food with me? You brought so much for one person."

"Oh, no, dear. You enjoy it. We have to be going, it's almost time for bridge. But thank you for the delicious coffee and welcome to town. It is so lovely to have young people move here." Veronica moved toward the kitchen door. The other ladies followed her like a trail of baby ducks. Gracie followed the procession and waved them off. They were so cute, delightful, really. Gracie knew that she was going to love this town!

Chapter Eleven

Gracie called and arranged an appointment with Maria Scully. Ms. Scully seemed genuinely delighted to share information and suggested that she come by Gracie's house that afternoon.

Gracie's internet was turned on that morning as well, so she decided to check the web for information on the Mallory plantation.

She was shocked at how much information there was. There was general information about the property, what year it was built, architecture and so on. Then the ghost sightings! And Ms. Scully was not the first to write a book. There were at least five others - three on the paranormal events on the property. There were pictures of the plantation taken in the forties and fifties and pictures of family members, as well. The Mallory plantation had withstood a great many tragedies, including the civil war. There was a lot of information, but most of it was centered on those who died with strange happenings surrounding their death.

When Gracie saw Ms. Scully's site, she clicked on it. It was much different. It was factual and definitely more realistic. It gave a list of the Mallory family, the dates of births and deaths. Gracie only recognized two names on the list; Edgar and Belinda. Oh, my! It was listed that Belinda died in 1951. Well, someone must have known the truth or Gracie wouldn't have inherited the Mallory fortune.

Could Edgar have been so quiet about leaving his will that no one had suspected? That seemed unbelievable in this town, especially considering the public eye on the plantation. There must have been some servants in the house. It sure didn't stand to reason that no one knew that Belinda left that night. Someone would have seen her.

There may be some elders in town that remember the it. They might have their own story to tell. She also wondered who Edgar's attorney was. Possibly from a neighboring city, perhaps Atlanta. If he wanted to keep it quiet that his daughter was alive, anyway. And exactly who was Billy? Gram didn't give a last name to her great-grandfather. She could still have family here, even if it was distant. She would like to know.

*****

Gracie decided to make a run to the grocery store before Ms. Scully arrived. She usually required little, but she realized that she had nothing in the house suitable to offer guests.

She was in the aisle at the town's only grocery store, looking at the display of goods. She chose a package of shortbread cookies, cheese, and wheat crackers. She was looking through the herbal tea selection when she heard a voice behind her.

"Oh, hello, Miss Lawson."

Gracie turned to see the blond waitress from the café. "Oh, hello. Mary Joe, isn't it?"

"You remembered!" She gave Gracie a huge grin. "I heard you bought a house from Brett, after all. It's nice that you decided to stay."

"Thank you. Swanson seems like a lovely little town."

"Oh, for sure. I've lived here forever. Do you have time to go for lunch? The drug store serves the most scrumptious little sandwiches."

53

"That sounds great!" Gracie returned her smile. She half expected the woman to clap her hands and jump up and down. Her exuberance was appealing. "And, please, call me Gracie."

Mary Joe followed her to the check-out, chattering all the way.

*****

Lunch proved to be very enlightening. Mary Joe was quite a fount of information. Nothing about the plantation, but a lot about the town's people. And surprising, nothing negative. Seemingly, Mary Joe only relayed good gossip. Gracie also learned that her new friend had a six-year-old son that she adored.

Sitting at the counter at the drugstore, eating sandwiches and drinking old-fashioned milk-shakes had its own charm. She was having such a nice time that she nearly forgot her appointment with Ms. Scully.

"Oh, no. I really have to go," Gracie told Mary Joe, reluctantly. She hopped down from the barstool and slipped some bills under the empty plate. "Thank you so much. It was nice." She gave her companion a smile.

"It was fun, wasn't it? Maybe, we can do it again. I'm off on Tuesday if you would like to go shopping or something."

"That sounds great. Sorry to run," Gracie told her as they quickly exchanged phone numbers.

Gracie barely got home before Ms. Scully arrived. She heard the car in the drive as she was putting her few groceries away. She pushed the button on the coffee maker and put the cookies on a plate right before the doorbell rang.

Chapter Twelve

She opened the door and peered down at the little blond woman. Ms. Scully was much younger than Gracie had expected, maybe in her forties, and dressed nicely in a plaid skirt and pink blouse. Her short, blond hair made her appear youthful, yet demure.

"Ms. Scully?" Gracie asked and the woman nodded, with a slight smile. "Please come in." She led the woman to the living-room and offered her a seat. "Would you like some coffee?"

"Sure. That sounds nice. You have a lovely home."

"Thanks," Gracie said, and left toward the kitchen. She came right back with a tray. She handed the woman a cup and sat the cream and sugar on the coffee table with the plate of cookies.

"I am so glad to finally meet you, Miss Lawson. The whole town is all aflutter," she said, with her calm little smile.

"Yes, I have got that impression. I am glad to meet you, too. I saw your website," Gracie told her politely.

"Yes, well, I started that site mostly for the school kids. They always want to write papers on the plantation; that gives them a little background."

"I was curious about one thing in particular, Ms. Scully," Gracie said. "It reports that Belinda Mallory died in 1951. I wondered about the cause of her death."

"I wondered if you would ask. Since you are here, it is obvious that the reports of her death were either wrong or fabricated, but since you ask, she supposedly died of a fall down the staircase at the house. It was accidental, of course. It fell in line with the ghost stories. Supposedly, There is a ghost child who pushes people down the stairs. Would you like me to document the truth?" She asked eagerly.

"You can document the fact that she ran away from home and ended up in Nebraska. She ran away in 1951 with a friend and died in childbirth not long after. She left a daughter, Susan. Susan died in childbirth in 1971, and her husband committed suicide. Susan's daughter was my mother, Anne, who died of complications from childbirth a few months after I was born. That pretty well catches you up."

"How tragic that they all died so young. I am sorry," Ms. Scully said, sincerely.

"It is tragic, but I didn't know any of them. I didn't even know of them until my grandmother, or rather the woman I thought was my grandmother, died a few weeks ago. She left me a letter explaining it all," Gracie said.

"Sometimes impending death is the easiest time for such confessions," Ms. Scully said soothed.

"Well, Gram had done nothing to feel guilty of. She simply cared for those that had no one else," Gracie said, a little irritated by the insinuation.

"Oh, I'm sorry. Confession was the wrong word to use," the woman said, instantly contrite.

"It's all right. I suppose I'm a little touchy on the subject," Gracie admitted.

"Well, I brought you a copy of my Mallory file," she said and pulled out two large, thick folders. "These contain probably more than you will want to know. I included the documented hauntings of the property. I try not to include that in my factual material. They are a part of the history, nonetheless. I hope you are not superstitious. There have been over fifty deaths on the plantation since it was built and those are only the documented ones. Of course, there were slaves' deaths that most certainly weren't documented. It is to be expected considering that it was built in 1820. Almost two hundred years ago. Amazing that it still stands." Ms. Scully sipped her coffee.

"I am most definitely not superstitious. I think the place could be a lovely home again. Mr. Galeman and I have discussed making a retirement home out of it," Gracie told her.

Ms. Scully smiled brightly, "I think that is a lovely idea. Though I wouldn't expect many of the locals to be interested. Still you might get out-of- towners. After it is open for a few years, the people here may become more receptive."

"Well, I'm glad we have your support." Gracie smiled. "Also I have thought that there might be a few items still left that the museum might be interested in."

"I would appreciate it if you would keep us in mind for donations."

"Of course," Gracie said, "The heritage belongs to the town of Swanson as much as it does to me."

"It is nice to know you feel that way. I have a feeling that you are going to be a real asset to this town, Gracie," she said.

"Thank you. What a nice compliment," Gracie told her. "I really like this town. It feels more like home to me than anywhere else I've been. The people here are lovely."

"Well, they seem to like you, too. The bridge club is singing your praises all over town." She gave a high tinkling laugh.

"I like them, too. They are so sweet," Gracie said.

"Everyone was shocked when you bought a house. It was almost comical the way they went on, talking over each other."

"Well, I didn't really expect that either, but when Brett showed me this house, I fell in love with it. Now, I'm so glad that I did. I feel like I have a real home now."

"So when are you going to start on the plantation?"

"Brett is going to have his crew here Monday. We can't even see the inside until the windows are uncovered. If you would like, you are more than welcome to come out to have a look. Though you might want to wait until we know that the structure is safe, Ms. Scully," Gracie told her.

"Oh, I would love that! I've been dying to see it for years! And please call me Maria."

"I would enjoy someone to share it with. Especially considering your knowledge. I am really excited. I do hope there were some good people among my ancestors. I have a feeling that Edgar wasn't a nice person at all," Gracie said, thoughtfully.

"There were, of course. Every family is full of good and bad. I believe Jameson Mallory, who built the plantation was indeed a good man. You have some you can be proud of, I promise," Maria said, and then, "I had better be going. I have to open the library this afternoon. If you have any questions, feel free to call me. I'm available most of the time." She handed Gracie a business card with her number on it.

Gracie walked her to the door and thanked her again for the files. She felt that she had made another new friend.

After Ms. Scully was gone, Gracie eagerly ran back to the table to look at them. The large folders contained smaller ones that were dated for every ten years. Gracie took out the one for 1820-1830 and sat down.

She spent the next several hours poring over the files. Maria had been right about one thing, there were some of her ancestors that were very good. Unfortunately, there were those that were not so good. The worst of them by far was Alfred Mallory, the third son of Jameson. He cruelly beat the slaves and many of them died from his abuse. One story included a small child. He had killed her to teach her parents the lesson that children didn't belong in the cotton field unless they were old enough to work. How horrible!

Really, after his thirty-year reign on the plantation, there was peace for a time after his son took over. Peaceful until the civil war hit. The Mallory plantation was left alone. Its remote location protected it from the Yankees. After the war, a couple of Yankee soldiers happened across the plantation. The two young daughters of the house, one only seven and the other, twelve, were out playing that day. They were raped and killed by the soldiers. Before the two could get off the plantation, they were both shot by Jerome Mallory, himself.

The plantation changed after the war, but many of the free blacks stayed on for a fair wage and board. It was about this time that Jerome invested a good amount of money in the railroad. It proved lucrative and he added a substantial amount to the family fortune.

During the latter part of that century, the Mallorys turned to horse breeding, as well as cattle. All seemed well. There was a couple of accidental deaths in the family and, of course, a lot of natural ones over the years.

Edgar Mallory was born in 1900 and married his wife, Beatrice in 1925. He was reported to be more private in nature though he was highly religious and was also a deacon in the Catholic Church. The older he got, the more eccentric and strange he became. He was excommunicated from the church for his harsh treatment of parishioners. He was also known for his cruelty to servants in his home. There were several that disappeared from his service mysteriously. In

1935, he had a daughter named Belinda. Belinda died of an accidental death, falling down the front staircase. Beatrice never got over her daughter's death and fell ill. She died in 1953 of her ailment. Edgar Mallory remained alone in the house with only a few servants left. He died from a stroke in 1960.

After that, the house was empty and remained so to this very day.

It was late when Gracie had finished. She dressed for bed and made herself comfortable on the couch, reminding herself that she really could afford a bed now. She would have to buy beds for the rooms upstairs if she expected Jeanette to visit.

Chapter Thirteen

Monday morning, the alarm went off at 7:30 am. Gracie reached out to turn it off, sat up on the couch and stretched. She grudgingly went to start a pot of coffee and then went upstairs to shower and dress. She dressed casually in blue jeans and a tank top and pulled her hair into a ponytail. She was ready to go to work at the plantation. She slipped on a pair of tennis shoes and ran downstairs in time to pick up her ringing phone. It was Brett. Strangely, her heart jumped at the sound of his voice.

"Hey, thought I'd come pick you up in a few if you are ready," he said.

"Yeah, okay. I'll just grab a couple of muffins for us to eat on the way," she told him.

"Sounds good. Be there in a minute," he said and hung up.

Gracie quickly poured them each some coffee in to-go mugs, and bagged up four of the apple muffins that she had bought at the bakery downtown on Saturday.

She had just finished when she heard him honk. She grabbed her bag and balanced the coffee under her chin as she opened the door. He saw her hands full and immediately got out and grabbed the coffee cups from her. She ran around the truck and got in.

"Hi, thanks", he said and took a sip of the coffee.

"Hi," she said, a little too breathless.

"We'll probably be a little early. It'll give us time to eat real quick before the men get there," he said as he backed out of the drive and headed toward the plantation.

Gracie sipped her coffee as he drove. Ten minutes later he pulled into the plantation drive. There was no sign of anyone yet. She found herself looking at Brett while they were eating. His bouncy blond curls seemed childlike. They didn't match his manly face. It made her smile. What was it about this man that took her breath away? His skin was roughened by working out in the sun and his nose was rather pronounced. The vivid blue of his eyes assailed her senses. She quickly averted her gaze only to make matters worse when her eyes met his muscled arm in his tight t-shirt. It felt odd being alone in a vehicle with him. Rather awkward.

After they were finished eating, she said, "We could wait in the house. There is light enough in the foyer."

"Okay, let's go then," he agreed. They got out and went to the door. Gracie unlocked it and they entered. The early morning light streamed in through the large windows.

"Wow! Looks like this room gets the best light in the morning," she said, looking around. She sneezed twice. "I wonder if some of these windows open."

"Let's see," Brett said and walked across the room. None of them had screens on them, but two of them did open. "There sure is a lot of dust in here." They could see the dust glittering in the sunlight.

"Yeah, sixty years' worth," Gracie said, running her hand over the fireplace mantle. Her hand came up black.

"We are going to have to have help cleaning this place," Brett told her, looking up at the high ceilings.

63

"Probably so, but I just don't want anything in here damaged. We might be able to use some of the authentic decor. It would be nice, don't you think?" she asked him.

"Yes, it would. I would bet those chandeliers would clean up. The tarnished brass should. What about Bambi?" he asked her, mischievously. The large deer head looked horrid.

"Uh, I think that can go," she told him, and laughed.

Just then they heard trucks pull up outside. "Ah, the reinforcements have arrived," he said and pulled her toward the door.

There were about a dozen trucks parking along the drive. Three of the men came forward to speak to Brett.

"Gracie, these are my foremen. Jack Trainer, Eric Logan, and Mike Williams. Gracie is the co-owner of the property, but please keep in mind that everything inside belongs to her alone. A lot of things in there not only are irreplaceable antiques, but also family heirlooms and historical documents. Just be careful. And make sure your teams watch for structure damage. We want to insure everyone's safety.

Okay, first on the day's agenda is uncovering every window. It is pitch black in there until we get sunlight in. Right now, there is no electricity. Evidently, modernizing was not important to the last occupants. We will need to check for a septic system and well water. We have a long road ahead of us on this one, but it will be worth it. It is a privilege to get to work on an historical landmark such as this. Now, chop chop!" he said, and they all laughed good-naturedly and sped into action.

One of the men returned with a stack of flat cardboard boxes.

"Where do you want these, boss?" the stocky man asked Brett.

64

"There in the foyer, I guess," he told him and then turned to Gracie, "I had them bring some boxes to pack up all of the loose stuff in there. I thought that if we boxed and labeled them by room, it would make it easy for you to go through later." She followed him back inside.

"That makes sense," she told him. "I told Maria Scully that she could come and see the house after we were sure that it is safe enough. I thought that she might be the proper person to have to help go through all this. She might know the value of the antiques here. I also told her that I would donate some things to the museum. Who do I call to hire some cleaning help?"

"Well, we had better inspect the whole building first, but there are some places in Atlanta that might come this far. You could advertise around town, as well. There might be some that are willing." He walked into the room and began to unfold boxes and tape the bottom with duct tape.

Gracie grabbed the first box and walked to the book shelf behind the piano. She started filling it with music books and papers from the shelf. She tried to be careful, but several of the books fell apart in her hands. She decided that there was little she could do about it as she packed the box with the dust-coated books. On some of the shelves were glass bowls and trophies and valuable china ornaments.

"I am going to need some newspaper or something to wrap the breakables in."

"We'll just get the non-breakables for now. We can run into town for lunch and stop by the newspaper office. I'm sure we can buy all we want in back copies. By the time we get back, we should be able to explore the bottom floor, anyway," he said, smiling.

"Do you think there is a basement?" she asked him, curiously.

65

He nodded, "Yep. I could see a few small windows from the back of the house. Maybe we'll get lucky and find some blueprints for the house in here somewhere. That would be great!"

Gracie taped the top of the first box. "We better stop and get some markers, too. I didn't bring anything to label these with."

He pulled a marker out of his pocket and tossed it to her. "I came prepared," he said, with a bright smile.

She laughed as she labeled the top of the box.

They worked quickly and had most of the large room boxed up by lunch-time.

She had just finished labeling box number twenty when Brett walked up behind her. "You look really cute covered in dust," he said, mischievously.

"Really?" she asked, and grinned at him. "Well, it's definitely a new look for me

"It's lunchtime, what do you say we take our dusty selves out to the cafe for lunch?" "Well, it's definitely a new look for me." He reached up and brushed a cobweb from her hair.

"Oh, no, Brett. I look horrible." She backed away and shook her head emphatically.

"You look great. Just brush yourself off, no one will notice. I'm sure some of the guys will be at the cafe, too. We can see how far they have progressed." They had heard the noise from the workers coming from various areas of the house.

"Well, maybe I can brush some of the dust out of my hair on the way."

He chuckled, "Come on." He grabbed her hand and pulled her to the door.

She saw that most of the men were sitting outside eating their lunch, but a few of them were heading to their trucks to leave.

Chapter Fourteen

The three foremen that Brett had introduced her to that morning shared their table at the cafe. The four men joked back and forth, while Gracie listened, quietly.

Gracie learned that the bottom floor was indeed all open and half of the second story, as well. They had seen no real sign of any structure damage, other than the roof. Apparently, having no plumbing had saved the house from frozen and leaky pipes.

Gracie's mind wandered as the guys talked business. Renovating that huge home and refurnishing it seemed like a daunting task. Perhaps they would have an estimate by the end of the week, but it would be a long time before the place was finished. It was exciting, but at the same time, she realized that she had no idea what she was doing. She felt a little useless to the project. She could box up and clean. That was about it. By the time lunch was over, she realized that she had missed most of the conversation.

When they returned to the house, the windows were all open and Brett and Gracie explored the bottom floor. Off the main foyer that they had been working with were four rooms. They chose to search the left side of the house first. There was a doorway behind the grand piano; they entered to discover a large parlor. Filthy drapes framed ceiling to floor windows covering the entire back wall. It was more of a woman's domain, with peeling, floral wall-paper. The floor was covered in a rotting elegant area rug. There was an antique couch and two wooden chairs upholstered with deteriorating tapestry material. There was a tear drop chandelier in the center of the room, and gas lights in each corner. The room smelled of dust and mold. It must have been lovely at one time, though, and could be beautiful again.

68

A set of French doors graced the center of the windows, leading out to the veranda.

Gracie's eyes fell on a great antique curio cabinet in the corner. She walked over to have a look. The massive cabinet was about four feet wide and a good seven foot tall. There were trinkets of all kinds inside, all labeled by various countries. Someone's traveling souvenirs. Everything from Faberge eggs to Grecian vases. There were items from all over the world. It was an impressive collection, probably worth thousands of dollars. She noticed that one thing was missing, from Istanbul, Turkey. There was a bare spot where a necklace should have been. A gold, square shaped one with a ruby? Gracie wondered.

She turned to find Brett inspecting the wooden molding. The gold paint had flaked off in places, but it did give the entire room an added elegance.

They left through another door to the left and it opened into a drawing room. This room was larger than the last and contained a billiard table, a well-stocked bar, and several high-backed chairs. It was easy to imagine several cigar-smoking men standing around the room.

"This would still make a nice recreation room for our retirement home," Gracie told Brett.

"Yes, it would. That pool table could probably even be refurbished," Brett said, seriously. "Look at that gun collection!" He walked to the wall on the right hand side. A large gun cabinet stood with a real arsenal. There were a dozen rifles, and at least that many handguns.

"Well, none appear to be missing," he said and opened the doors on the bottom of the cabinet. It contained plenty of ammunition.

"Odd that it isn't locked," Gracie observed.

"The top part is. You will have to get a key to get in there, or break the glass," Brett said, "Gracie, you would have to get a gunsmith to tell you for sure, but I would bet that some of these date back to the civil war."

"We will have to get an expert in here, anyway, to appraise a lot of the antiques here. Maybe Maria Scully could recommend someone."

The next room was a front parlor, similar to the other one. To the right was a library. The entire room was lined with shelves filled with books. In the center was a huge desk, still littered with dust covered, yellow papers. There were two stuffed chairs in front of the windows facing the front of the house with a small table in between. Gracie couldn't wait to see what that desk contained.

From there they came out through the door under the stairs back into the foyer and crossed directly into a formal dining-room. The huge table seated twenty-two, Gracie counted. The back wall was decorated with several paintings. There was a large chandelier in the center over the table. It looked suitable for royalty, other than the dust and grime. They went straight through to the other end of the room. There was a wide door. Brett opened it and went through.

Gracie followed him into a huge room. It could only be a real ballroom! There were tables on one end of the room with chairs stacked on top of them. It was really beautiful. The front and the side walls were lined with windows like the other rooms. The north, interior wall was entirely mirrored other than several doors. Gracie counted six large chandeliers hanging from the domed ceiling.

Gracie walked across the room and curiously opened the French doors at the back. It opened into a long sun-room with old wicker furniture. Long dead plants decorated the room, and a couple of bird cages were on the end of the narrow wall. She walked through that room to another door that led to the kitchen and a back stairway. The kitchen was huge. The ovens were like nothing Gracie had ever seen before. They covered one entire wall, huge, iron monsters that looked to be fueled by wood. *You would think they would have updated some by 1951*, Gracie thought. There were huge cabinets filled with crystal, china, silverware, napkins. There were also two food pantries with three old ice boxes. All the food had, at least, been cleaned out. Evidently, Edgar didn't care much about modernizing.

The kitchen had a large wooden table and chairs in the center that looked centuries old. It was a place only inhabited by servants, no special decor here. Looked more like a sweatshop than a kitchen to Gracie.

That completed the tour of the downstairs. Brett and Gracie returned once more to the foyer. The great window above the back balcony had been uncovered. It was stained glass. It looked like a coat of arms, the shape of a shield with a golden sword.

"Can we go upstairs, yet?" Gracie wondered.

"I don't see why not. We will stay where it is already well lit." Brett said and led her up the front left stairs. "Be careful, I'll go first and test each step." He did so and they slowly made their way to the top. They had apparently opened all the windows on this floor, as well. They entered a wide hallway. There were four doors, leading to four different suites on this end of the house. Gracie chose the first door on the right and went in. There was a large parlor, three bedrooms, and a study. Curiously, no bathroom. But each bedroom contained a chamber pot. Well, perhaps this suite hadn't been used in more recent years. *Where did they bathe?* Gracie wondered.

All four suites were similar -- the last one with only two bedrooms. They were all full of the last occupants' personal items and clothing. Gracie felt as if she were invading someone's privacy. She couldn't tell if any of these rooms were Belinda's. There was a sun-room similar to the one at the back of the house, in the center front, leading out to the balcony. The other side of the house contained four suites, as well. One filled with religious-looking pictures and objects. It must have been the one Edgar and his wife shared.

There were stairs leading to the third floor on both ends of this one. Brett went up, and Gracie followed. They could see that not all the windows up here were open yet, but there was enough light coming in. There was a long, plain hallway with six, almost cell-like rooms. *Servants quarters*, Gracie guessed. All of the rooms were void of personal items and clothing. They all contained a bed, chest of drawers, a chamber pot and a small set of shelves.

The other side of the third floor appeared to be simple attic space used for storage. It was filled to the hilt with items of the past. A treasure trove to go through when the time came.

They had explored the entire house except for the basement.

They headed back to the foyer, quietly. They were each lost in their own thoughts.

"Well, there are no bathrooms in this entire house!" Gracie finally said and laughed.

"Yeah, not really unusual, except that the wealthy usually modernized."

"Will it be hard to plumb?" she asked.

"I don't think it will be especially hard. We will just have to make a blueprint before we will know where to plumb. That and we will have to get some electricity in here. You and I will have to sit down and look at it, plan it down to the last letter before we start," he said, thoughtfully.

"Well, we'd better see the basement. Do you have flashlights?" she asked.

Sure, he pulled two out of his tool belt. The basement stairs were just off the kitchen. It was pitch black as they descended. When they got to the bottom, they could see that there were a few small windows letting in a little light.

They stepped down into a large room with stone walls. They walked into the room and realized that the basement was made up of a series of rooms. There were five large rooms. The floor down here was dirt, though. The rooms were full of discarded things of all kinds. Gracie would have to go through all of this stuff, too. *Lord, it would take months to do all this*, she thought.

They went back upstairs. It was 5:00 already and time to go home for the evening.

Chapter Fifteen

For the rest of the week, Gracie stayed busy clearing out the bottom floor, room by room and stacking boxes in the ballroom. Brett helped when he wasn't busy with overseeing the work crew. They had already started reroofing. He hadn't said anything more about estimates. She had resisted his urging for her to hire someone to help clearing the house. She wanted to feel as involved with it as possible.

She had collapsed on the couch that Friday night and was thinking about dragging her aching body up to soak in the tub in the master bathroom when she heard the doorbell.

Sighing, she pulled herself up and answered the door. It was Brett.

"Wow, you look beat!" he said. "Sorry to bother you." He cleared his throat as he stepped inside.

"It's okay. What can I do for you?" She looked at him curiously. He must have come directly from the plantation. He was still covered in dust.

"I heard you say something the other day about needing beds. I was planning to go into Atlanta tomorrow for supplies. I thought maybe you might like to ride along." He looked at Gracie, expectantly. "So you can do your shopping – for beds, I mean."

Gracie had forgotten about her bed problem. She was perfectly happy sleeping on the couch. If Jeanette came out, though, she would definitely need beds. "That sounds great," she said, gratefully.

"Good, I'll be here around ten in the morning, then?" he asked, nervously.

"Yeah. I'll be ready. Thank you for thinking of me," she said, awkwardly.

He left quickly. Gracie wondered if she had just been asked on a date or just a shopping trip. He had certainly seemed nervous about it. Either way, he wanted to spend the day with her. Closing the door behind him, she felt her heart fluttering.

The warm water relaxed her tensed muscles as she soaked in the tub. She couldn't help feeling attracted to Brett, but she reminded herself that she shouldn't get her hopes up. Looking over their interaction that week, it did seem that he was subtly flirting with her. It was likely her imagination. He was probably just being friendly. Anyway, she wasn't going to make the mistake of falling for the first man that came her way – again.

*****

Neither of them said much on the way to Atlanta. Gracie realized that it didn't seem as awkward as she had feared being in such a small space with him as the cab of the truck for the road trip. It was nice to enjoy the ride and the landscape without a lot of conversation.

Gracie spent the afternoon at the mall while Brett went to the construction company to take care of business. At 4:00 they met in the food gallery of the mall.

"Well, did you finish your shopping?" Brett asked, looking at the dozen bags beside her.

75

"Oh, yes! I think that I am set up now. It isn't really that much. Just a lot of bedding." She laughed at his incredulous look.

He helped her carry her bags out to his truck and loaded them. On the way back home, Gracie took the opportunity to pump him for information.

"Brett, how long have you lived in Swanson?" she asked.

"Well, a few years now. Oh, wait, I guess it's been about thirty-four years." He grinned over at her. "Swanson, born and raised, my dear."

"There must be a lot of people in town that remember the last Mallorys that lived at the plantation," she prodded.

"Well, I imagine there are still some that worked on the property. Art Grandy is one. He worked there as a gardener. He is pretty proud of the fact. You could talk to him. I believe that his wife was a housemaid, too. I think that is how they met and married. There are probably at least a few more, but I don't know who they are." He looked over at her. "You know the whole town is buzzing about you. Everyone had thought that the family had died out. Is it true that Belinda is your great-grandmother?"

"Yes. She ran away with a friend. They ended up in Nebraska, and built a life together. That friend raised her daughter after Belinda died. That daughter had a daughter that was my mother," she told him.

He thought about that for a moment. "So why didn't your mother or grandmother claim the plantation?"

"I'm not really sure. In any case, they all died very young. I guess, I am the only one that has lived long enough to claim it." Gracie looked down the gray highway, thoughtfully.

"Well, at least one of you returned. I don't know much about the family. Just never had much interest, I guess. We had to tour the museum several times in school. Edgar didn't exactly have the greatest reputation. He was something of a religious fanatic, but also didn't seem to remain faithful to his wife. There were rumors that he had fathered more than one illegitimate child in town," he told her.

"Well, that doesn't surprise me. According to Gram, that wasn't the worst of his deeds. Anyway, I already know more than I want to about him. But there had to be some good people in the family. What happened to Edgar's wife?" she asked, curiously.

"I think she died of some illness. I don't really remember. The stories all seem to center around Edgar. Well, the past is past, anyway."

"I really want to know about my family. I do love the town, too. There is something about it. It seems so innocent and pure. There can't be many places like Swanson left in the world.

"Well, sometimes change is good. I lived in Atlanta for ten years. I finally realized that I really liked living in Swanson much better. The people are caring and neighbors are still neighbors. The place has a charm all of its own. I had to leave and come back to recognize it. It's easy to take what you have for granted, I guess. Well, it worked out for me. I started my company and built it up. Now I can afford to live how I want."

"It's wonderful what you do with the old houses. You make them real homes again. It really should attract a lot of people to the small town life. I know I love my house. I knew the moment I saw it that it was mine. It was as if you had had me in mind when you renovated it, and I could feel the love that you put into it," she told him.

"I lost my wife a few years ago to cancer. She used to say the same thing, that I put love into it. I suppose I do love it. Somehow the houses become like living things to me. Every crack and damage, feel like old wounds that haven't healed. They all have a personality. I enjoy bringing them back to health. Just call me the house doctor." He laughed.

"I'm sorry about your wife, but she was right. It's a gift to love what you do. I just haven't found that yet. I thought I wanted to go to graduate school. Now that doesn't seem what I want at all. My head has been spinning since Gram died. I have had too much to digest, I think, and too quickly. Perhaps I shouldn't be making such life decisions right now - like buying a house and staying in Swanson. But somehow it feels right. I feel like I belong here. Maybe it's the family connection that I am starved for. I don't know, but this is right for me. At least for now, anyway."

"Well, I don't think it is ever wrong to go with what is in your heart. You may learn some things that aren't pleasant. Every family has skeletons in their closet, but I would bet that you will learn good things, as well." He gave her a sideways smile.

Chapter Sixteen

When they got back to Swanson, Brett pulled in her driveway. He helped her in with her bags.

"Would you like a cup of coffee?" she asked him, gesturing to the couch.

"Sure," he said and instead of sitting, he followed her to the kitchen. He glanced at the table and the barstools that she had bought. The room was void of other furniture. "So, have you found some furniture at the plantation? You could use a bigger table in here," he suggested.

"I know that the house looks kind of empty. I guess, I should do something about it. I just don't need much for myself." She shrugged as he took a seat at the counter. "There will be beds here, though, when my cousin comes to visit. At least, I hope she comes to visit. I don't want to take things that we might need at the plantation."

"The entire basement out there is full of antique furniture. I don't think we will need so much. If you find some pieces you like, it doesn't take much to refinish and make them look new."

She handed him a cup of coffee and poured some for herself.

"What do you think of concentrating on just the main floor and the second floor suites? That way, we can get the house functional a little faster. With a little landscaping, we could be ready for guests in about six months." He took a sip of coffee.

"That sounds fine, except one thing that I think you've missed," she said, and he looked at her indignantly. She returned his look pointedly, "I've been thinking this over, Brett. Everyone in town is convinced the place is haunted. Who is going to want to live there? Art Grandy wouldn't even set foot on the property."

"Well, there is that," he said, thinking, "But if the place were renovated and no longer looked like the scary ghost house, perhaps the attitude would change. There are some who might even like the idea of living in a haunted house."

"Yes, perhaps, but are you willing to gamble on it?" she asked.

"Oh, absolutely! I just want to get in there and work. I don't care if it's never lived in. I want to uncover its glory," he said.

"You know, I think you may take this saving houses thing a little too seriously," she said, teasing. "I would love to see it restored to its former 'glory', but we are apt to lose money on it," she added seriously.

"Well, I really think it would be a success. I know people. If I build it, they will come," he said and chuckled, his vivid blue gaze meeting hers.

"All right, Mr. Costner, we will do it," she said, smiling brightly, "Why not? We both want to. If it doesn't work, we can always live in it. You in your half, and I in mine." She laughed.

"You know, I think I'm falling in love with you," he teased, flirtingly.

"Do you love me for my house or my mind?" she teased back, laughing loudly.

"Both," he said, laughing just as hard. Then he turned serious, reached out and pulled her against him. The kiss was light and playful at first, but deepened quickly as she responded. He suddenly pulled away, shocked at his action.

"I'd better go," he said, with a vague expression on his face and suddenly ran out of the kitchen. She heard the door slam on his way out.

Gracie sat, bewildered at his quick departure. She didn't move until she heard his truck start and drive away. She slid from the chair and walked to the sink to rinse their coffee cups. That was certainly odd. They didn't exactly know each other well, but after all, it was just a kiss.

She decided that her purchases could wait until tomorrow to be put away. She went upstairs and ran herself a bubble bath. Soaking in the tub, she went over the evening in her mind until she got the part with the kiss. She wondered if she had done something wrong, offended him somehow. He sure left quick enough. Well, it was all good on her end. Maybe it was his wife. Could he still be in love with her? Kind of hard to compete with the dead.

It was only one kiss, it shouldn't mean so much!

Gracie tried to put it out of her mind. She got out of the bath and dressed for bed. She went downstairs and made up the couch to sleep. *Tomorrow night, she would be sleeping in her own bed*, she thought. The beds would be delivered in the morning.

In her dream, she was Belinda.

Belinda thought she had slipped into her room unnoticed just as her father, Edgar, cornered her.

"How nice of you to come home again!" he bellowed.

Belinda nearly jumped out of her skin as she turned to see him in the doorway. She laid her bag on the bed without taking her eyes from him. She had learned the hard way how fast he could pounce.

"And I heard a wretched story only a moment ago about a rendezvous between you and that lowly farm boy up the road. Oh, yes," he said, as he crept closer. Belinda, instinctively, backed away. "Amazing the tales someone will tell while under duress. I heard about how you had gotten yourself pregnan, as well."

Belinda cringed at his words. He must have been horribly cruel to have extracted that information from Lydia. She began to panic, momentarily forgetting her own plight, wondering what he had done to her dearest friend.

Edgar was now standing over her, his face nearly touching hers with a murderous glint in his black eyes. "Do you have anything to say for yourself? Do you have any idea what you have done?"

Belinda dodged the first blow by ducking and rolling onto the bed. As she stood up, Edgar's arm caught her right across her shoulder blades, causing a blazing pain as her head bounced off the bedpost. Slowly, she sank into oblivion.

Belinda woke on the floor of her bedroom, her head reeling and her eyes unfocused. She was lying on the cream colored area rug and she stared at the swirling golden design, trying to remember what had happened.

It all came back to her in a rush, and she finally pulled herself up on the side of the bed. She had to find Lydia. She knew without a doubt that Edgar had done something to her.

Chapter Seventeen

Ignoring the throbbing in her head, Belinda went to the closet and packed her smallest suitcase. She didn't worry about neatness as she haphazardly threw some clothing into the case. Then she went to her dresser and with one quick swipe she pushed the entire contents from the smooth chestnut surface. Quickly, she stuffed the clothing that hang over the sides into the case and had to sit on it to get it zipped.

She didn't have much of a plan. She would find Lydia and then go to Billy. Billy would know what to do.

Surprisingly, the suitcase wasn't as heavy as she expected. She peered out her bedroom door, making sure that Edgar was nowhere in sight. Quietly, she snuck down the curved staircase, terrified that her father would hear her and it would be over for her.

Thankfully, the foyer was dark. She could see the light from Edgar's study and gave the area a wide berth. The light made it much easier to see and she ran as quickly as she could to the kitchen. The room was completely dark, but Belinda had made this trek in the dark more times than she could count. She opened the door to the basement and rushed down the stairs.

The light in Lydia's small room almost blinded her, but she saw Lydia sitting in the corner of the room, shaking.

Belinda dropped her suitcase in the doorway and ran to Lydia, whose face was already beginning to swell.

"Lydie, I am so sorry!" Belinda slid to the floor beside her friend and wrapped an arm around her.

"I told him, Belinda. I told him everything." Lydia looked at her through her half closed eye. "I'm so sorry." Belinda's heart broke at the girl's tear-stained face.

"It's okay. We have to get out of here. We have to get to Billy."

"Y-you don't hate me?"

"How can I hate you, Lydie? I know you had no choice. Is it just your eye or did he hurt you anywhere else? Can you walk? We have to hurry." Belinda hurriedly checked her over for injuries.

"I'm okay, I think." Lydia stood up and gave Belinda a hand up off the cold floor. "Jeepers, Bel, you have a great lump on your head. Are you okay?"

"Honestly? I don't know, but we can't worry about it now." Belinda touched the knot on her temple. It did feel huge and really sore. "Let's go. Do you need to pack your stuff?"

"Naw. I only keep my uniforms here, anyway. The rest of my things are at home." Lydia followed Belinda to the door.

They made their escape from the house, out the back kitchen door without incident. Once outside, Lydia turned to Belinda.

"Where do we go?" Lydia looked around. "What is that?"

Belinda looked in the direction Lydia was pointing. There was a light in the field. It took a moment before they saw the orange cast.

"It's a fire!" Lydia said.

Belinda took off at a run, forgetting her fear. The fire was close to the area that Billy had been working earlier that evening.

Lydia trailed after, limping a little from an injury.

The fire was contained in a metal bucket not far from the combine. Billy lay a couple of feet away. Belinda fell down beside him. The light of the fire illuminated Billy's lifeless face. His eyes looked toward the sky as if enraptured in the stars.

There was no scream, no yelling, no real shock. Belinda simply lay down beside him, ignoring the blades that protruded from his middle. She slid her hand into his. She could still feel his warmth. She let her gaze drift upward into the vast expanse of the universe, quiet tears sliding down the side of her face. She stayed that way for a moment and made a silent promise to Billy to keep their baby safe.

Gracie woke, shaking. The dream had felt so real. She was sweating profusely. She got up and went downstairs. She adjusted the temperature of the air conditioning and looked at the clock in the living-room. It was just past three. She went into the kitchen and poured herself a cup of the cold coffee, still left in the pot, and microwaved it. Then took her coffee back to the living-room and curled up on the end of the couch.

She remembered the dream vividly. She knew something else, too. It must have been in her dream, yet it was a part that she didn't remember. She only knew that there was a box buried under a great oak tree. Of course, it was just a fabrication of her mind, like the dream itself, but it was odd. She didn't know where this tree was, in the field or near the house, but she could see Belinda's hands as she put the box in the hole and covered it with dirt.

Well, no more caffeine before bed, she thought wryly. She went to her desk and checked her Facebook account. There were three messages from Spencer. How many times did she have to tell him that she quit? He was begging her to come back. He would even include that raise that she wanted. *Too bad, so long, sucker*, Gracie thought with satisfaction. Now he would know what it was like to do his own dirty work.

There was nothing else of importance and Gracie turned off the computer.

Chapter Eighteen

Gracie had arranged for some pieces of furniture that she had chosen from the plantation to be delivered at the house. Also, her new beds would be arriving. Her needs may be small, but she wanted her house to look like a real home.

That afternoon, she was making the beds with new linen. She was digging in one of the shopping bags for pillow cases when her fingers felt a small piece of metal in the bottom of the bag. She grasped it and pulled out a small tarnished key. *Where had that come from? Had the saleswoman had accidently dropped it in by mistake?* She decided that she would call later and check, and went back to her bed making.

The room she had set up for the children now looked cozy with the two twin beds and chest of drawers. The brightly colored quilts looked cheerful, but not so childish that an adult would be uncomfortable sleeping there. It could still use a few personal touches; a lamp for the small round table between the beds and maybe some pictures on the walls. The dresser and table cleaned up nice and with a little furniture polish gleamed like new.

By the end of the day, the house looked much better with the added furniture. Gracie stood, admiring her dish hutch that she had found in the basement at the mansion. She had also found the buffet and table and chairs that gave the dining-room a distinguished, yet homey feel. The phone rang and she sat down in a high-backed chair and answered.

"Hi!" Gracie answered when she saw that it was Jeanette. "I was going to call you tonight."

"Hi, Grace. How is everything? I'm sorry for being so negative before."

"Oh, that's okay. I know you were just trying to look out for me. Are you okay, Jeanette?" Gracie thought she detected some trepidation in her voice.

"Yeah, yeah, I'm okay. Gracie, I'm calling because a man showed up here looking for you. He was kind of strange. When I told him you weren't here, he said to tell you to 'find the box'. If you want to know who Billy is, you have to find the box. That was all he said and then left. It was creepy."

"Huh. What did he look like?"

"Well, he was an older man. Maybe in his fifties. He was wearing a suit, but it was all wrinkled and dirty. He kind of looked like a homeless person or something."

"I don't know who it could have been. Strange that he would know about Billy. He sounds like some kind of kook. I'd make sure to keep your doors locked."

"For sure. I just thought I would tell you. Do you know anything about a box?" Jeanette pressed.

"No." But she did, didn't she? She remembered her vague recollection of burying a box in her dream. Dreams aren't real, she reminded herself.

*****

Brett showed up on Gracie's doorstep that Sunday morning, bearing flowers and an apologetic smile. He was dressed in a dark blue suit and tie.

Gracie grinned at him and invited him inside.

"Uh, I am sorry for running out on you the other night," he said, nervously and handed her the flowers.

"Well, now you are forgiven," she said, her nose buried in the lilacs and daisies. "Lilacs are my favorite." She walked into the kitchen and filled a large glass with water and arranged the flowers in it. She then carried them to the dining-room table and set them in the center. They looked lovely.

He had followed her and now stood in the dining-room doorway, admiring her handiwork.

"I came to invite you to church. I thought that maybe we could set all the tongues wagging by showing up together," he said, his eyes dancing mischievously.

Gracie chuckled. "Well, I am not ready. What time does it start?"

"You have time. The service doesn't start for another hour," he said, grinning, "I'll wait."

"All right. I'll have to hurry, then." She ran upstairs to her room. What should she wear? She really wanted to make a good impression. She looked through her closet. There were several new dresses she had bought with attending church in mind. She selected the lavender one. It was a dressy sun-dress with a white crocheted jacket. She had bought a white straw hat to match.

Gracie showered and dressed quickly, but took extra care with her hair and make-up. It was the shoes that were the real problem. None of the heels she had bought really looked good to her with the dress. She finally decided to wear the plain white flats that she had worn to her grandmother's funeral.

She added a squeeze of her favorite cologne and inspected herself in the mirror. Satisfied with her reflection, she finally returned downstairs.

Brett was still waiting for her in the dining-room, looking at the papers that she had strewn across the table. He glanced up as he heard her enter the room.

"Wow!" he said, looking her up and down, "You look beautiful."

She felt herself blush, pleased at his response. "Well, you look nice, too," she said, and glanced at her watch. "Should we go, now?"

He was still perusing her with his piercing blue eyes. "Uh, yeah," he said and looked her in the eye. "It's only a couple blocks away, I thought we could walk."

"That sounds nice," she said, and walked toward the door. He followed her through the door and into the morning sunshine.

Gracie found it pleasant walking down the pretty little street lined with trees, white fences and freshly mowed lawns. She was slightly surprised when he slipped his hand into hers. It felt good and natural to hold his hand and charmingly old-fashioned.

"You smell good," he observed, giving her a sideways glance.

"I bought this cologne at the mall the other day," she told him, with a smile. She had, of course, bought it with him in mind.

"You smell good, too," she returned the compliment. He smelled of Stetson. He had overdone it a little and Gracie was surprised that he could smell her cologne over his own.

He squeezed her hand, lightly, as they neared the church.

There were people standing on the front steps. Gracie recognized Rhoda, from the furniture store. She was dressed attractively in a blue blazer and skirt. She greeted Gracie and Brett with a smile and shook their hands. On the other side of the door was an older, slightly balding man in a suit. He was the pastor and greeted them both warmly, as Brett introduced Gracie.

They went inside and Brett led her to a pew halfway toward the front. The church was filled with people already seated and Gracie could feel at least a dozen eyes on her. Several members of the bridge club came over and greeted them, welcoming Gracie into the fold.

The church itself was lovely. Stained glass windows lined each side of the sanctuary. Another large one behind the pulpit, depicting a huge, beautiful cross. The pews were nicely padded.

The service was pleasant and not overlong. After the service, many came to greet Gracie, and there were a lot of introductions. All of the church members seemed sincere and Gracie found their friendliness endearing.

On the walk back home, Brett told her a little about a few of them. Gracie felt that it was really cute how he staked his claim on her that morning. He held her hand during service and even put an arm around her shoulders as they left the church. He was telling them all in his subtle way that Gracie might be single, but she was unavailable.

She certainly didn't mind, but was curious of his actions after the other night. They walked back to her house after the service, hand in hand. They waved at others that they passed along the way.

When they got back to the house. Brett gestured to the truck.

"Hop in," he said and let go of her hand to walk to the driver's side. Gracie had no idea what he had in mind, but decided to do what he wanted. She got into the truck, careful not to get her dress in the door.

"I wanted to take you somewhere special. Do you mind a picnic?" He looked at her, questioningly.

She laughed, softly. "No, a picnic sounds lovely." It did seem a perfect idea for this beautiful day.

"We have to stop at my house for a minute," he said and backed out of her drive.

Gracie wasn't sure what she expected, but she sure would never have guessed that the house they stopped at was his own. It was a very small, run down house. Nothing like the one he had sold to her. *He surely could afford something better*, she thought curiously. She said nothing as he left her to run into the house. He came back out ten minutes later. He had removed his jacket and tie and carried a large cooler in one hand and a brown paper bag in the other. He dropped both in the bed of the truck and got back behind the wheel.

Chapter Nineteen

She was quiet as he drove, and was surprised when he turned in at the plantation. He skirted around the house, driving over the grounds and back through a path in the trees behind the house. He stopped the truck in the clearing, in front of a beautiful little pond. It was a lovely spot; the trees framing the pond with the sun shining joyful on the water.

"So, what do you think?" he asked, looking over at her.

"It's wonderful. Like an oasis, hidden from the rest of the world," she said, with a bright grin.

"I've been coming here for years. It's become my thinking place. I like the tranquility."

"Thank you for sharing it with me," she said, sincerely.

"Well, we own it. It goes with the property. Come on," he said and got out of the truck. "You grab the blanket and I'll get these," he said and pulled out the cooler and brown paper bag. She grabbed the blanket and followed him. They found a shady spot and spread the blanket.

They sat down and Brett opened the chest. He pulled out a soda and handed it to Grace, and pulled out one for himself. He reached over and pulled off her hat. The breeze blew through Gracie's hair.

"You should take off those shoes and get comfortable."

She chuckled and did as he suggested.

"Now", he said and opened the bag. "We have, egg salad, bologna, peanut butter, or chicken salad."

"Wow. That seems like a lot," she said, grinning.

"Well, I figured you should like one of those, at least. And I brought Doritos and Hohos. The best I have to offer," he said, winking at her.

She shook her head in mock exasperation. "Well, truthfully, I like all of those."

"Good, I knew you wouldn't be hard to please. I may not be the classiest guy you know, but I do aim to please."

He handed her the chicken salad and picked the bologna for himself.

"The church service was lovely, thank you for inviting me," she told him and nibbled on the sandwich.

"It is nice. I go every week. The ladies are always bugging me about not bringing a lady friend, so I thought I would oblige them, for once." He gave her a shy look.

"Well, it was nice. The people here are so different. Friendly, gossipy even, but at the same time, you feel real concern and caring."

"They are good for the most part. We have had some bad eggs in town, but they usually leave when they can't seem to bait anyone into a fight."

He finished his sandwich in no less than three bites and drowned it down with a long drink of his soda.

They finished their meal in companionable silence. Then Brett wordlessly, pulled her over to him so that she leaned back against his chest. They quietly watched the water. They could see a fish jump now and then.

94

After a few minutes, Brett wrapped his arm around her holding her gently against him. He whispered softly in her ear.

"I'm sorry for the other night. That kiss scared me that bad."

She turned in his arms and faced him. "It surprised me, too." He traced her face lightly with his finger.   "I thought that maybe I did something wrong, or maybe it was too soon for you after losing your wife. I don't usually throw myself at men."

The kiss that came next started softly just as the last one had, but neither of them could keep it light. After it was over they both laid back on the blanket each lost in their own thoughts.

Finally, Brett reached out and grabbed her hand. He asked softly, "Does this mean we are dating?"

Gracie looked at the blue sky through the tree limbs above them. "I guess so." She felt a thrilling shiver rush through her at the thought. After a moment, she glanced over at him. He was looking at the sky, just as she was.

Suddenly, the smile left her face as she wrestled her hand away from him. She jumped up, her eyes filled with terror.

He pulled himself up on one elbow and looked at her in surprise and confusion.

Gracie started shaking from head to foot. Brett looked bewilderedly up at her, seeing that something was wrong. He stood up and pulled her trembling form back into his arms.

"Hey, what's wrong? Are you okay?" He framed her face with his hands and looked into her face. He saw real terror in her eyes.

"I'm okay," she said, though he could see that was a lie. "Can we please get out of here?" she asked him.

"Sure, honey. Let me grab this stuff." She could see that he was disappointed to cut their outing short.

They got back into the truck and headed back to her house. He parked the truck in her drive and turned off the ignition.

"Please don't leave. Come in with me," she told him. She didn't want to be alone with her thoughts.

"Okay, let's go in. Then you can tell me what just happened." He walked in and sat down on the couch. She sat on the other end quietly.

"Hey, you want to come down here so I can hold you?" he asked, gently.

"Yes." she said, "No. I don't know." But she did anyway, she needed his comfort. He pulled her into his lap.

"What happened? Something back there spooked you bad. You are still shaking! Was it me?" He held her tight.

"No, uh, yes. It wasn't you exactly. I had a dream the other night. A real nightmare. It was so very real," she started and told him about the dream. By the time she was finished, she had started to recover. "Brett, when I looked at you today, lying on the ground beside me, you had the same expression as Billy did in my dream. It was as if I had had a premonition of some sort."

She moved from his arms.

"I am so sorry for freaking out on you," she said. "The tree-line was even the same. And your face. It was exactly what I saw in that dream. I am not normally superstitious, but I can't explain that. Was it some kind of warning or omen?"

"I don't believe in omens or ghostly warnings. It does seem that we can't kiss without one of us freaking out," he chuckled.

Chapter Twenty

It was a week later when Maria came out to the plantation and showed Gracie how to tag and log everything. It had been a busy and productive morning. It was nearly noon when Gracie got a strange phone call.

"Miss Lawson, this is Meredith Grandy. Dear, I know you don't know me. I really need to speak with you, if you don't mind coming here. I don't get out anymore." The woman's voice sounded shaky and strange, yet warm.

"I can come to visit you, Mrs. Grandy," Gracie said, thinking it was strange how these people seemed to obtain her number. "How about Thursday evening?" She was really so busy this week, but perhaps the woman had some information about the plantation.

`"Thursday will be fine, dear. Oh, and she says to wear the necklace."

"Who says?" Gracie asked, wonderingly. How did she know about the necklace?

"Never mind, just please wear it. You should wear it whenever you are near the plantation. I will explain when you come." There was a click as the woman hung up.

Wear the necklace? Whatever for?

"Everything okay?" Maria asked. She was looking at Gracie with concern.

"Yeah. Fine. Mrs. Grandy asked to see me." Gracie smiled across the table.

"Ah. Meredith Grandy hasn't left her home for about ten years. Art comes to the café in town every day to get them food. Sometimes people take groceries and prepared meals out to them. Rumor has it that they are both near a hundred years old."

"Really? And he still gets around?" Gracie asked, shocked.

"Well, he drives to town nearly every day," Maria said, bending her head to read the print on a document in front of her. Her blond head was nearly touching the paper.

"I have no idea why she wants to see me, but I suppose I should be neighborly," Gracie said, and reached to wipe the dust from her nose.

"You know, Gracie," Maria paused and pushed her blond hair from her eyes. "I think this is a marriage certificate. I can't make out the names or dates. Perhaps if we can darken the image on the computer…"

"That would be great," Gracie said, enthusiastically. She glanced down at her watch. "It's about lunchtime. I packed plenty if you want to join me and Brett."

"Actually, I had a late breakfast. Why don't you two go on? I'd like to finish this box." Maria grinned up at Gracie.

"Okay. Don't work too hard. We have plenty of time." Gracie returned her smile and went to find Brett.

Gracie walked into the foyer, now void of furniture and contents. She went to yell up the stairs when she noticed someone standing in the entryway of the front door. As she came closer, she saw that it was a girl. Her blond hair hung around her head, looking as if it were combed with a rake and with pieces of twigs stuck in it. Her head was slightly askew as if her neck had been broken. She glared at Gracie with a radiating hatred that was overwhelming.

Gracie was standing, unable to move or tear her eyes away from the dreadful image. After a moment, the girl opened her mouth abnormally wide and gave an earthshattering scream that resonated through the empty room. Gracie unconsciously covered her ears and finally broke eye contact.

When she looked back up, the girl was gone. Either everyone was already outside or she was the only one that heard the scream. No one came running. Cautiously, she inched her way to the door, shuddering as she passed the spot where the girl had been. She flung the door open and ran for her car. The workers were all sitting around on the lawn and the tail gates of their trucks eating lunch and a few noticed her pass. It wasn't long before Brett found her, sitting in her car, shaking and crying.

Brett got in on the passenger side of the Honda. "Hey, Baby, what's wrong?" He pulled her hands away from her face.

"I need to go home. I think you should send everyone home. Can you tell Maria to go home?" Gracie gave him a pleading look.

"Honey, talk to me. What's happened? Did one of the guys do something? Say something?" Brett took her face in his hands.

"No. Nothing like that. I just don't think we need to be here. I want to go home." She was shaking all over, just like

100

after the carriage house incident. Now she knew that that had been real, too.

"Do you want me to come with you?" Brett asked, confused.

"Yes." She looked at him and cried, "Yes. I want you to come, but not until everyone is gone from here. Right now, Brett."

"Okay. I'll tell the guys to take the rest of the day off and I'll get Maria. Stay here. I'll be right back." Brett gave her arm a squeeze and jumped out of the car.

Gracie watched him walk to the door of the house while biting her lip. He was gone for only a few minutes before emerging with Maria. Maria glanced toward Gracie's car in bewilderment before getting into her own and driving away. Brett stopped and spoke to his foremen. Then, a moment, later he was approaching Gracie. He opened the driver side door.

"Want me to drive? You don't look like you're in any condition." His eyes were full of concern.

"Yeah," Gracie said and stepped out. In seconds, she was buckled into the passenger seat. "Let's get out of here," she said, recovering, but still shaky.

Brett drove to Gracie's house in silence. Gracie was wondering if he was angry with her. His face seemed more mystified than angry, she decided.

Back at her cottage, Gracie made them coffee. She knew that he deserved an explanation, but she wasn't looking forward to it. Her hands were still shaking as she added sugar to her cup. She sat Brett's cup in front of him on the kitchen table.

"Are you going to tell me?" Brett asked as he watched her sit in the chair across from him.

"I think the plantation is really haunted," she said, weakly.

"Was it something you found? You have to tell me more than that, Gracie."

Gracie took a sip of her coffee, bolstered her courage and told him about the carriage house incident and then about the girl in the entryway.

"You think this girl was a ghost," he said, unbelievingly.

"I don't know. She looked very real. I thought she was a real person, at first. She didn't look see-through or anything like that. She was just there, glaring at me, then she screamed and was gone. It was enough to scare the crap out of me."

"You have listened to too many stories, Gracie. Maybe you are scaring yourself," Brett said, skeptically. "You can stay away if you want, but I have too much invested. I have to go on with the renovation."

"I guess, I didn't expect you to believe me," Gracie said, coldly. She knew she would feel the same if the situation was reversed, but it still hurt.

"Gracie, you can't expect me to. I don't know what you saw. I know that you really believe what you are saying, but you've had a lot of changes in your life, pretty suddenly." Brett stretched his arm across the table to her.

"So, the stress of losing my grandmother along with this move has pushed me over the edge of sanity!" Gracie ignored his hand and stood up. "I'm not crazy, Brett!" She dumped her coffee into the sink and stomped from the room. She was half-way up the stairs when she heard the front door slam.

Chapter Twenty-One

All Gracie wanted to do was to chase Brett down and apologize, though she had nothing to apologize for. What would be the point when he thought she was crazy, anyhow? Instead, she cried for a while.

At nine pm, she turned off the TV and stood to go upstairs when a tap came at the door. Who would be there this late?

Gracie peeked out the window to see Brett standing on the other side of the door. She gave a deep sigh, knowing that she really didn't need more stress. It wasn't possible for her to turn him away and she opened the door and gave him a defeated look.

"Come in," she said and left him to follow her to the couch.

"Gracie, I'm sorry," he said, shamefaced.

"I'm really not crazy, you know," she told him as he sat down beside her.

"I know," he said, and looked down at his hands, searching for what to say. "Two of the men left today. One didn't say a word. He just walked off the job. The other kept ranting about hearing voices."

"I'm sorry, Brett."

"I've seen some things, too. I just chose to ignore it. Yesterday, my tools kept disappearing and reappearing. I don't know what is going on." He shook his head, wearily. "I am really so sorry, Gracie. Can you forgive me?" His sad look nearly broke her heart.

"I forgive you. Brett, what are we going to do? I don't mind reimbursing you and will gladly pay for the work your men have done, but I don't know what to do with the plantation now."

"I don't want to give up, Gracie. I'm going to continue to work. There is no reason to think that what is there is dangerous. If it is ghosts, how can they hurt us?" He slipped her hand into his and squeezed.

"You might be right, but that girl sure scared me. Her scream is still echoing in my brain. I don't want to think about it tonight." Gracie gave a shiver and Brett put his arm around her.

Gracie's phone rang just then. She grabbed it off the coffee table and answered.

"Hello."

"Gracie, it's me," Jeanette said, sounding agitated.

"Hi, Jeanette. What's going on?"

"Grace, I'm coming out there. We are leaving in the morning. I'm driving out so it will be a couple days."

"Jeanette, that's wonderful, but don't you think you should fly? That will be a long trip for the kids."

"Well, I'm bringing too much with me to fly."

"You could fly and have the rest shipped. What on earth are you bringing with you?" Gracie asked, curiously.

"Well, your china, and then there were some things that I thought you could use for the plantation house. I really can't explain so much until I get there. I guess I could hire a moving company to bring it out."

"Jeanette, what in the world are you talking about?"

"Gracie, most of the stuff Gram has here; I think it belongs to the plantation house. I think she brought it all here. The antique furniture and I found a lot of old papers. I can't explain over the phone. I'll have it shipped and see if I can get a flight within the next couple of days, okay?"

"Okay, honey. If you can fly into Atlanta, I'll come get you at the airport. Be safe," Gracie said, confused.

"I will. You, too. See you soon," then she hung up.

Brett was looking at her curiously.

Gracie relayed the conversation to him.

"I really don't know why Gram would have things from the plantation," Gracie said, perplexed. And why was it so important to Jeanette to ship it all here.

"Well, it seems that you will have some company," Brett said.

"Yeah. I can't wait for you to meet her and the kids. I didn't like the way she sounded, though. She was upset. Something has happened. She wouldn't tell me over the phone."

Brett pulled her back into his arms. "Well, I guess you will find out soon."

"She sounded really strange. But it's more than that. I think she had been crying."

"Well, she will be here soon," he said, "I was thinking that we need a larger vehicle for the plantation. Maybe a van. Comfortable enough to ride in, but big enough to haul supplies."

"Yeah, it will be tough to fit all five of us in my Honda. I hadn't really thought about it," Gracie agreed.

"Well, we could go van shopping in the morning. If we found one, we could use it to pick up your sister."

"Okay. That sounds like a plan. If we are going to go ahead with the renovation, maybe we should open a business account. Are you sure you really want to?"

"Well, if it comes down to it, we can call a ghost extermination." He laughed, softly.

"Hmm. I haven't heard of such a thing," she laughed and turned her head just in time to receive his kiss.

Gracie felt it was time to fill him in on all of the incidents - the episode at Gram's funeral, the carriage house, and the man looking for her in Maytown. Separately, they could all be dismissed. Together, it was obvious something was going on.

She told him all of it, then added, "I just don't understand what it all means. Then I got a call from Meredith Grandy. She needs to talk to me and told me to make sure I wear Belinda's necklace when I am at the plantation. I'm supposed to go see her on Thursday."

"Well, we will just go on as if nothing happened for now. If you want to stay away from the plantation, I understand." He squeezed her hand, but she got the feeling that he would be disappointed if she didn't.

Chapter Twenty-Two

That evening, Meredith opened the door at Gracie's knock.

"Hello," she greeted Gracie. She was wearing a long gray dress with a white ruffly apron and a smile.

"Hello, you must be Mrs. Grandy. I'm Gracie Lawson. I've come to ..."

"Oh, I know why you are here, dear." Mrs. Grandy cut her off. "Please come in. Art isn't here just now. We can talk freely."

What an odd thing to say, Gracie thought and stepped inside.

"What a lovely home," Gracie said, looking around.

"Thank you, dear. We do like it here. Come in and sit down. Would you like some lemonade?" the old woman asked.

"Oh, yes, thank you. That would be nice," Gracie said. Merideth left the room and came back a moment later with the lemonade.

She handed the glass to Gracie who had sat on the divan.

"I'm so glad you came. I was afraid that I would have to come to you and, well, I just don't get around like I used to," she said, in an apologetic tone. "Belinda keeps at me all the time now that you are here in Swanson. I know that she won't let me rest until I've told you."

Gracie was beginning to wonder if the woman was in control of her faculties. "Uh, Belinda?"

"Of, course. She has been here every night this week. It is truly unsettling to continually get visits from the dead, you know. Though you would think I would be used to it by now." Meredith shook her head in resignation.

"What is it that she wants from you?" Gracie asked, curiously.

"Well, to warn you, of course, and to tell you where that silly box of hers is," she said, as if Gracie should have already known this.

"The box?" Gracie prodded.

"Yes, yes, the box. Her pretty little box that she used to keep on her bureau. She buried it in the field before she left. I have no idea what is in it, but it is important for you to have it. I've drawn you a map." Meredith stood and grabbed a sheet of paper from the bookshelf and handed it to Gracie.

It was roughly drawn, but Gracie could see the pond marked and a jutting rock. According to the map, the tree was eight feet south of that rock.

"Please find that box. Belinda won't leave me alone until you do. Also, she says for you to wear the necklace. You must wear the evil eye when you go to the plantation. It will keep you safe." Meredith looked relieved that she had delivered the message.

"The necklace? Evil eye?" Gracie asked, not understanding.

"Yes, you have Belinda's ruby necklace. She says so, anyway. It is from the middle-east, what they call an evil eye. It is a talisman to keep you safe from evil. Belinda says that you are to wear it when you go to the plantation," Meredith

109

explained patiently. "Edgar was a very superstitious man. Whether or not the necklace has real power, he will likely leave you alone if you wear it."

"So, Edgar is still at the plantation?" Gracie asked.

"Of course, dear. Don't you know the story? Everyone who has died on or near the plantation resides there. Until the curse is broken at any rate." She was speaking as if Gracie was a simple-minded child.

"I'm sorry, Mrs. Grandy, I don't know about a curse," Gracie told her.

"You don't know of the curse of Dahlia?" she asked, and shook her head in exasperation. "Well, listen closely, because this story is very important. This is why Belinda wants you here. She believes that you have the power to break that curse. Back way before the civil war, when the plantation was still worked by slave labor, there was a young slave woman by the name of Dahlia. She and her husband lived and worked in the cotton fields. They had a small child, who would play beside Dahlia while she worked. One day the master came out to the fields to check the progress and saw the child. Who knows what really angered him, the man was evil through and through, but he picked the boy up and just snapped his neck like a twig. He told the screaming mother that the cotton field was not the place for children too young to pick cotton and strode away after tossing the lifeless child on the ground like it was a piece of filth.

Voodoo was a common practice among slaves at that time and Dahlia put a curse on the Mallorys and the plantation. Ever since, whoever dies on that cursed ground, is enslaved forever. Their souls are imprisoned. Make no mistake, the plantation is haunted. There are, at least, a hundred or more souls trapped there. Most are innocent, but there are two strong evil forces, as well. Edgar had already been taken over by Alfred years before his death. He is most likely still in

110

servitude to that demon. Though the lesser of the two evils, Edgar is a force to be reckoned with on his own. Alfred, I believe, has tainted a few of the spirits there and they may give you some trouble. You will have to be very careful, Gracie. They see and hear all. If you do any planning, do not do so at the plantation. And Billy will be there to help you." Meredith was finished and stood up. "Would you like some more lemonade, dear?" she asked, cheerfully, as if she hadn't just told such a horror story.

"Uh, no thank you. I think I'd better be going," Gracie said, and stood up nervously. She suddenly had a lot to think about.

"All right, dear. Thank you for coming. I know it will take you a while to digest this information. And get that box, but wear the necklace when you go to get it. I have a feeling that Edgar will try to stop you," she said as she walked Gracie to the door. "And Gracie, don't go alone. I know Brett will go with you. You shouldn't try to do it by yourself."

"Okay. I'll see if Brett will go with me," Gracie said to reassure the old woman. "Oh, one more thing, Mrs. Grandy. You said that Billy would be there to help me. Did you know Billy?"

"Yes, dear. I knew Billy. Billy was my son, and you are my great, great-granddaughter. But for now, no one must know. Only Art and I know about Belinda and Billy and we should keep it that way until the curse is broken. The answers that you seek are in that box. When it is all over, come back. I wish to get to know you, Gracie. You are all that is left of our Billy." She reached out a hand and touched Gracie's cheek.

So, Billy was the son of Art and Meredith Grandy, a housemaid and gardener in 1941 at the plantation. So Billy, likely, had spent much of his life on the plantation. Perhaps he and Belinda were playmates before they were lovers. Did he even know about her pregnancy before his death? What a sad and romantic story.

Gracie would have sworn a week ago that she didn't believe in ghosts or curses, but now? She would never forget that girl in the entryway and those cold dead eyes glaring hatefully at her.

Chapter Twenty-Three

The next day turned out to be a very busy day. Jeanette and the kids were flying into Atlanta.

They arrived at the airport thirty minutes early and easily found Jeanette's gate. Jumping up and down, the kids saw Gracie and she waved at them and Jeanette.

"Oh, Gracie!" Jeanette said and hugged her. Brett helped collect their luggage, just two suitcases and followed them outside to the van. They all loaded in.

"This is nice, Grace, is it new?" Jeanette looked at the van's interior.

"Yeah, bought it just yesterday. We needed something to haul things to and from the plantation."

"Aunt Gracie, do we get to see the big house?" Aubrey asked.

"Sure, sweetie, but you have to be careful there. There are a lot of people working inside just now," Gracie answered.

"Who's him?" Jasper asked, pointing at Brett.

"I want all of you to meet Brett. He is my boyfriend and we are working on the plantation house together."

"Boyfriend?" Jeanette asked, meeting Gracie's eyes. "We certainly have some things to catch up on, huh?" She looked at Brett, curiously, "Nice to meet you, Brett. I am truly happy for you both. Please don't mind me," Jeanette said, and started to tear up.

"Mommy's sad," Jasper said.

"Well, sometimes we all get sad," Gracie told him, wondering just what was going on. "I am so glad to see you all. I bought presents for you." She hoped to change the subject.

"You did?" Aubrey asked, excitedly.

"I did. When we get to my house, you can open them."

The kids chattered all the way home, but Jeanette was quiet.

When they got there, the kids got out, hyper from all the traveling.

"I'll bring in the suitcases," Brett said.

Gracie put her arm around Jeanette. "Come on, sis. Whatever it is, we will work through it together. I'm here for you."

"Thank you, Gracie," she said and followed the kids into the house.

Brett held Gracie back a moment. "It's obvious that you and Jeanette need to talk. Why don't I take the kids down to the park for a while?"

"That sounds good. Thank you." She kissed the corner of his mouth.

"Come on, guys, I'll show you your room real quick. Then Brett wants to take you to the park. If it's okay with you, Jeanette."

"Yeah, sure," she agreed and followed the kids up the stairs.

The wrapped gifts were placed on each bed in the kids' room. They ran to them immediately and tore them open. A toy car for Jasper, and a doll for Aubrey.

"Thank you, Aunt Gracie," Aubrey said and gave Gracie a hug. Jasper gave her a hug, too.

"You are both welcome. Now, Brett's waiting downstairs for you." They took their gifts with them and went down to find Brett.

"That was nice of you, Grace," Jeanette said.

"Well, I haven't gotten to spoil them. Come on, I'll show you your room." Gracie crossed the hall to the other guest room.

"Wow! It's really nice. Thank you for welcoming us." Jeanette sat down on the bed.

"You don't have to thank me, silly. You are my family. 'Sisters by circumstance', remember?"

"Jim left me, Grace. He just called me and said that he had found someone else." Jeanette was crying again. "And now, I don't know what to do. I haven't told the kids. They don't know the difference; he hasn't been home much in the last couple of years. They hardly know him, anyway."

"Oh, honey, I'm so sorry." Gracie sat down beside her and held her while she cried.

"I'm so sorry, Grace. I'm really a mess right now." And then, "Oh, God, Gracie, you are not going to believe what I found out!"

Jeanette stood up and lifted her suitcase on the bed. She unzipped it and pulled out an old photo album. I found this under Gram's bed. She opened the album and sat back down with Gracie. "See this picture?" It showed a pretty young

115

woman holding a little girl of about three years old. It was labeled, Lydia and Susan, in Gram's handwriting. "Now look at this one." Jeanette pulled a picture out of the book. "I found and printed it out from the plantation web-site." It appeared to be the same girl only a couple of years younger. The caption was labeled Belinda Mallory.

"This has to be a mistake," Gracie said looking at both pictures. "Gram simply labeled it wrong."

Jeanette shook her head, "Nope, I did some checking. Gracie, Gram was Belinda Mallory. There never was another woman. I called the granddaughter of the woman she had worked for in Nebraska. Lydia did not have a sister. She came to work there alone and pregnant. Most of the story she told you was true, except that she really was your great-grandmother. The scariest thing to me, though, is who am I? Belinda never had any siblings. So who was Sophie? She wasn't really her niece, that's for sure. I thought maybe I could find out. If Sophie was really from Swanson, maybe someone knows."

"So she lied to us?" Gracie was trying to comprehend this.

"I don't know, Grace, I don't think so. I think she was delusional. She really believed her story."

"How do we know how far her delusion goes, then?" Gracie said in horror.

"Well, I know that you are truly her great-granddaughter. But also she was married for a short time. Her husband had some kind of disease. He died and left her his money, which presumably, is where my inheritance came from. According to the ladies of the church, there really was a Sophie and Lydia introduced her as her niece. So Sophie had to come from somewhere. Maybe she was the daughter of a childhood friend or something. But this on top of Jim leaving, it just makes me feel like the whole world is shifting under my feet."

"It makes no sense. She was delusional, but lucid enough to set up an account for me with the Mallory fortune? Just when did she become delusional, if that is the answer?" Gracie asked.

"There is no telling. Perhaps she was from the beginning. She suffered the abuse of her father," Jeanette said.

"Well, would someone have kept her on a job if she was crazy enough to believe that she had her friend with her? Surely, she couldn't have been at that time. Or at least part of her knew the truth. She was very good at hiding it. Perhaps she had just decided to be Lydia Mason and made herself believe that was so. She lied to cover any holes in her story. Maybe, by the end, she had convinced herself so well that she no longer knew the difference."

"Well, whatever the reason, it amounts to the same thing. My identity has been tossed by the way-side," Jeanette said and started pacing.

"Honey, you know who you are! You are the same person you have always been. You have never known much about Sophie, and well, now, you know that she wasn't related to Gram. So what? Gram loved you, whether or not she was Belinda or Lydia. You will always be my sister, no matter what. And together we will look for the truth, I promise. Okay?"

Jeanette stopped and looked at Gracie. "Okay. I know you are right and this shouldn't matter so much. It might not if it hadn't been for Jim. You make me feel better."

"That's what family is for. You are welcome here as long as you want. I've been so anxious for you to come. I can't believe Jim. What a creep! Well, he doesn't deserve you, then," Gracie told her. "I was hoping that you could help me shop for the plantation house."

"Sure, I really can't wait to see it. I hope we don't, well, interfere with you and Brett."

"Why would you?" Grace asked, then seeing the pointed look on her face, "Oh. No, don't worry about that. If we want privacy, we can always go to his house."

"This house is really cute. I see why you liked it so much," Jeanette said.

"Brett renovated it himself. He even carved the trim by hand," Gracie bragged.

"It's really good," Jeanette said, admiringly. "He seems really nice, Gracie."

"I adore him completely, I can't seem to help it," Gracie said.

"Well, I am really happy for you."

Gracie stood, "Let's go make some dinner. The kids will be hungry when they get back. I know Brett will be. He is always hungry."

Jeanette was joking with Brett by the end of the evening. It was good to see her come out of her misery. The kids spent the evening playing in the back yard.

At nine, Jeanette took the kids upstairs to settle them into bed. Brett took the opportunity for a long kiss and goodnight.

"Thanks for watching the kids. It really helped," Gracie said.

"I had fun with them. They are really good kids. Did I mention that I want at least a half dozen myself?" he teased.

"On second thought, three seems fine to me." He gave her a parting kiss and disappeared out the door.

Chapter Twenty-four

Gracie woke up the next morning to the smell of bacon frying. She showered and dressed quickly and was almost half-way down the stairs when Jeanette shouted.

"Gracie! Gracie, come here," she cried.

Gracie came down the rest of the way to see Jeanette staring at the table, in horror. Gracie had left the papers strung over the table from Maria's files.

"I'm here, what is it?" Gracie asked, concerned.

"Gracie, it's him. My God, this is him," Gracie looked over her shoulder at a black and white photograph of Jameson Mallory.

"Jeanette, I don't understand," Gracie said.

"Gracie, this is the man that came looking for you in Maytown. The one who told me about the box, remember?"

"Jeanette, this is Jameson Mallory. He has been dead since, like the 1800's," Gracie told her.

"I don't care, that is him. Ask the kids, Grace. They saw him." Jeanette yelled at the kids to come in there and she showed them the picture.

"That's the weird man with the cane," Aubrey said. "The one asking for Aunt Gracie."

Jasper nodded.

Gracie looked at Jeanette. "I don't know what this means. If it was him, and he is dead, why wouldn't he just find me here?"

"I don't know, Gracie. It's very strange," Jeanette said. Then she realized that the kids were both looking at her oddly. "Come on, let's go eat. I cooked bacon and eggs."

*****

That evening, Gracie felt it was time to discuss everything with Brett. She wasn't sure if Jeanette could deal with any more stress and she had to talk to somebody. Gracie would have sworn a week ago that she didn't believe in ghosts or curses, but now? She would never forget the terrifying figure of the girl in the entryway of the plantation house.

Gracie drove to his little decrepit house. At ten pm, it was a little late to go visiting. She hoped he was awake.

She could see lights on inside as she pulled in the drive. She bolstered her courage and got out. He answered her first knock at the door. He pulled her into the house and into his arms.

She let him hold her for a moment, savoring the feel of him so close.

He listened intently, letting her vent.

"Jeanette told me yesterday that she had found out that my grandmother, Lydia Mason, was actually Belinda Mallory. She was either delusional or was completely lying about her identity. We really don't know which. But this only complicates matters worse," she continued and told him about Meredith, the curse, and Billy.

His eyes widened at the mention of Billy. "I've known them all my life, but I didn't know that they had had a son. Well, I think that after everything that has happened, maybe

121

we should call a halt on the renovation until we get all this resolved. I don't want my men added to the ghost collection. When they are safely gone, we will go dig up that box. Why don't I just do that on Monday? I'll tell the men to go home Monday morning and bring the box back here with me. Okay?"

"No! I don't think that is okay. I'm not sure you should even go with me to get the box. I think that dream was a warning to me that if you tried to help me, Edgar would kill you! You are sure not going without me." She was adamant.

"Okay. We will go together, wait until the men have left, then go get the box. But I think we shouldn't open it until we get it off the plantation," he said.

"It's a plan, then." She slipped her arms around him in a hug. "Thank you so much." She felt much better at having confided in him, and gratefully relieved that he had believed her.

He pulled her into his embrace and they sat for a long time, each lost in their own thoughts. It was then that Gracie took a long look at Brett. It wasn't as though she hadn't already memorized his face, his deep blue eyes, and blond wavy hair, but it did just now occur to her that he really looked a lot like Jeanette. Especially in the dim lamp light.

She pulled away from him, slightly. "Brett, you have never mentioned your family. Where are your parents?"

He gave her a half-smile. "My father died years ago. I never knew him. My mother fell ill when I was seven. I went to live with a neighbor. Then, one day, my mother came and told me that she was leaving. She wasn't well and had to make plans for us. That was the last time I ever seen her."

Gracie's eyes were tearing up, thinking about it. It had to be Sophie. "What was her name, Brett?" Gracie held her breath at his answer.

"Sophie. Sophie Galeman. I used to wonder where she was and if she would come back for me. She never did. No matter, really. I ended up with a good home."

"You never knew what happened to her?" Gracie was beginning to really cry now.

"I stopped wondering about it years ago, Gracie. Don't cry, honey. It doesn't matter in the least, now." He gave her a squeeze.

"Yes, it does," Gracie said, softly. "Jeanette is your sister."

Suddenly, he let go of her and jumped off the couch. "What?" he shouted.

"I'm afraid that it's true. Her mother's name was Sophie. She came from here. She had a baby and was ill. Perhaps she was planning on coming back for you, but she died, Brett. I am so sorry."

"This is impossible."

"Brett, you and Jeanette look alike. I didn't realize that until tonight, but your features are very similar. You have the same blue eyes, blond hair and it doesn't stop there. Your smile is the same. I don't know how I didn't see it before."

He sat back down. "I don't know what to think. I would be proud to claim Jeanette for my sister." He hesitated a moment. "Do you think she would agree to a DNA test? I think we both deserve to know, for sure."

"I'm sure she would. She is really feeling lost right now, not knowing who her family is. I think she would be thrilled. Do you want me to tell her?" Gracie asked.

"I don't know. Maybe we should do it together. What if you are wrong, Gracie?"

123

"I don't think I am. And I am so thrilled for both of you. You are the two people I love most in the world." Gracie kissed him quickly. "I'd better get home. Jeanette will be worried."

"Okay. See you in the morning, then."

*****

Monday morning, Brett and Gracie waited outside for everyone to get there, so they could announce the temporary halt on construction.

The crew arrived. Brett was talking with them when Gracie noticed someone standing by the carriage house. Whoever he was, he had her attention and motioned for her to go over there. She looked over at Brett and saw that he was deep in conversation. She decided to walk over. The boy seemed to want something. He must have been from a neighboring farm or something.

As Gracie neared, she saw him enter the carriage house. She walked in after him. She didn't see anyone in the dim light, and called out. She walked forward and felt the floor under her give out and she fell through. She would have expected only a couple of feet, but she fell in a hole more than ten feet deep. She hit hard enough to knock the breath out of her and felt her arm snap and it was bent under her. A wave of pain hit her and she heard her scream echo. She looked around her, but it was pitch black down there. She moved her legs. They didn't seem hurt. She thought maybe she could stand up. She tried, but the movement sent more pain washing over her. She started yelling though she was sure that Brett and the guys wouldn't hear her.

Out of the dark, she saw a white mist form in front of her. It turned into a small black boy, just a baby. He was the most beautiful thing that she had ever seen. He smiled sweetly and reached out a chubby little hand to Gracie. He touched her on the shoulder. He just stood near her, patting her shoulder to
124

comfort her. Gracie was so enthralled with him that she forgot her pain and forgot to yell. She just looked in the sweet, innocent eyes of the child and let him ease her pain.

"Gracie! Gracie!" She heard Brett yelling and the boy dissipated as the shouting began. Gracie found her voice.

"Brett! Brett, I'm down here!" she said, coming back to the real world.

"Gracie? I can hear you, sweetheart. How far down are you?"

"About ten feet, I guess. Brett, my arm is broken."

"Are you okay? Other than your arm?" he asked.

"I think so, but Brett it's really bad. I think I might pass out." She was really feeling faint and sick to her stomach.

She could see a flashlight flashing far above her.

"Honey, stay awake! I need you awake, okay? I'm coming down to get you," he told her.

"Okay, I'll try. Please hurry." She felt the pain throbbing strongly now.

He threw down a rope. He climbed down easily. His light found her face.

"Oh, baby! I see." He was looking her over with the light. "Honey, listen to me carefully. I'm afraid that we will have to wait for a stretcher to get you out. He walked to her good side and knelt down beside her. He caressed her hair. "Mike called fire and rescue. They should be here real soon. Just stay as still as you can."

He was really scaring her. She must have been hurt worse than she thought.

125

He saw the fear in her eyes. "Oh, you will be fine, sweetheart. It's looks to be just your arm." He wasn't going to tell her that the bone was sticking out and she was bleeding badly. He wasn't going to tell her just how scared he was that she would bleed to death before the paramedics got there. She did finally pass out. He was trying to put as much pressure as possible on her upper arm, but she was still bleeding.

Chapter Twenty-five

Gracie opened her eyes slowly. She didn't remember ever feeling this bad before. Where was she, anyway? She looked around the room. She saw Brett sleeping in a chair beside her bed. She was in the hospital.

Then, suddenly, it all came rushing back. She had fallen through the floor in the carriage house. She didn't remember anything after that. *Probably a good thing*, she thought. She tried to sit up, but pain shot through her arm. She gave a little shriek.

"Honey, it's okay," Brett said and she looked up to see him leaning over her. "It's good to see you awake." He smiled tenderly and kissed her on the forehead.

"What happened?" she asked.

"Do you remember falling in the carriage house?"

"Yeah. I saw this boy. He was young, a teenager, maybe, with red hair. He was waving to me. I thought that he must be from a farm around there or something. He went into the carriage house and I followed him. But when I came in, he wasn't there. I walked forward trying to see where he went, and then I fell. I don't remember anything else. How did you find me?"

"You won't believe it," he said with a smile. "A young, red-headed boy or ghost, if you prefer. Art thinks it was Billy." Then his eyes turned serious, "Honey, you were really hurt. You lost a lot of blood. Your arm broke and the bone went straight through an artery. They had to do several surgeries and gave you blood twice."

"Wow. Am I okay now?" she asked fearfully.

"Yes. You are okay. You have to be careful with that arm, though. The doctor thinks it will heal just fine. I was so scared. You've been out of it for days. The nurses said that you were just sleeping, but..." he squeezed her hand. Gracie saw his tears.

"Well, I'm okay now," she said and returned his squeeze. "I love you, Brett."

"I love you, too. He kissed her gently on the forehead. "I need to call Jeanette. I promised that I would call as soon as you were awake." He dialed the number and walked away from the bed. He talked for a couple of minutes, then came back to the bed.

"I'd better call a nurse to let them know you are awake," he said and hit the call button.

"All right, Brett, why did you walk away from me to talk to Jeanette? What are you not saying?" He looked like a fly caught in a spider web.

"Honey, there are things that you just aren't in any condition to hear right now. I promise you will know everything soon," he said, gently.

"Brett Galeman, I swear you'd better tell me right now!" Gracie tried again to sit up.

"All right, but don't hurt yourself," he said and propped up her pillows so she could sit up.

"Brett, what has happened? Is Jeanette and the kids okay?" Gracie was starting into hysterics.

"They are all just fine, Gracie, I swear," he said, and she calmed down a little.

"Then, what?" she asked.

"It's Meredith Grandy. She had a heart attack the other night. She died," Brett said, sadly.

"Oh," Gracie said, and burst into tears.

"I am so sorry," he said and put his arm around her.

"I-It was Edgar. It was, wasn't it?" she asked, searching his eyes.

"I don't know. She was an old lady. It could have been natural," he said, gently.

"But you don't think so," she said, knowingly.

"Art believes it was Edgar. He is scared for you, too. He knows that you are his great-granddaughter. That is why he helped you that first day. He didn't want you going to the house alone. He told me that the other night."

"I have to stop this. Meredith told me. Only I can break the curse. As soon as we get out of here, Brett, I have to get that box."

"Or we can simply burn the place down. Doesn't fire purify?" he asked.

"I don't know. I don't think that would work. The curse covers the entire property, not just the house. I have to stop it for good."

"I'm not sure we should even go back onto that property. Though, I would like you to see what you found."

"Found?" she asked, curiously.

"You fell into a tunnel. I went back to check it out. It is a series of tunnels under the plantation."

129

"You shouldn't have gone there alone." She shook her head.

"I'm not sure we should go back at all."

"Yes, Brett, we have to. Don't you see? There are so many innocent souls trapped there. They deserve to be released. If we do nothing, it will never end. Besides, I want to cleanse that beautiful house. It was built to be a loving home. One day it will be again, I swear." Gracie said, determined.

"Well, not until you are far better, Gracie. You will have to give yourself time to recover. Honey, I almost lost you. I can't go through that again." He grabbed her hand again.

"Is Jeanette coming?" Gracie asked.

"Yes. She had to go home for the kids. I promised I would call when you woke. She should be here in just a little bit."

The nurse walked in just then. "Well, it's good to see you awake, Miss Lawson." She came over to the bed and checked Gracie's vitals. "You appear to be just fine. The doctor said only a liquid diet for a couple of days. Can you rate your pain level for me? From 1-10."

"About three, maybe," Gracie told her.

"That's very good. You are getting some pain medication along with antibiotic through your IV. Please don't try to stand up by yourself for a couple of days. You could get dizzy and fall. You are much weaker than I'm sure you realize." The nurse turned to Brett, "Mr. Galeman, now that she is awake and doing well, you should really go home and get some rest. We will take good care of her."

"Thanks for your concern. I think I'll stay for a while longer," he told her.

"The doctor will be in to talk with you, shortly," she said to Gracie, "He has already given the order for some food."

"Thank you," Gracie said, as the nurse left.

"I hate that nurse!" Brett said.

"Well, she is right. There isn't anything you can do here, for now. How long have you been here?"

"I've showered here. I slept at night. I'm fine."

"Brett, go home. Get some rest. Please, for me. You can call me and check on me from there. Get a good rest and come back in the morning," Gracie told him.

He leaned down and kissed her, gently. "If anything happens, you will call me. I will be back later tonight."

Chapter Twenty-Six

Jeanette arrived only minutes after Brett had left.

"Oh, Gracie! I'm so happy you are awake." She ran toward the bed, smiling.

"Hi, Sis. I'm sorry if I scared you. How are the kids?"

"They are fine. They love it here. I think I've decided to stay, Grace. I'm going to sell Gram's house. I thought maybe Brett might have a house for us, too."

"That's wonderful, Jeanette. I am so glad you will be close," Gracie said. She could feel herself growing tired already.

"Gracie, I found out about Sophie. Brett told me. There really was a Lydia. She was a house maid at the plantation. Lydia and Sophie's mother were sisters and Gram and Lydia were best friends. The real Lydia was killed the night Gram left the plantation, according to Art. Gram had stayed in contact with Sophie. When Sophie had no one else to care for her when she got sick, she contacted Gram. I really don't know why she would leave Brett behind. She must have thought she would get well and come back for him. We are going to do a DNA test to be sure, but Art told us the whole story."

"I'm glad you know now," Gracie said, trying to take it all in, but she was too drowsy. "Jeanette, I'm so sorry, but I have to sleep now. When the doctor gets here, will you please wake me?"

"Don't be sorry, honey. And I will wake you, I promise," Jeanette said and patted her arm.

The doctor showed an hour later. He woke Gracie up, gently.

"Gracie, I am Dr. Jones. I am going to check your eyes and reflexes real quick." He shone a light in her eyes. He did this as he talked to her. "Your fall did a real number on your arm. You had artery, muscle, and tendon damage. Honestly, when we got you, there was little holding it together at all. We performed three separate surgeries. We are hoping for minimal damage. Truthfully, we won't know how successful we were until it heals. Afterwards, physical therapy will be recommended. In the meantime, you must be easy with it. No carrying, lifting, nothing. I don't want you to so much as pick up a pencil with that hand. It will likely take a few months to heal. I'm going to keep you here for another couple of days. If you seem strong enough on Friday, you can go home.

You will probably get full use back, but it might be a while. Luckily, your fiancé stated that you are right-handed. Right now, the hope is that you will eventually be able to carry with your left arm. Beyond that, we just don't know. You will be surprised how quickly you will adapt to being one-handed." He patted her right arm. "I will be by to see you tomorrow."

As he left the room, a young woman came in with a tray of food. Broth, applesauce, apple juice, and gelatin.

Jeanette walked to the bed to adjust Gracie's pillows for her so she could sit up.

"Well, at least I'm alive, I guess," Gracie said.

"It could have been so much worse, Grace. You had lost so much blood, they weren't sure that you were going to live."

"I'm sorry, Jeanette. I'm angry right now. I have something I have to do. I don't have months to wait. Edgar already got to Meredith. Who could be next? I have to find that box and end this thing before more people are hurt."

133

"Gracie, Meredith was an old woman who died of a heart attack. You don't know that it was Edgar. This curse has been going on for centuries. What difference can a few more months make?"

"It does, Jeanette. When I came here, I stirred it all up again. I am the last living Mallory. If I don't break the curse, then all those souls will be trapped of eternity. I can't allow that, Jeanette."

"They almost killed you, Gracie. How could you want to go back?" Jeanette was pacing the room.

"They didn't, Jeanette. It was an accident. I fell, but even if it had been deliberate, I would still have no choice. I have to find out how to break that curse," Gracie said, and started eating the lukewarm broth.

After Gracie ate, she needed to sleep again. She sent Jeanette home to be with the kids. True to his word, Brett was back at 10:00 that night. Gracie was awake when he arrived.

He looked much better and had showered and shaved. He walked to her bed and bent down. He caressed her cheek and tucked a strand of hair behind her ear.

"Hi," he said, softly, and kissed her. He pulled the chair close to the bed so he could hold her hand.

"Hi," she answered, and smiled slightly.

"Jeanette called me. She is upset over the plantation thing. Don't worry, honey, she just doesn't understand. She loves you, though."

"Oh, I know. This has been hard on you both. Getting hurt was my fault for not watching where I was going."

"I think Billy was trying to show you the trap door. I don't think he knew you would fall through. It was a piece of

134

pipe that your arm landed on, its sharp edge must have cut right through you. But what he was showing you was a tunnel. I didn't follow it, I thought we should do that together. Where you fell is a larger space, like a small room."

"I wonder where the tunnel goes?" she said.

"I think the tunnel is important. Gracie, I felt different down there. Lighter somehow. I think that the tunnels are where the good hide from the bad."

"I don't understand. You mean that only good spirits are down there?" she asked, confused.

"Yes. I think that Billy was trying to show you a safe place to go to."

"Oh. I had forgotten," she said, "There was a boy, Brett. Down in the hole with me."

"Was it Billy?" he asked.

"No. It was a very small boy, maybe two or three years old. He was a little black boy. He came to me and smiled, a sweet baby smile. He stood beside me and patted my shoulder. He was trying to comfort me. That's why I can't give up, Brett. I have to break that curse - for that child and all the others that are imprisoned." She gave him a mischievous look and changed the subject. "Did you tell the doctor that you were my fiancé?"

He grinned, "Well, they wouldn't let me in here otherwise."

Chapter Twenty-Seven

Home from the hospital, at last, Gracie came in and sat heavily on the couch. Brett left her there and went into the kitchen. He was back in less than a minute and handed Gracie a can of soda.

"Thanks", she said gratefully.

"We are going to have to put off our trip to the plantation, honey."

"No. We are going in the morning. I have to get that box. Do you have the necklace?" She looked up at him, daring him to argue.

"Yes, I have it," he said, looking grim.

"I wish we had a second one. Maybe we could find a talisman for you to wear tomorrow." She looked worried.

"I don't think that I'm the target. It's you that can break the curse. Why should they want to harm me?"

"Why did they harm Meredith? It was because she was helping me. I really don't like this. I think I should go alone."

"I'm not letting you go by yourself. Besides, you can't handle a shovel. Anyway, you are as weak as a kitten. I don't think you could make it by yourself."

He sat down and put his arm around her.

"We do it quickly, then," she said, "We will drive the truck directly to the field and park near the tree. We'll get out, dig it up, and be out of there in minutes. Then we will come back here to open the box. Later, we can explore the tunnel,
136

okay?"

"Okay," he agreed, reluctantly.

"I'll tell Jeanette that if we aren't back within thirty minutes, she should call the police department to come look for us."

"I don't think anything will happen, but better to be safe."

*****

Gracie was wearing the heavy necklace, but really, it was Brett she was worried about. She couldn't convince him to wear it instead.

All was quiet at the plantation. It was strange to see it deserted again, with no workers. They drove around the house and to the back field. Brett had brought Meredith's map along, and the tree was easy to spot. As they got out of the truck, the wind started to pick up. Brett grabbed the shovel from the truck bed and they walked to the tall oak tree. Gracie closed her eyes, trying to remember the exact spot from her dream. It had been about a foot from the base of the tree.

"Here," she said and kicked the grass in the correct spot. Brett started to dig. As he disturbed the ground, the wind started to blow stronger. By the time he struck the metal box, Gracie had to hold on to him to keep her balance. It had turned into a great storm. The tree limbs were bending toward the ground. Gracie looked up just in time to see a large tree limb falling toward Brett. She gave him a quick push just before it would have come down on his head. He looked startled as he saw the branch lying over the hole. He pushed it away with a heave, grabbed the box and grabbed Gracie's good arm to pull her back to the truck. The hurricane-like wind fought them for every step. They reached the truck and Brett pushed Gracie in first, thrust the box at her and got in. He had to struggle against the force of the wind to shut the door.

137

He started the truck and slammed it in gear. Dust and debris was flying everywhere as they flew down the drive and back onto the high-way. As soon as they left the property, the wind died down. They were both shaking as they drove back to Gracie's house.

They didn't say anything as they walked into the house. Gracie collapsed on the couch; her arm was aching from all the activity.

"Are you all right?" Brett set the box down on the dining-room table.

"Yeah, my arm just aches." Gracie grimaced as she changed positions to get comfortable.

Brett yelled up the stairs to Jeanette who came flying down the stairs at the sound of his voice.

"You got it? Already?" Jeanette asked and then looked at Gracie in concern. "Are you okay, Grace?"

"I'm okay. Let's just see what is in that box," Gracie said, determined.

"How do you intend to open it?" Jeanette asked.

Gracie went to her room and got the key she had found in the shopping bag weeks ago. For some inexplicable reason, she was sure that it fit that box. She went back downstairs with it.

Brett set the box on the coffee table. He gave Gracie a bewildered look as she held out the key. Taking the key from Gracie, he struggled to unlock it. The rusty metal was resistant, but finally opened.

All three of them looked eagerly inside. The contents seemed pretty random. There were three brightly painted stones, a feather, and what looked like two locks of hair; one black and one red. In the bottom was a book. Upon closer inspection, it was a journal. Belinda's journal.

"What is all this?" Jeanette asked, bewildered.

"I think maybe it is a Voodoo starter kit," Brett said, and grinned.

"This is hardly something to joke about," Gracie said, glaring at him. "But, yeah. It kinda does look like that."

"You need some aspirin, Grace?" Jeanette asked.

"No. I'll be fine. Just need to rest. Sorry for snapping."

"Well, now that the box mystery is solved, why don't you rest?" He led her to the living-room and helped her onto the couch. He sat beside her and said, "You can read that journal later."

"No, we'd better read it now. Jeanette, why don't you read it aloud," Gracie said, and lay back down, resting her head on Brett's knee.

"Okay. Just let me run up and check on the kids before starting," Jeanette said, and sprinted up the stairs.

Chapter Twenty-Eight

In the beginning, Belinda talked lovingly about her father, Edgar. It seemed that they were close. The journal had been a gift from him for her thirteenth birthday. It read like any typical teenage diary. Belinda did, indeed, have a best friend who was a maid in the house. Her name was Lydia. It seemed that Lydia, Belinda, and Billy were a trio, doing everything together with Belinda always the instigator in their mischievous adventures.

Then the journal stopped for several years and continued the year Belinda turned sixteen. Something was wrong with her father and had been for a while, and now Belinda was seriously worried. The kind and gentle man that he had been was turning mean and contemptuous. He had gotten into an argument at the church where he had been a deacon for many years. Suddenly no one in the family was allowed to attend. He spent more and more time shut in the den and came out only to chide the servants or yell at his wife.

Belinda had grown up with the stories of ghosts on the property and had heard all about the slave Dahlia and her ancestor, Alfred Mallory. It was intriguing, but Belinda had yet to see a ghost on the plantation. Not until now. Not until her father began to act strangely.

The first thing that was out of the ordinary was the whispering. It started one day and could be heard throughout the house on a daily basis. It was a muffled sound that could be heard in various parts of the big house. Belinda and her mother were both afraid and when they brought up the subject to Edgar, he called them superstitious fools. He told them that they were imagining it. He heard nothing. Then things began to move in the shadows during the night. Belinda was terrified to even sleep. It wasn't until she saw a real apparition that Belinda finally confided in her friends.

Lydia admitted to hearing the voices, but she hadn't seen anything else. It was Billy's idea to visit a Voodoo Queen in Atlanta. The three of them went together.

The woman gave them instructions, but didn't seem very positive about them breaking the curse. In order to break a curse like that there had to be blood from both sides of the curse -- Dahlia's and Alfred's. Billy was a descendant from the slave Dahlia as Belinda was from Alfred's. Their best bet was to intertwine locks of their hair and dip it in boiled blood root. She gave them a chant, but told them that it had to be done in the place the curse had been originally enchanted.

They left without much hope. How were they to find exactly where Dahlia had done her Voodoo?

It was Billy who told his mother about the trouble at the plantation and about their plan. Meredith had seen firsthand how haunted the plantation was when she was a girl working in the house. She also knew a secret that was passed down the generations from Dahlia. There was a series of tunnels under the plantation. They included several large rooms where slaves once gathered. One of these was Dahlia's Voodoo temple.

Belinda, Billy, and Lydia found the tunnels and did as they had been instructed. Instead of the desired effect, it seemed to worsen and the supernatural activity increased. Also, Edgar's behavior seemed even more bizarre. Several servants had left due to his abuse. Belinda feared the worst.

Billy and Belinda went back to their Voodoo queen and told her that their ceremony had not worked. It was then that she told them of the only way she knew to make it work. There had to be a union between the families. Only a child from that union would be able to remove the curse.

Belinda had loved Billy for years, but didn't think her father would let them marry. It was Billy that suggested that if she got pregnant, Edgar would have to give his consent. The father that Edgar had been a couple of years ago would have done that, but Belinda had her doubts about this new Edgar. This would also mean that the curse wouldn't be removed until the child was old enough to perform the ceremony. That would be years. It would be too late for Edgar. Or would it? If the story was true, then he would be trapped along with every soul that had died on the plantation since Dahlia first issued the curse.

In the end, they went ahead with their plan. They met every evening in the field by the pond. Within a few months, Belinda was pregnant.

That was the last entry in the journal.

Gracie was crying silently while Brett was caressing her hair.

"What I don't understand is what happened?" Jeanette said, laying the book on the table. "Why didn't your grandmother or mother come back to break the curse?"

"I think they died before getting the chance," Gracie said, quietly. "I wonder at what point Gram lost her mind. Was it Billy's death that caused it or being alone and pregnant?"

"So, can we safely say that Edgar was being influenced by Alfred or whatever evil force is on the plantation?" Brett asked.

"If it was Alfred, wouldn't he want the curse broken?" Jeanette asked, confused.

"Not if it would put an end to his reign on the plantation," Gracie observed, "I'm sure that it was not Dahlia's intention to give Alfred immortality." Another thought was growing at the back of her mind, but Gracie didn't dare give voice to it. If Edgar had been influenced by Alfred, could Belinda have also? Could she have murdered her daughter and granddaughter to keep them from what she had at first intended? It somehow made sense. Had her anger been unnatural when Gracie left? Had Gracie actually saved herself from the same fate by moving away when she had? Surely not!

143

Chapter Twenty-Nine

"You know, we could still burn it down and sell the property for farm land," Brett told Gracie later that evening. They were sitting on the couch at his shabby little house.

"I'm not going to lie to you, Brett. I'm really scared about this. I know that you think that my fall was an accident, but I'm not so sure. How am I going to get down in that tunnel with my arm in a sling? Sure is convenient for me to be suddenly handicapped."

"I will be right there with you. If you decide to do it. You really don't have to."

"I do have to and we both know it. Those people trapped there are my family. Both sides of my family. They are being forever tormented by Alfred. Meredith said so." Gracie noticed the strained look on Brett's face. All of this was taking its toll on him. It really was unfair of her to drag him into this. "Honey, if you don't want to do this, I understand."

"I know that the plantation means a lot to you, but I think you should wait a while. It's not going anywhere and you need time to heal. Do some research on voodoo. See if you can get more information on the plantation."

"Brett, what about Art? He is all alone now. We need to see that he is all right. I can't believe that I didn't get to go to the funeral. Art is my only living family."

"Art is staying in town at Rhoda's house. I can take you there tomorrow if you like. Right now, you need to get some sleep."

"I slept all afternoon." Gracie yawned.

"Well, sleep some more," Brett said and adjusted the blanket for her while she stretched out.

Brett waited until she was asleep, then grabbed the phone and took it into the other room.

Pouring himself a cup of coffee, he dialed and listened to it ring as he sat down at the kitchen table.

"It's about time! What happened? Did you find the box?" the creaky voice asked, excitedly.

"Ya, we got it. I don't like it, Art. It feels like we are using her. I didn't think it would be this dangerous. I was almost hit by a falling limb while digging that thing out of the ground."

"But you convinced her. She believes the story."

"She believes it. It wasn't hard. It is true, after all. I don't want to see her hurt, Art. Why aren't we just telling her the whole truth? I don't see your point in all this."

"She wouldn't believe it. Hell, I had a hard time believing it. Don't let your love blind you, boy!"

"And if she never forgives me for this?"

"This isn't about you or her; it is much bigger than that." Art gave a deep sigh.

"Art, you are wrong to think she wouldn't help if she knew the truth. She already loves this town and the people. She has cried for days over Meredith's death."

145

"She is an outsider! Even if she did buy your pretty little cottage and intends to stay, she cannot understand the gravity of it all. Alfred has to be stopped and by rights that plantation belongs to the town, not some naïve kid from Oklahoma. Brett, have you even asked yourself if she could handle the truth? She is just a fragile little thing. She just lost two grandmothers in a row. Alfred has killed her entire family. She and I are all that is left and I won't be here much longer. He has to be dealt with before we are both dead, too. If not, he will be truly immortal. That is how demons are born."

"And if he kills her? What then?" Brett asked, angrily.

"Then we are all doomed."

Those words resonated in Brett's mind late into the night as he tried to sleep. They were all doomed if the curse wasn't lifted. Alfred had to be banished, but were they just leading a lamb to the slaughter? What if the old man was just ranting? Was he risking losing the love of his life on something that may not even be real?

*****

Over the next few days, Gracie took Brett's advice and willed herself to heal quickly. She did some on-line research and found a practicing Voodoo queen living in Atlanta. It might be expensive, but she made an appointment to see the woman.

Chapter Thirty

Not being able to drive was the hardest thing about her arm, but Gracie had Brett drive her into Atlanta for her Doctor's appointment and to see the Voodoo Queen, Almira Hayes.

The doctor was impressed with how well she was healing, but insisted that she not attempt to use the arm yet.

Almira Hayes was something of a surprise. She was an older woman, possibly in her sixties. Other than her moon and star earrings that hit her shoulders, she looked more like a farmer's wife than a mystic. Her southern accent seemed a little too dramatic as she introduced herself to the two of them.

"So, what is it I can help you with?" she asked, giving Gracie a once-over.

"We have a curse to remove," Gracie said, looking around the shop at all the oddities.

"Okay. Well, I generally charge by the nature of the curse. First, are you positive that you have actually been cursed? If not, sometimes it can go awry and do damage to an innocent party."

"Well, it's not that I have been cursed, personally." Gracie went on to explain the situation. Almira listened intently until she was finished.

"Hmm. A generational family curse. I haven't had much experience in such matters. You will have to give me a few days to research this and find the best way to deal with it."

She turned and gave Brett a serious look. "This Alfred may be hard to deal with. Even after the curse is lifted, he may not leave without a fight, but you already knew this, didn't you?" Her eyes bore through him.

"I-a well, I had thought about it somewhat," he answered nervously.

"You have more than thought about it. If you intend to work together on this, your honesty is imperative. You cannot fight evil with deceit in your heart." She was still glaring at him as they left.

Gracie didn't say anything until they were both in the van and on their way home.

"What did she mean, Brett? And don't try to lie to me. The guilt is written all over your face." *Why would he be holding back on her?*

"I promise that I will explain, but there are others involved, Gracie." He glanced over and gave her a pleading look. "When we get back to town, we will pick up Art. He and Jeanette should both be present."

Brett looked back at the road. His heart was in his stomach. *It was all over between them now*, he thought. *She had trusted me so unconditionally and I betrayed her.*

*****

Everyone was seated in Gracie's living-room. Jeanette had arranged for one of the bridge club to watch the kids. Gracie was trying to brace herself for what was to come, but she knew that it was bad by the way Brett kept eyeing her guiltily.

She was surprised when it was Art that took over the meeting.

"Gracie, I am sorry to say that all of this was my doing. Brett was only doing as I asked." He looked puzzled for a moment as if wondering where to begin. "You see, my Meredith had inherited some of nature's spiritual gifts. She could see things and even speak to the dead. I know this may be hard to believe, but it is true.

We knew that you were coming before your arrival because Belinda had told Meredith. Belinda told Meredith many things. Some of which will shock and upset you to no end, which is why we didn't want to tell you the whole truth. Everything you know now is only part of it. You have suspicioned that Alfred had influenced Edgar, but the reality is so much worse." He hesitated and his grey eyes took on a haunted look. "Alfred actually possessed Edgar. Edgar was a good man, strong-willed and stubborn, but good. By the time of his death, he was stark raving mad and had murdered Billy and his own wife. He would have killed Belinda if she hadn't escaped." Art paused to let that sink in.

"If that were true, then why wasn't Edgar prosecuted?" Jeanette asked, unbelievingly.

"There wasn't enough evidence to convict him for it. Belinda was lucky that she escaped. Though she really didn't. You see, Alfred found that he could leave the plantation through Edgar. As a spirit, he was tied to the plantation, but with control of Edgar, he could roam at will. When Edgar died, that was all over for him. There was no one on the plantation left to possess. At least, not until Belinda showed up a few years later.

It seems that Belinda was better at fighting Alfred than Edgar had been, but still she shared a body with that demon.

149

He made sure that her offspring didn't live to break the curse, but was careful to make sure that it looked natural. He didn't want to lose his Trojan horse. When Gracie left Oklahoma, Belinda rejoiced, but Alfred was enraged. Belinda was strong enough to keep him from going after her, but in the end the fight was just too much for her heart. When she died, she was set free and Alfred returned to the plantation. She was so worried about you and came straight to Meredith."

Gracie didn't know how to process this information. Jeanette looked just as perplexed.

"Anyhow, though her urgency was to end the curse and weaken Alfred, I worried that you would suffer the same fate as Belinda. After all, he had already possessed two of his descendants. I don't think it is possible for him to possess anyone other than his own bloodline or he would have done it by now."

Jeanette looked in horror at Gracie.

"Don't worry, I'm still me," Gracie said, at her look. "So, how does Brett fit into the grand scheme of things?" she continued, bitterly.

"I asked Brett to keep an eye on you. Distract you, if you will, while we figured a way for you to break the curse and keep you dispossessed. If Alfred or Edgar get to you, you could really wreak havoc in this town. It would be letting a murderer on the loose. That curse has to be broken and you are the only one with that ability."

Gracie didn't hear a word after it sunk in that Brett was distracting her. How far did he go to distract her? Was their entire relationship fabricated to distract her?

"I think I've heard enough," she said, her pain-filled eyes met Brett's and then she ran up the stairs to her room.

Jeanette turned to her brother with cold eyes that could kill. "How could you use my sister that way? You couldn't just take her to the movies or invite her to church? Instead, you tell her you love her? I think you'd better leave."

Brett cowered under her gaze. He knew she was right. When he got to the door, he turned to face her. "I wasn't playing her, Jeanette. I truly love her. Come on, Art. I think we have done enough damage here." Art followed him out the door

Chapter Thirty-One

Gracie wasn't sure who to mourn first -- Belinda, her mother, her grandmother, Meredith, Billy? Just how many people had died at Alfred's hands? Maybe even Sophie. And then there was Brett! How could he have betrayed her that way? Why not just tell her the truth? Was it all a lie?

For the first time in days, Gracie took a pain pill for her aching arm. She lay back on the bed, too emotionally stressed to even sob.

She felt like she had been pulled into a vicious nightmare and she couldn't wake up. Ghosts and demons were not supposed to reside in the real world. She would never forget the look in Almira Hayes' eyes when she had looked at Brett that day. It was that moment that her world started to completely unravel.

What was she going to do now? Part of her wanted to pack up and leave it all behind. The other part wanted to stomp Alfred into the ground for good.

A thought then occurred to her. Belinda wasn't tied to the plantation because she hadn't died there. Jameson Mallory died before the curse so he wasn't tied either. If both of them were willing to stay of their own volition, then how could she walk away? Billy had died for nothing if she didn't complete this mission. With or without Brett, she had to stay and see it through.

The evil eye necklace may have fooled Edgar, but not Alfred, assuming that Belinda had worn it as well. She needed

protection. Hopefully, Almira would come up with
something.

*****

The next morning, a red rose appeared with a note
attached. It was from Brett. The note read, "I will send a rose
every day until you understand how much I love you, even if it
is for the rest of my life."

Gracie sighed and put it in a vase of water. She set it in
the center of the table and pondered it, thoughtfully. She
wasn't ready to deal with him just yet.

A week went by and the vase filled up. Still, Gracie
didn't call him.

"Gracie, it is obvious that the man loves you," Jeanette
told her that Friday. "You should have seen his face when he
left that night. If I hadn't been so mad at him, I would have
realized. You need to call him."

"I don't see a bunch of roses as proof of his love. How
can I trust him again? I'm not asking you to hate him,
Jeanette. He is your brother and I respect that."

Gracie's phone gave a shrill ring and she answered it,
glad to get out of the conversation.

"Miss Lawson, this is Almira Hayes. I think I have come
up with a plan to remove the curse. I will come there in two
weeks. It's better in the full moon. Let's make it Tuesday,
June 22. I will bring everything you need."

"Ms. Hayes, I need protection from possession. Is that
possible?"

"Yes. Actually, I've already thought of that. Your colored stones should help, as well. I will see you then."

Well, that was easy enough, Gracie thought. She just had to cool her heels for two more weeks.

"Who was that?" Jeanette asked, curiously.

"It was the Voodoo Queen from Atlanta. She says that she is coming here in two weeks to help me break the curse."

"Well, that will give you time to make up with Brett," Jeanette said, slyly.

"I have no intention of making up with Brett! Why do you think I should? Because of his roses?" Gracie gestured to the vase.

"Well, you aren't throwing them out, are you?" Jeanette said, pointedly.

Gracie rubbed her left arm, relaxing the ache.

"Grace, I know you love him. How long are you going to punish him?"

"How do you know he feels punished? He may be out on the town every night." Gracie had to giggle at her statement. Being out on the town in Swanson wasn't exactly a wild time. "You can go see him if you want to."

"I'm not going to go spy for you! If you want to see, go for yourself." Jeanette stomped out of the room.

Why should she go to see him? If he really wanted to see her, loved her, then why didn't he come here? Instead, he sent a note and roses.

154

*****

It was that night that Gram came to her. It was the real Belinda, not the mix of good and evil she had known. This woman was a softer version of the other.

Gracie was in that state of half-sleep and at first thought it was a dream. Gracie opened her eyes wide at the apparition. Not so much afraid but rather in a state of wonder. Gram looked at her in a loving manner that she had seen only on rare occasions. Then, two other ghostly images appeared behind her. She recognized Meredith right away. The other one was a beautiful black woman. It had to be Dahlia.

"We will all be with you, Darling. We will all be with you. You do not have to stand alone." Gram reached out and gently patted her hand before they all dissipated into nothingness.

A feeling of peace and comfort flowed over Gracie as the truth set in. If this was a war, then Alfred was very much outnumbered.

Chapter Thirty-Two

Gracie was up at dawn on the day that Almira Hayes was due. Tonight would be the full moon and whatever happened would be over soon. Almira was going to be here by one o'clock. They had a lot to go over before they actually did the ritual. Strangely, Gracie felt as she had when she had gotten the lead in the school play in the sixth grade. Her stomach was fluttering with nervousness.

It had been three weeks since she had spoken to Brett. The vase was full of roses in different stages of deterioration. She couldn't bring herself to throw any of them out though many were shriveled and dead.

Jeanette had informed him of the ritual and he, apparently, intended to attend. Gracie was almost as nervous about that as she was about the ritual altogether.

The extra couple of weeks had been good for her arm and the constant ache had left. Now it only hurt when she bumped it on something, which she did habitually.

Almira showed up on time and the woman, strangely was dressed more for a work-out in a gym than for a mystical ceremony. She had brought a large grocery back containing things that they needed. After setting it on the dining-room table, she looked around the room.

"Where is Mr. Galeman?" she asked, with a concerned look.

"He isn't here. He is coming to the plantation tonight, though," Gracie told her.

"No, no, no. He needs to be here. We can't plan this without him. Can you get him here?" Almira said, shaking her head.

"Well, we aren't really speaking just now," Gracie said, not making eye contact with the woman.

"Not speaking? Honey, I don't care if you are fighting or what you are fighting about, but you need him. He is part of your protection. Please, get him here."

Gracie turned to see Jeanette come into the room. "The kids are down for their naps," she said, cheerfully and smiled at Gracie.

"Jeanette, Almira thinks Brett should be here. Would you give him a call?" Gracie asked, her large, green eyes, pleading.

Jeanette gave her a disapproving look. "All right. You do know that you will have to talk to him once he is here, right?"

"Probably," Gracie said, noncommittally, and turned back to Almira, who was pulling things out of her bag and laying them out on the table.

"You don't have to worry about most of this stuff, Miss Lawson," Almira told her. "I'll do the mixing and most of the chanting. Removing the curse should be fairly simple--a little blood root mixed with some herbs with a lock of your hair. You will have little part other than your presence." She looked up into Gracie's face. "It is Alfred that you will have to manage mostly on your own. I will show you how and give you the protection, but defeating him will be up to you. I will tell you no more until everyone is here." She turned back to her work.

Gracie left her to it and joined Jeanette in the living room.

157

"Did you call him?" Gracie asked.

"I called him, Grace. He and Art will be here in a few minutes." Jeanette leaned back in the chair.

"Why is Art coming? I thought he was too afraid to go to the plantation," Gracie asked, surprised.

"I don't know. Maybe he just wanted to be here. He feels responsible for what happened between you and Brett."

"I suppose in a way, they were trying to protect me, too. I do love Brett. You know that, but I am afraid to trust my own judgment, anymore. I feel stupid, Jeanette."

"You aren't stupid, Gracie. Brett and Art were wrong for what they did, but they didn't set out to hurt you."

Gracie almost panicked when she heard the knock on the door, however, she answered it herself. Brett stood in the doorway and they just stared at each other for a few seconds. Gracie looked away first and stood aside to let them in. Art kept his eyes downcast as if ashamed to look at her directly.

They all went to the dining room and sat around the table to hear Almira's plan.

"This ritual tonight will be done in three parts. Who is actually going to the plantation?"

"All of us, aren't we?" Art answered.

"I have a babysitter coming, so I can go," Jeanette said, which was news to Gracie. She had assumed that it would be just herself, Brett, and Almira.

"I don't think anyone should put themselves in unnecessary danger," Gracie said.

158

"We want to be there, Grace. Don't worry. We won't interfere."

"Actually, the more the better," Almira said. "The more positive flow we have, the better the chance of cleansing. Now, the first part will be removing the curse. It should be a simple endeavor. All I ask is that you be silent during the ritual.

The second part will be between Gracie and Alfred. Have any of you heard of protection possession?" Almira looked at them curiously. When no one responded, she continued, "Well, what it pertains to is letting a spirit take possession of your body in order to protect or help yourself. This is what I am asking Gracie to do tonight. I will call out spirits to help her banish Alfred for good. I believe it will work."

"I don't like the sound of that!" Brett objected. "What if her body can't handle it? What if her mind can't?"

"She will have you to ground her and she will be protected. It will only last for a few minutes," Almira answered.

"How is this going to banish him? Exactly what am I supposed to do?" Gracie asked.

"After the curse is broken and the trapped souls are released, he will become much weaker. Not so weak, though, that he will be easy to handle. He will be angry and still quite a force to be reckoned with. You and Brett will leave the tunnel. You will place the painted stones in a circle around you with Brett as part of the stone ring. Together, with the others residing inside you, you will simply force him to leave. When that is accomplished, I can do a spiritual blessing and cleansing."

159

Well, that sure sounds complicated enough, Gracie thought. She had to become possessed to keep from being possessed. Her eyes roamed over toward Brett, who was seated at the opposite end of the table. He was looking at her intently. She wondered if she looked as terrified as she felt.

Chapter Thirty-Three

Brett drove them out to the plantation. Everyone was so silent that it felt like going to a funeral.

Almira had given each of them a carved wooden talisman to wear. Gracie wasn't sure if it was for added protection or just her version of a souvenir of the ritual. Either way, it seemed ridiculous to wear the ruby amulet with it.

"No one waste any time getting to the tunnel entrance," Almira was instructing. "If Brett is right, we should be safe once we are down there."

Gracie felt dread rise up as the plantation came into view. It was dark, but the moonlight lit the place well enough to see. It was 11:00 now. Almira wanted time to set it all up and finish the 'removing the curse' part before Gracie's midnight rendezvous with Alfred.

Brett slipped his hand into her right one and gave it a light squeeze as he helped her out of the vehicle.

The plantation was utterly still. There was not even a breath of wind, no chirping crickets, nothing but silence and a sense of being watched. It was a creepy sensation, but it was as if they were surrounded by people who were staring at them with invisible eyes. The heaviness in the air was stifling.

Brett had parked a few feet from the carriage house and he had to practically drag Gracie into the space that had held so much trauma for her, already.

Jeanette and Art followed with Almira in the rear. Brett, turned on his flashlight and descended first, then turned and helped Gracie, who was awkwardly climbing down using her one arm. Other than that one stream of light, it was pitch black down there.

One by one, they each turned on a flashlight and followed Brett. Gracie wondered how they would know where to do the ritual.

"Aww, God!" Jeanette shrieked. She had just walked into a cobweb and was wiping it from her face. "It's awful down here!"

"You can go back up if you like," Art said, amused.

Even for the cobwebs and dust, the atmosphere was significantly lighter in the tunnel than above.

"Uh…That's okay," Jeanette said, trailing behind.

The tunnel narrowed and they had to go single file for about ten minutes before the tunnel opened into a large shadowy room.

"This is it," Almira said, waving her flashlight around the room. Finally, it rested on what looked to be an altar of some sort that had been carved from the rock. She seemed unperturbed as she went directly to it and began to unload the contents of her paper bag.

Brett and Art had wisely brought along a couple of small lanterns and lit them. They sat them on either side of the long table, giving Almira more light to work by.

Jeanette and Gracie sat down on the dirt floor and watched the preparation. Almira filled her black pot with water and various unknown herbs. Likely, one of which was

162

the blood root she had mentioned earlier. She lit the white and black candles, and began chanting softly to herself. When she was ready, she motioned for Gracie to come forward and positioned her directly in front of the altar. Then she clipped a small piece of Gracie's hair and added it to the pot, which contained what now was a bright red liquid. Almira's face seemed to glow in the candlelight as she closed her eyes and continued her chant.

The rest of them watched as the candles created jumping shadows on the wall of the cavern and Almira stood shaking her hands in the air. As her voice, now reaching a maximum crescendo, echoed through the old tunnel walls, a sudden draft came from somewhere. It snaked through the tunnel and hit them like a blast of cool fresh air, blowing out the candles.

Almira's glowing face settled into a bright smile and she opened her eyes. The silence seemed deafening at the sudden cease of her chanting. "It is done. They are free."

*****

The first part was over and now, Gracie's fear had doubled. In only a few minutes she would have to face Alfred. She had no idea what to expect.

The Voodoo queen handed Brett the stones and reminded him of what his part was. She grabbed Gracie by her good hand and her large brown eyes looked into hers.

"There is no reason to fear. You are protected. These spirits that will enter are not going to harm you. Just don't fight them. Let them help you."

The entourage headed back the way they had come. And up the ladder. What had been a silent, still night when they had went underground was anything but that now. The wind was reminiscent of the day they had unburied the box. It was blowing hard enough that they had to fight to stay upright. Brett held on to Gracie's hand and pulled her along. The group gathered in front of the mansion.

"Brett, the stones!" Almira shouted, her voice nearly lost in the sound of the storm. Brett had to let Gracie go in order to set the stones. He made a small circle around Gracie with himself as part of the link. When he looked back toward Gracie, he no longer saw the fragile girl he had pulled through the tunnel. She suddenly seemed taller, stronger, and she had lost her fear entirely. She stood glaring into the wind with an anger and purpose he had never seen before.

Chapter Thirty-Four

As soon as Brett let go of her hand, Gracie felt a different swirling around her apart from the wind. Almira's chant wasn't necessary this time as she felt each of the entities enter her body. She immediately recognized each of them-- Belinda, Meredith, and Dahlia.

As the wind continued to whip around her, she felt anger like never before building inside her. All of the tragedy that Alfred had caused flickered through her mind like a movie strip gone mad. She let all of it flow through her being.

She could hear the chanting, but didn't realize at first that it was coming from her own mouth. It was Dahlia, at first, but soon the other three spirits encased in the small body joined her. What came out was a chorus, drawing out Alfred.

The others, Jeanette, Art, Almira, and Brett watched in wonder as a brilliant blue aura began to surround Gracie. Her eyes turned to focus on something in front of the house. Whatever she saw was invisible to the rest.

Gracie saw the demon, Alfred, stumble out of the house as if pushed from behind by an unseen force. The apparition gave an angry roar that frightened Gracie and she lost her focus for only a moment. She looked around, bewildered and her eyes met Brett's. His eyes sent her the message she needed. She centered in on Alfred once more and let the spirits surge through her. Alfred was caught and doubled his efforts sending tree limbs and dust flying, but Gracie was safe within the circle. The ground beneath them began to shake.

Alfred was twisting violently to get loose of an invisible restraint and Gracie could see that they weren't going to be able to hold him for long. To her right, she could see Jeanette, Art, and Almira, clinging to each other in order to stand against the wind. Alfred saw her distraction and raised a hand in their direction.

Dahlia took over the reins and held up Gracie's good hand. A blue ball of light appeared in the open hand and projected directly at Alfred. The ball hit him square on and both exploded in a brilliant blue and white light.

Gracie went limp and fell to the ground as the maternal souls left her. The plantation seemed darker in the night after the blinding flash. She felt Brett's arms around her and heard the voices of the others as she went into a dead faint.

*****

She woke up hours later with the morning light streaming in her bedroom window. She looked over and saw Brett sleeping in the chair by her bed. It reminded her a little of waking up in the hospital. She didn't want to wake him, but she wanted to know what had happened.

She looked down at herself and realized that she was still fully dressed and filthy from the tunnels. She decided to get up and take a shower before waking him.

When she stepped out of the bathroom, fully dressed in clean blue jeans and a t-shirt, Brett was awake and waiting for her.

"That's totally unfair. You look as fresh as a daisy while I am still covered in dust," he said, grinning at her.

"We did it, didn't we?" Gracie asked, giving him a serious look.

166

"Oh, yes, you certainly did it, babe!" He stood and pulled her into his arms. She put her arms around his neck to receive his kiss, but he pulled back and looked at her quizzically. "Are you sure you are alone in there?"

Gracie couldn't help, but tease. She gave him an empty, cold stare and said in a monotone voice, "I'm sure. The question is, which one am I?"

"Gracie, that isn't even funny!" he said, in consternation.

*****

A year later, they were celebrating the opening of the Mallory Plantation Retirement Home with a Grand Ball. The room sparkled with newly restored blue and gold and hummed with the voices of guests.

Gracie stood behind the punchbowl, watching as Art swept Veronica Brewer across the floor in a graceful waltz. Her great-grandfather was looking rather handsome and dapper at his age. He had promised to dance only one round.

Gracie was amazed at the turn-out. Half the town was there. She spied Brett dancing with a giggling Jeanette. She looked lovely in a blue gown.

The orchestra played the last few strands and Gracie met Brett's gaze across the expanse.

"You'd better go dance with your prince." Gracie hadn't noticed Mary Joe coming up behind her. "I'll take over. Go on."

Gracie grinned at her friend and went to join Brett. The pearl colored tile seemed to glow beneath their feet as they glided across the room.

167

"You know, for a carpenter, you are pretty light on your feet," Gracie whispered in his ear.

"With that heavy stone around your neck, it's a wonder you can move," he teased, his blue eyes dancing. She had decided to wear Belinda's necklace tonight for luck.

"It's the one on my hand that is weighing me down." She held up her hand in evidence, the diamond glittered under the light of the chandelier.

"Too bad, that one stays on." He gave her a stony look and tightened his hold.

Standing within the arms of the man she loved and surrounded by the warmth of friendship and family, Gracie felt that more than the curse of Dahlia had been lifted.

Part 2

Lydia's Legacy

Chapter One

The bridge club met three times a week and it was getting tiresome. It was Marilyn Marrs turn to host. Marilyn lived in a small house a few doors down from Grace.

"You know, I'm getting bored with bridge. Why don't we find something else to do?" Gladys McCarthy said, looking around the table at the rest of her friends.

"My grandkids left a few games in the closet, years ago," Marilyn offered. "I've never really looked at them. They might be fun."

"Let's get them out and see what you have," Lucy said, curiously, smiling a big false-toothy grin.

Marilyn looked away quickly, thinking that she sure hoped her own teeth didn't look that grotesque. She stood and went to the other room, coming back moments later with two boxes of old board games.

She set them on the table and pulled the games out of the first box, one at a time while the others looked eagerly on. There was a Monopoly game, Aggravation, Sorry, Clue, Scrabble and dozens more.

"Hey, what's that?" Veronica asked, looking into the next box. She pulled a strange-looking board out and blew off the dust. The rest of them coughed and waved their hands at the dust in the air.

"I've seen one of those before," Gladys said. "It's one of those Ouija boards. My son had one. I made him throw it out. They are dangerous. Calling out to dead spirits and stuff."

"It looks like fun," Lucy said. "It's not real, you know. It's just a game."

"We could call on all of our dead friends. I'll call Paula Miner. You remember how angry she'd get when some poor kid would trample her daisies? I swear little Charlie Brewster used to do it once a week just to hear her holler. He-he-he! " Marilyn laughed, shaking her gray head.

"It's not kind to speak ill of the dead," Gladys reminded her and Marilyn suddenly looked contrite.

"I say, we give it a try. We deserve a little thrill in our lives," Veronica piped up. "We need to get some candles and close the curtains. Gotta get a little atmosphere going in here."

"Oh, this is gonna be good. I'll grab the cookies and get some more coffee started," Lucy said.

"This can't be a good idea," Gladys said as she closed the draperies.

"Turn off the lights," Veronica said.

"Not yet. We haven't read the directions," Lucy objected.

"What directions? All we found was the board and this triangle thingy taped to it," Veronica said.

"I saw it in a movie once," Marilyn said. "All we have to do is everyone touch that piece and it moves over the letters to spell things out. We ask questions and it answers."

"Sounds silly to me. I'll take notes while you old fools do what you will," Gladys said.

"Don't be a stick in the mud," Lucy whined as Gladys fetched a notepad and pen out of her purse.

171

Lucy set a tray with four cups of coffee and a plate of cookies on one side of the table. Marilyn had dug a few fat candles out of the buffet and set them on the other end. With the Ouija board in its place of honor in the center, they were ready to begin.

Marilyn lit the candles and Lucy turned off the lights.

They tried several questions directed at people that had died recently and got no results that seemed accurate. The answers they got were just a jumble of letters that didn't make sense, each of them pulling the marker in a different direction. They were having a good time, though, and laughing at the nonsense. They were ready to give it up when Lucy stopped them from turning the lights back on.

"Let's try one more. We have done several people that we know, but what about someone important. Like a forefather of the town," she said, and paused to think. "Oh! I know, let's do Alfred Mallory." It seemed just naughty enough to appeal to them all. None of them were aware of the incident at the plantation only a few months ago.

"Okay," Marilyn agreed and they all resumed their positions as all three fingers touched the marker. "It's your idea. You ask the question."

"Alright." Lucy hesitated a moment to let a question form in her mind. "Alfred Mallory, come to us here. Tell us if you can hear us," she said in an oddly spooky voice.

Immediately, the marker moved under her fingers. It moved directly to the 'yes' written on one corner of the board.

"You moved it," Marilyn accused her.

"I did not!" Lucy denied it.

"Well, someone moved it," Veronica said, looking at them both unbelievingly.

172

"Well, let's ask another question. It's your turn," Lucy said and elbowed Marilyn.

Marilyn thought for a moment. "If this is really Alfred, what is your middle name?" Hopefully, none of her friends would know this and they could look it up later to confirm.

The marker moved, seemingly of its own accord around the board. The word 'Thomas' was spelled out with no mistake or hesitation.

All of them looked at each other questioningly.

It was Veronica's turn next and the candle light gave her wrinkled, skeletal face an even scarier look than normal. "If this is Alfred, appear to us." There was a collective gasp around the room at her boldness.

Suddenly, the table began to shake. A moment later, a black smoke began to seep out of the center of the board and a putrid smell filled the room. A white flash like lit up the room and Gladys screamed and fell back in her chair clear to the floor.

Marilyn jumped to her feet and turned on the light. Everything looked perfectly normal except the smell that remained and Gladys lying motionless on the floor.

Lucy and Veronica leaned over their friend in concern. Marilyn could see the glazed look in Gladys' face, and gasped, knowing immediately that her friend was dead.

Chapter Two

Nine months later, Jeanette was at the opening ball for the Mallory Retirement Home. Her brother, Brett, was dancing with the girl that she had always thought of as her sister. *They make a beautiful couple*, Jeanette thought. The curly blond hair that made Brett look rugged and handsome, made Jeanette feel unkempt. Her mop of unruly curls never did what she wanted it to.

Six-year-old Aubrey was wearing a yellow, satin dress and looked just like the little princess she was pretending to be. Jasper looked adorable in a light blue suit and bow tie. They were both sitting at a table, stuffing themselves with cake. Aubrey dropped icing on her skirt.

"Oh, Aubrey," Jeanette said, wetting a napkin in her water glass and dabbing at the frosting.

"Sorry, Mommy. Look! Uncle Brett and Aunt Gracie." The couple stopped at the table.

"My, don't you look lovely," Gracie said, bending down to talk to the children.

As Jeanette looked up at Brett, a man sidled up beside him. "Charlie, I'd like you to meet my sister, Jeanette," Brett introduced his friend.

"Charles Maxwell," the man said, holding his hand out for a shake. He was taller and thinner than Brett. He had short dark hair and a neatly trimmed beard. She looked up into warm brown eyes. "Would you do me the honor?" He motioned to the dance floor.

"Oh, thank you, but I can't leave the kids," Jeanette replied.

"Oh, go on," Gracie urged. "I'll watch my adorable niece and nephew for a few minutes." She sat down at the table and grinned at Jasper whose mouth was covered in white frosting. "Looks like you have a white beard and moustache."

With no way to get out of it gracefully, Jeanette accepted.

Charles Maxwell, quite skillfully, twirled her into a waltz. She was facing him, suddenly with a smile, his hand on her waist.

"Your children are adorable," Charles told her.

"Thank you. They're my pride and joy." She smiled back. "So, have you known Brett for long?"

"Actually, all my life. We've been best friends for years. I've been working in Oklahoma for the last few years. Brett is the happiest I've ever seen him. He was thrilled to find that he has a sister. I was surprised to find him remarrying. Gracie seems to be a nice girl, too."

"Gracie is a nice girl. We were raised together, you know," Jeanette said.

"Really? No, I didn't know. Brett and I haven't quite finished catching up."

Jeanette nodded in understanding, feeling unbearably shy.

"So, where is your husband?" he asked, innocently.

"Oh, I'm divorced," Jeanette said, a little embarrassed.

"Well, whatever man let you get away must have been insane," he said, flirtatiously.

Jeanette could feel herself blush though she knew he was just being nice. The music stopped and she stepped away. It was Gracie and Brett's night to shine. She thought she had better get back to her kids.

"Thanks for the dance, Mr. Maxwell. I imagine the children are ready to go to bed." She smiled at him, politely and went back to the table. Jasper was already nodding into his cake.

"Why don't you put them down in the lounge," Gracie told her. "That way you can rejoin the party."

"Thanks, Grace," Jeanette said and picked her son up, carrying him over her shoulder. She took Aubrey by the hand and led her across the ballroom.

She laid each child on the wide sofa in the lounge, taking off Jasper's jacket so he could be comfortable. They were both asleep within minutes. She kissed them both and went to join the party.

She noticed Mary Joe working behind the refreshment table and went to relieve her for a while.

"I saw you dancing with Charlie Maxwell," Mary Joe said with a smirk. "He is looking rather dashing tonight, isn't he?"

"He seems nice enough," Jeanette answered.

"He was in our class at school. Always teasing the girls with his charm. I don't think there was one of us that wasn't half in love with him," she giggled.

"Why don't you ask him to dance?" Jeanette suggested.

"It's obvious that I'm not the one he is interested in," Mary Joe replied, not seeming jealous in the least. Several times, he had glanced their way.

"He's just curious because I'm Brett's sister."

"If you say so," Mary Joe said, looking amused.

"It's your turn to go have some fun. Shoo!" Jeanette told her, but couldn't help one last glance at Charles before turning her attention to the task at hand.

From her vantage point, she could see the entire ballroom. Brett and Gracie had done a beautiful job restoring it. It was like stepping back in time into a dream. The blues and gold on the walls reflected on the cream colored tile. The added touch of mirrored inside walls made the huge room look even larger. It was truly gorgeous.

Sadly, the place wasn't nearly as full as it should have been. A few new residents that had come from other towns and their families along with Brett, Charlie, Gracie and Mary Joe. Maybe thirty people altogether. Jeanette hoped for Gracie's sake that the town would lose its fear of the plantation.

*****

Belinda Mallory watched the party from her own private corner. Of course, no one could see her. When Dahlia, Meredith and all the others at the plantation had gone, Belinda had stayed behind. She had some unfinished business. This child, who was her dearest friend's great niece and so very close to Belinda's heart was still floundering for her place in life.

Belinda had failed both girls in life. In death, she would be sure they were taken care of. Oh, she had made sure they both had money—enough that they no longer had to be dependent on any man, but happiness was something that was much harder to attain.

Gracie was easier. She had a natural enthusiasm for life that Jeanette lacked. Her sweet, timid Jeanette had been crushed like a dainty flower by her husband's indifference. It

177

would take time for her confidence to build. She had a lot to learn and she would have to do it very soon.

Alfred was gaining power fast and Jeanette would have to find the inner strength that she had no idea she possessed. It wasn't just the plantation at stake this time; it was the entire town of Swanson. Belinda would do what she could to help, but ultimately, it would be up to Jeanette to finish it.

Chapter Three

Jeanette rode home with both kids laying across her lap. The ball had been lovely. She had taken a hundred pictures of everyone. Gracie and Brett had already rented to several residents. They were doing pretty well. Their wedding was coming up and she had been thinking about things all evening. She and the kids needed to find a place of their own.

It was really awesome to have her brother marry the girl she considered her sister. After finding out that she and Brett were siblings, there were all kinds of questions that she just couldn't get straight in her mind. Finally, a year later, it was beginning to sink in. Their mother, Sophie, was the great niece of the real Lydia. Lydia was Belinda's best friend and a maid at the plantation who had disappeared on the same night that Billy was killed. Belinda took over Lydia's identity. Maybe because of a psychosis due to the trauma or maybe it was deliberate so that Edgar couldn't find her. Apparently, she convinced herself of it and that belief lingered until her death. Jeanette wondered vaguely if the real Lydia was laying in Belinda's grave in the cemetery in Swanson. It seemed that Lydia's family had never contested the fact that Belinda wasn't Lydia. Perhaps they had known the truth and didn't want to expose her.

Gram (Belinda) had come home a few times over the years. On her last trip in the eighties, she had brought Sophie, along with her baby daughter, Jeanette, back to Oklahoma with her to take care of. Brett had already been staying with a neighbor so he was left there to attend school, but Sophie had promised to return after she was well. When Sophie died, Brett's foster parents had wanted to keep him and Gram kept Jeanette.

Their father had left Sophie and took off for parts unknown as soon as he realized she was sick. Gram must have felt obligated as she was still claiming to be Lydia, the great aunt. Jeanette was upset that Gram had hid from her all those years that she had a brother. Perhaps she had thought that she would leave her if she'd known. Who can tell?

It is nice to find some people who had met my mother, though, Jeanette thought.

She felt as though she belonged here and intended to stay in Swanson with the little family she had left. According to Brett, the rest of the family had moved to Florida years and years ago. He had never met any of them. It didn't seem to bother him in the least, but it did bother Jeanette. She didn't have Gracie's knack for accepting everything at face-value and living in the moment. She kept wondering what family she still had left out there.

They pulled up in front of the house and Gracie helped her carry the kids upstairs and into their beds. Jeanette tucked them in, lovingly knowing that in just two days, they would be gone. Her, now, ex-husband, Jim had been granted joint custody and they were to spend the summer in Oklahoma with him and his new girlfriend. It was tearing Jeanette apart. She had never been away from them for more than a few hours since they were born. Maybe, it would give her time to get their lives in order.

Jeanette knew that Brett had several houses for sale in town. She would talk to him about it soon. She had all of their stuff in storage and it would be pleasant to have her own things around her again. Gracie's house was nice, but they all needed their privacy. She and Gracie had taken the last year to get to know each other again and the kids had loved it, too. Now, it was just time to move on.

Back in her own bedroom, she took off the powder blue ball gown and hung it back in her closet. Aubrey wasn't the only princess at the ball that night. Thanks to Gracie, Jeanette had felt like one, too. Gracie had helped with her make-up and hair, pulling Jeanette's unruly curls into a neat bun with tendrils to frame her face. Jeanette had actually felt pretty tonight. Although she was sure that Brett had suggested it, it had made her feel good when Charles Maxwell had asked her to dance.

She gave herself one last smile in the mirror before disassembling her hair and taking off the make-up.

Chapter Four

It was really sweet of Brett to take a day off to show Jeanette a few houses. There were three that he thought would be most appropriate. When she made her choice, he insisted on gifting it to her and wouldn't take no for an answer.

They stood in the living-room of the house of her choice. It was the perfect location, only a block from the elementary school. It had four bedrooms. One downstairs and three upstairs so the kids could each have their own room with her own close by. The back yard was as big as Gracie's, if not a little bigger—plenty of room for a swing-set and sandbox. The kids would be so excited.

"Oh, Brett, thank you so much!" She gave her brother a hug. She didn't usually show affection that way with anyone but her kids, but she was overwhelmed by his gift. He had done an amazing job on the house and like Gracie's his attention to detail was evident.

He grinned and blushed slightly with pleasure. "I'm happy I could do something for you. You can move in whenever you like." He handed her the keys. "I'll have the deed fixed up for you in a few days. Do you need help getting your things out of storage?"

"Thanks, no. I didn't bring much. Mostly clothes and the kids' things. I let Jim have most everything. I thought it would be easier to replace it than move it." She gave him a half-smile. "Maybe, Gracie or Mary Joe would like to go shopping with me."

"Do you want a ride back?" he asked.

"Naw. It's only a few blocks. I'd like to spend some time here to look things over, if it's okay."

"Sure. It's your house." He whistled a light tune as he walked down the steps.

When he was gone, she went back through the rooms, one at a time, and made a mental note of what she would need. She would enjoy surprising the kids with brand new bedrooms. They would be happy to have all their toys and things that have been in storage, too.

*****

The next day, Jeanette was out with Gracie and Mary Joe for a shopping day. She concentrated on appliances and furniture, but she had sprung for outdoor play equipment for the kids and patio furniture so she could be comfortable outside with them.

They took a break for lunch and ate at the café. They met Art on his way out. He was looking even more frail than usual, Jeanette thought, but he greeted them in his usual chipper fashion.

After they had ordered, Mary Joe turned to Jeanette.

"I saw the bridge club the other day. They all seem so sad since Gladys died. She was kind of the leader of the bunch. It's been a long time and they still seem to be in mourning."

"It's been a while back, but they were awfully close. All like a family, really," Jeanette said, reaching for a menu.

"When do you have to take the kids?" Mary Joe asked, realizing the reason for Jeanette's preoccupation.

"Tomorrow. They are flying out of Atlanta," Jeanette told her.

"Brett and I are going to the airport, too. To see the kids off," Gracie said.

"So, what are you going to do with all this time on your hands?" Mary Joe asked Jeanette.

Jeanette hadn't thought about it much. Really, she had no idea. "I don't know. I thought about finding a job—volunteer work or something."

"What about going back to school?" Gracie asked. "You were great in photography. You could take some classes over in Atlanta. Maybe, even open up a photo shop here in Swanson. They don't have one here."

Jeanette let that idea settle over her for a moment. Could she really do that? She would love it. Wasn't she a little old to go back to school, though?

"That would be just the thing here," Mary Joe said, exuberantly. "I heard just the other day that the Cathers had to take their daughter to Atlanta to have her senior pictures done. There hasn't been a photographer in Swanson since Old man Redding died fifteen years ago."

"What do you think, Jeanette?" Gracie asked. "I think you'd do great."

"Well, I've never considered myself professional, but if I did take the classes, I could be, right?" Jeanette said, a little unsure.

"Of course," Mary Joe said. "I've seen some of the pictures you've taken of the kids. They are gorgeous."

It was certainly something to think about. She had to do something with her life. Why not something she loved?

*****

Jeanette, Gracie, and Brett stood about ten feet away from Jim at the airport.

The kids were already crying though Jeanette had tried to prepare them. Jeanette hugged them with a promise to call them every night before bed. She did her best not to shed tears in front of them. She didn't want them to think that it was a bad place they were going to.

Jasper wouldn't let go of her and finally Jim gave her a glare while he ripped Jasper from her arms.

Brett started forward, but Gracie held his arm. Jeanette waved at Aubrey while she walked away with Jim, Jasper howling all the way to the gate.

"They'll be okay," Gracie said and put an arm around Jeanette.

"They don't know him at all," Jeanette said, regretfully. "Even when he came home, he paid no attention to them and then he was gone, again. I hope he spends some real time with them." Really, she knew that it was more about revenge than wanting to have the kids. He was angry because Gram had fixed it so that he couldn't touch her money. Jeanette seriously wondered if he'd been waiting for Gram to die before divorcing her.

She was over her hurt from the divorce, or at least, she wasn't upset about his absence at all. Now, watching him walk away with her babies was the hardest thing she had ever done.

Chapter Five

Jeanette spent the next couple of days packing up her things from Gracie's house. Going through the kids toys, she was amazed at what they had accumulated in a little over a year. Gracie and Brett had spoiled them relentlessly, she realized. With what they had in storage, they would have way too much.

Gracie came into the room as she was boxing things up.

"I'm gonna miss you guys being here so much," Gracie said.

Jeanette looked up and grinned. "We'll just be a couple of blocks away. Besides, you'll be too caught up in wedded bliss to notice."

"Speaking of the wedding, I hadn't gotten the chance to ask you to be my maid of honor. I was thinking of Mary Joe and Maria for bridesmaids. What do you think?" Gracie asked, happily.

"I think that sounds perfect," Jeanette said. "I would love it, thanks." *Gracie will make a beautiful bride*, she thought to herself.

"What about blue and cream for the dresses. That way, I could have a bouquet of blue flowers. I want to go dress shopping next week."

"Are you having the wedding at the plantation?" Jeanette asked, thinking that Gracie had chosen colors to match the ballroom.

"Would anyone show up if I did?" Gracie said, looking glum.

186

"Well, too bad you couldn't spread the word that the place has been cleansed," Jeanette said in sympathy.

"They wouldn't believe it. They like the idea of having a haunted mansion. It will be years before the place loses that reputation, if ever. At least, we were able to get a few residents from out of town."

Jeanette taped the top of the box she had just fillied with stuffed animals and set it aside. "Where, then? The church?"

"I thought about central park. It has that lovely gazebo," Gracie said. "Then having the reception at the plantation. The people that matter aren't afraid to come there and the tenants might really enjoy it."

"That will be nice," Jeanette agreed, taping the bottom of another box to fill.

"When will your stuff be delivered?" Gracie asked.

"This afternoon. I can be pretty well moved in tomorrow. I just have to get household items. You know, like dishes and silverware."

"Well, that shouldn't be too hard. Are you moving all this stuff in your car?" Gracie asked in disbelief.

"Oh, no. A couple of teenagers from the church offered to help with their pick-up. They will be here in a couple of hours. I'm almost finished, anyway." She grinned up at Gracie. "You are planning to come with me to see the house this afternoon, right?"

"Yep. Mary Joe is taking care of things at the plantation. I'm all yours for the afternoon. I thought you could use the help."

"Thanks. I really want the house to look perfect when the kids see it for the first time." She was starting to feel melancholy all over again.

*****

That afternoon, true to her word, Gracie helped Jeanette get her new house in order. The furniture and appliances arrived and before she knew it, the house looked like a real home.

Jeanette had chosen a cranberry colored sectional couch with extra wide cushions that the kids would love to curl up on. There was a huge square ottoman and a recliner to match.

With everything set up and new beds upstairs, there was really no reason why she shouldn't stay there that night, she decided, looking around her with a sense of pride. She could get her things out of storage tomorrow and finish unpacking.

After Gracie went home, Jeanette finished hanging her clothes in the closet and looked around at all the empty boxes. She stacked them together and went downstairs to take them out to the garbage. As she did, a man came out of the house next door.

He turned and looked at Jeanette. His brown hair hung over his eyes and he gave a half-wave and pushed his glasses up the bridge of his nose before he looked down at his feet and wandered slowly back to his door.

He looks a little creepy, Jeanette thought, wondering why any man would think that plaid shirts were in style. She reminded herself to lock her doors at night.

That night, Jeanette slept fitfully, with dreams that she didn't quite remember. Then, near morning, she dreamed that she was in a field, lying in tall grass. Hovering over her was a dark form with a scythe in his hands. His horrific face became clear and his eyes glowed red. She screamed as she saw the blow coming.

She sat straight up in bed. It took a moment for her to realize that it had only been a bad dream. A very realistic bad dream, she thought as she remembered those eyes. She got out of bed and took a quick shower to wash the sweat from her body.

Jeanette pulled back the shower curtain and wrapped a towel around her middle. She began to step out of the shower when she saw a shadow standing in the corner of the small room. She backed into the shower with no other place to go. The shadow stepped into the light.

Jeannette recognized Gladys McCarthy, but she looked much different in death. Her gray hair was no longer in a bun, but hung around her head in a stringy mass. Her skin seemed to sag everywhere and her eyes were wild.

"Go, he's coming," Gladys said, in a broken voice, then she screamed it, "Go! He's coming!" And then the apparition disappeared.

Jeanette cowered in the shower, crying, muffling the sound with her arm over her face.

Chapter Six

Later that morning, Jeanette had recovered from her episode in the bathroom. She was convinced that somehow the apparition had been leftover from her dream and she hadn't been quite awake yet. Terrifying, but not real at all.

Jeanette was working on getting the kids' rooms decorated. She was doing Aubrey's room in butterflies and rainbows and Jasper's room in rockets and spaceships. She had found some stick on murals for the walls and was adding a matching border in Jasper's room when the doorbell rang.

She got down from the ladder and went downstairs. She peeped through the window and saw that it was the weird guy from next door. She opened the door and he stood there awkwardly with a plate of cookies in his hand.

"I came over to welcome you to the neighborhood," he said in a mumble and handed her the plate.

"Thank you," Jeanette said, feeling obligated to let him in. "Why don't you come in? I'll make us a cup of coffee, Mr...uh?"

"Truit. Josh Truit." He stared at his feet as he walked in the door.

"Nice to meet you, Mr. Truit. I'm Jeanette Galeman."

"I can't stay. I-I just wanted to say hello." He backed out of the doorway and didn't even look back as she watched him cross the yard.

How strange, Jeanette thought, looking down at the plate of cookies in her hand. They were homemade chocolate chip. Well, at least she had a name. Maybe, Mary Joe knew
190

something about him. Honestly, she was glad that he hadn't come in.

She put the plate on the kitchen counter and resumed her work on Jasper's room.

It was later that evening that she got on her laptop looking for online schools. It was a pleasant surprise to see that the University of Atlanta gave online courses. With almost two years behind her, she could graduate in only three more. Less than that if she took summer classes. The only courses open for enrollment at the moment were biology and beginning photography. It was a start, anyway and she filled out the applications and paid the tuition by credit card. She would have to wait until the next day to order her books from the campus bookstore.

Feeling very accomplished, Jeanette cooked herself a small dinner of chicken fetticini and ate one of Josh Truit's cookies. It was very good, actually. Her first real meal in her own home. It felt good. Maybe, a little lonely, though.

After dinner, she went outside on the back patio. The boxes still sat unopened for her patio table and playground equipment. *There is still enough light to put the table together*, she thought and opened the flat box. She went inside to fetch the necessary tools, a screwdriver and a wrench. The design was pretty simple and she had it together in about thirty minutes. She gave it an approving look and sat down in one of the wrought-iron chairs that she had bought to match. Tomorrow, she would have her breakfast here.

While she'd worked, the sky had grown darker and the shadows cast by the trees were dark and foreboding. A chill went through her despite the muggy night air.

*****

The next day, she had some more shopping to do. She needed something to keep her occupied. Also, she had

191

decided to do some volunteering at the museum with Maria Scully.

She was at the downtown drug store picking up a few odds and ends when she ran into Charles Maxwell.

He was coming down the aisle as she was inspecting a box of adhesive bandages with cartoon characters.

"Hello," he said, with a suave smile.

"Hi," Jeanette said, pleasantly surprised.

"I'm so glad that I ran into you. Mary Joe told me that you were going to be Gracie's maid of honor. As the best man, I rather thought it would be appropriate if we got to know each other a little better. Would you be free Friday night, by any chance?" he said, looking far too charming.

Jeanette wasn't sure about accepting the date, but supposed it would be rude to decline under the circumstances. "That would be nice, thanks," she said, then regretted her decision immediately. What would she wear? She hadn't had a date in seven years.

"Great. I'll pick you up at your house, then?" he asked.

She was ready to back out when she heard herself say, "That would be fine."

He walked away whistling. She stood there watching him walk away in a panic. What had she just done? She pulled out her phone to call Gracie.

"Grace, I just agreed to a date with Charles Maxwell," she said, anxiously.

"How wonderful. That's great, Jeanette," Gracie said, sounding excited.

192

"But, Gracie, I don't know what to do on a date. What am I going to wear?" Jeanette knew she sounded hysterical.

"Jeanette, no one has a better wardrobe than you do. Want me to come over and help you decide?" Gracie chuckled.

"No. I'll be okay. It's not until Friday night. That's a few days away."

Chapter Seven

Jeanette entered the museum and the silence seemed to envelope her. In all the time she had been in Swanson, she had never been here before. She knew that Maria was in here somewhere and had probably heard the door chime as she came in. She took the opportunity to look at the exhibits in the room. There were several cases that were dedicated to the Mallory plantation.

Jeanette walked over and looked through the glass. There were all kinds of antiques from the plantation—several pairs of wire framed eye glasses were included and a couple of cameras as well. She was looking intently at the cameras when she heard Maria walking up behind her.

"So, are you ready to start?" Maria asked.

"I think so." Jeanette turned and smiled.

"There isn't much to it, really. Mostly, just babysitting the building. Not much traffic through here. Occasionally, we get an arranged tour, but mostly it is just walk-ins off the street."

Jeanette followed her through two more rooms and into an office.

"I've written a tour guide out for you in case you need it. Some people like to look around on their own and others expect a guided tour. Actually, it is sad to say that it will likely just be a nice quiet place to do your school work." Maria gave her a set of keys. "The odd round one is to set the alarm. I'll show you how to do that in a bit. The other is for the front door." Pointing to a calendar on the wall, Maria went on, "This is where we write down arranged tours. As you can see, we have a couple of history classes scheduled for next week. I intend to be here, but it would be nice for you to see how I do it." She smiled at Jeanette. "Any questions?"

"Is there an entry charge?" Jeanette asked.

"The museum is free to all students and seniors over the age of fifty-five. For everyone else, we ask for a donation of 2.50. You shouldn't have to worry about it too much. There is a slotted barrel inside the door that collects donations. I thank you so much, Jeanette for offering your time this way." Maria's blue eyes met hers.

"Oh, it's no problem at all."

"Well, I would bring your computer with you or a book. It gets tedious around here real quick."

Maria took her to the door and showed her how the alarm worked. Then left Jeanette on her own.

The quiet seemed to be tangible once more now that she was alone. Jeanette walked through the museum taking a close look at all the exhibits. Maria certainly had a flare for making them attractive. The first room had a case with a picture of a young Belinda Mallory along with a trunk of clothes from her room. Jeanette was surprised to see Gracie's ruby necklace among the pieces of jewelry.

Moving on, inspecting everything as she went, she suddenly heard a tinkling sound coming from somewhere. Wondering where the eerie sound was coming from, she walked through the rooms. The sound grew louder and she came to the last room before the office. There she saw what it was. There were several sets of old wind chimes hung from the ceiling. There was no wind to set them off, though.

Looking along the walls, Jeanette expected to find an air-conditioning vent or something, but found no such thing. The chimes continued to move, yet there seemed to be no draft

195

anywhere. The sound was haunting with the high-pitched smaller chimes and the larger, deeper sound from the large ones. It was almost like voices arguing back and forth. Sufficiently creeped out, Jeanette left the room and as soon as she did, the chimes got quiet once more.

Jeanette finished her self-guided tour of the museum. It wasn't a very large building, but it held a lot of things of interest. When she got to that last room again, the chimes were quiet. The afternoon went fairly quickly while she studied the notes Maria had put down for the guided tour. Maria had altered the story of the Mallorys and had included the tale of how Belinda's maid suddenly disappeared.

*****

It was late when she fell asleep that night. In her dream, she was Lydia. She lived with her family of six in a small, cramped house on the edge of town. Lydia had given up school to stay home and help her mother with the smaller children. Their father worked at a mill in town, but there was never enough money. The children were often sick and there wasn't money to take them to the doctor. On this day, her mother sat her down to have a talk.

"Lydia, your pa and I have decided that you are old enough to make your way. We just can't feed all the mouths around here, you understand? You are almost fourteen and nearly a grown woman."

Lydia sat, quietly, feeling a lump begin to grow in her stomach. Where would she go? What would she do?

"Now, I'd never just let you go with no place to go to. Your pa has fixed it up for you to go to the Mallory plantation. They need a maid. It is a good position."

Fear struck Lydia's heart. "But Ma, there is ghosts out there. Everyone says it's haunted."

196

"That's just gossip and nonsense. I would expect you to be more sensible than that after the way I've raised ya. You'll go and do as you're told. Be respectful and work hard and you'll make a good livin'. You can keep a little of what you earn, but you bring the rest here to help with these babies, ya hear? You won't need much anyways with the Mallorys feedin' and clothin' you."

"Yes, Ma'am." Lydia looked down at the potatoes that needed peeling on the table and picked one up. She had never disobeyed her ma and she wouldn't now, but just the thought of going to the plantation made her sick to her stomach.

Chapter Eight

The next day, Jeanette had an assignment to get some nature photos. She decided that she might try the woods behind the plantation and it was a perfect day to be outside. She went to the house to leave word with Mary Joe that she was on the property and then headed past the pond and toward the tree line.

The woods were much larger than they appeared and if there ever had been trails, they were grown over now. Jeanette made her way through in a zigzag pattern through the foliage. It was cooler below the canopy of trees and she took her time, enjoying the day as she snapped photos of wildflowers and trees.

She'd walked for an hour before she realized that she was lost. She wasn't too worried, though. She knew she couldn't be far from civilization. She was about to turn back when she came to a small clearing. There was a small building in the center. She was walking toward it when she tripped on something and fell to her knees. She wasn't hurt and looked down at what stuck out from the ground. It was a piece of stone with something carved on it. She looked around and realized that she'd stumbled across an old graveyard. There was even an old crypt not too far from the building. She walked over to read the inscription. It was unreadable, though, other than the Mallory name. It must have been a family crypt.

The building was locked, though the rotten door probably would have crumbled easily if Jeanette forced it. She would leave that up to Brett and Gracie. Walking to the side, she tried to see the interior of the building. She wiped the dirt off with her hand and saw that it was stained glass. It was a chapel, she realized.

Jeanette sat down on an old gravestone and was suddenly transported back in time.

Giggling, Belinda was pulling Lydia though the trees. "We are almost there. You have to see it, Lydie. It's unbelievably creepy."

"I don't think we are supposed to be out here," Lydia said, worriedly.

"Of course, we aren't. That's part of the thrill, silly."

"Easy for you to say. You can't be thrown out on your hiney if you get caught," Lydia said, grumbling.

"Father won't throw you out. He knows how much I love you, Lydie. Now, look." They had just stepped into the graveyard.

"Are-are those gravestones?" Lydia looked around, ready to run at any moment.

"Don't worry. Come on. Let's see what's inside the chapel."

"Ain't that like consecrated ground or somethin'? We oughtn'ta be here." Lydia knew that nothing she said would change Belinda's mind. She shivered in the cool evening breeze.

"There is nothing holy about this plantation. It's all cursed. My mother said so," Belinda said as she easily pulled the door open. "See? The spirits want us here. This door was locked tight yesterday."

"Do you s'pose they had Sunday services here?" Lydia asked, her curiosity getting the better of her.

"Well, it is a church. They could have. Or it might just have been for funerals or something." Belinda lit the lantern she'd brought with them.

"Why couldn't we have come durin' the day?" Lydia asked, getting jittery again.

"Because that would have spoiled the fun. Sometimes, you are such a baby." She stepped inside. Lydia followed close behind, too afraid to stand by herself.

There were cobwebs everywhere and everything was covered in dust. Lydia sneezed and the sound echoed. They walked down the center aisle with half a dozen pews on each side. She looked into the seats as they passed. There were bibles and purses and hymnals laying on each row.

"Belinda, why do you s'pose people would leave their things here?" Lydia asked, shakily. Something about this place was completely wrong.

"Look at this!" Belinda picked up a piece of cloth and held it up to the light. It looked like a baby dress with tatted lace around the collar. "Isn't it darling?"

"I don't think we should take anything."

"Why not? It's on our property, after all. I don't think Father even knows about it."

"Belinda, it's spooky." It looked just like the Rapture had come and taken everyone in the middle of a service. The preacher was always talking about the Rapture and how those left behind would suffer. Lydia would have bet that it was nothing Godly had happened in this place. "You can stay if ya want to. I'm gettin' myself outta here." Lydia turned and ran out of the chapel.

It had grown dark outside in the few minutes they had been inside. Lydia stood by the door waiting for Belinda to come out. All her young life she'd been told about the ghosts at the plantation, but after several months living on the property, she still hadn't seen one. Not until that very night. She was nervously shuffling her feet when a white form stepped out of the trees. It glowed in the darkness as it walked toward Lydia. Terror-stricken and unable to move, Lydia watched as the ghost woman approached. It got within two feet of her and opened its mouth showing abnormally sharp teeth. She gave a shrill scream as she took off running and didn't stop until she reached the house. She looked back over her shoulder, guiltily realizing that she'd left her friend behind.

She saw Belinda coming toward her, out of breath. She crumpled to the ground in relief.

*****

Jeanette stood up and realized that she was herself again—not a fourteen year-old girl. Where were the dreams and visions coming from? She took a few dozen photos of the chapel and the graveyard before heading back to the plantation. She wasn't sure why, but whatever was inside that church was important. No one had a vision like that without a reason.

Gracie was behind the counter when Jeanette walked in the plantation house. She looked up and smiled as she approached.

"Hey, I heard you've been taking pictures of our woods. I hope you'll share them. I wouldn't mind some framed ones in the lobby."

"How about ones of your little chapel and graveyard hidden in the woods?" Jeanette asked, slyly.

"You are joking," she said, looking incredulous.

Jeanette motioned her around the counter and showed her the photos on the digital camera.

"Wow. This is great. Did you go in?" Gracie glanced up at Jeanette.

"No. It was locked. I thought it should be up to you and Brett. I wouldn't mind going along, though. I thought all the Mallorys were buried in the city cemetery."

"They are, as far as I know. Maybe, the graves were moved for some reason," Gracie said.

"I'll ask Maria. You know, if you put in trails out there, those woods would make a beautiful place for hiking." Jeanette put her camera back in the case.

Changing the subject, Gracie moved back to her place behind the counter. "So, have you decided what to wear Friday night?"

"Not yet. I'm really regretting that I agreed to go. I don't know if I'm ready to date," Jeanette told her.

"I think you should go. You deserve to get out and enjoy yourself. Don't think about it as a date. Just go out and have fun."

Jeanette left the plantation feeling a little better. Maybe, the date would be okay.

*****

That evening, Jeanette had a lot to think about. It was one thing having a vivid dream and quite another to have a vision during the day. It had felt like a memory. Why would she see Lydia's life? Yes, the woman was a relative of sorts. She would have been her great aunt? And what purpose could it possibly have? Was something wrong with her? Was she going insane?

202

She took a long hot bath to soak the soreness from her muscles. After slipping on her pajamas and robe, she went down to heat herself a cup of coffee and she noticed that the trash can was full and tied it up. It was already late, surely no one would notice if she took the trash out in her robe.

She pulled the bag out and headed to the front door. There was no one in sight. She carried the bag to the road and put it in the can. She was about to turn back toward the house when she ran into someone.

"Sorry, Ma'am." In the dim light from the porch, she saw that it was that creepy neighbor guy. Josh something. He went on past her toward his own house. *Strange that he was out walking this time of night? Had he been watching me? Lord, I'm getting paranoid*, she thought, shaking her head as she entered her house and locked the door behind her, adding the slide lock.

Chapter Nine

Maria called on Friday morning just as Jeanette was getting ready to sit down at her computer to see what her class assignments for the day were.

"I did some research and I found that there was a great flood in 1870. It did a lot of damage including washing out several cemeteries around the area. Apparently, during the clean-up, they decided to rebury their dead in one place on high ground and the Swanson Memorial Cemetery was started. It was sad, though, that many of the bodies were feared to have been mixed up and no one was certain if their loved ones were in the correct grave. Some of the bodies simply washed away and only the headstones are there in memory. But that should clear up your mystery of the Mallory family cemetery."

"Thank you, Maria. I appreciate it. I don't know how you dig that stuff up." Jeanette smiled into the phone at her unintentional pun.

Maria laughed, lightly, "Well, there are records of all kinds of things if you know where to look. I would be interested to know if you all find anything in that chapel."

"I'll be sure to let you know," Jeanette said and hung up.

So, Gracie was right about a simple explanation. Then why did Jeanette still feel so unsettled about it? She put it out of her mind and concentrated on schoolwork. They would know soon enough this afternoon. Gracie had called her last night and invited her to go with them to check it out.

*****

Going through the woods with Gracie and Brett reminded Jeanette a little of Lydia's jaunt with Belinda. Of course, it

204

was bright daylight this time. Jeanette led the way, and hoped she was going the same direction she had gone the day before. It didn't take them long to find it.

"I wonder if this little graveyard could be fixed up," Gracie said, looking around at the crumbling stones. "We could add a memorial and put rock trails through the woods. It could be really nice."

"That chapel needs some work," Brett said, looking at the dilapidated building. "I don't know what has kept the roof from caving in."

He forced the door open. The inside wasn't as dark as it should have been. A window on the wall behind the pulpit had been broken out and sunlight came through, illuminating the one room space.

"It's larger in here than it looks from the outside," Gracie observed, as she knocked away cobwebs.

Everything looks just the same, Jeanette thought. The strange feel that something was wrong about it persisted. "In what case would people leave their personal things here?"

Gracie saw that she was looking at the pews. "It is odd, isn't it?"

"Knowing the plantation, something scared the crap out of them and they ran away screaming," Brett said, giving the girls a grin.

Neither of them found it humorous, though. Least of all, Jeanette. The image of a ghost woman with fangs entered her mind.

"I think the idea of a chapel in the woods is charming," Gracie said. "We should go through all of this to see if there are any records or anything of value, then tear down this

205

building and replace it with a new one. It would make a nice attraction for the residents."

"This is what you are looking for?" Brett picked up a stack of books off the podium in front and took them over to Gracie.

"Possibly, but they look like they've been damaged. I'll take them to Maria and see if she can get anything off of them." She studied the stack. "This one looks like one of the hymnals. We should collect them all and see if we can find one undamaged enough to copy."

Jeanette was looking through the items on a pew toward the middle. She saw the bag of clothes that Belinda had found all those years ago. Slung on the top was the baby dress. The material was rotten, but still recognizable. She still needed to deny that her vision had been real, but this little dress gave it a credibility that she didn't want to think about.

*****

Jeanette dressed carefully for her date with Charles. She changed outfits three times before settling on a yellow summer dress that could be considered casual and dressed it up with a pearl necklace and earrings. She pulled her hair into a tight bun, but some of the blond curls still resisted the restraint and fell around her face until she finally gave up and let it all loose again. She cursed her genes. Picking through the corkscrew curls, she decided that it didn't look too bad.

Charles showed up on time. Jeanette grabbed her handbag and, nervously, answered the door. He greeted her with the charming smile she remembered.

She was surprised and felt a little awkward as he opened her car door for her.

"I hope you like Italian. I found a nice little restaurant that I thought you would like. It's just on the edge of Atlanta

206

if you don't mind a little drive." He looked at her questioningly.

"That sounds fine," she said, realizing that he required a response, and then sat back to enjoy the ride.

Chapter Ten

After they were seated at the restaurant, Charles ordered wine as they looked the menu over.

Jeanette looked around the dining-room. The place had a charming old world atmosphere with adobe walls and candle lighting. The tables were solid wood giving it a little rustic look. Flowers and painted murals were the main touch of decor. There was live music as a three-man orchestra played in one corner.

"I have an ulterior motive bringing you here tonight," Charles told her, looking over the menu. "I thought it would be a wonderful place to have a pre-wedding dinner for Brett and Gracie—that is for the four of us the night before."

"That is a lovely idea," Jeanette agreed. "Gracie would love this place without a doubt."

"Might I suggest the shrimp linguini? It is excellent," Charles asked.

"That sounds great," Jeanette said, relieved to leave that decision to him and laid the menu aside.

He set his menu on top of hers and gave her a long look. "I was certainly surprised to find that Brett had a sister."

"Well, we were both surprised, too." Jeanette gave a slight smile.

"I knew that Brett's mother had left Georgia when she became ill. I always thought it was strange that he was left behind," Charles prodded.

"I think that Sophie intended to return," Jeanette said. "She died when I was just a baby. There is a lot about the ordeal that I don't understand and probably never will." It was difficult to talk about Gram and Sophie without having to explain Gram's influence of Alfred.

"Still, it's a shame that the two of you didn't get to grow up together. It is obvious that you have a close relationship now." Charles took a sip of the wine.

"I couldn't ask for a better brother and I am so happy for Gracie, too. She deserves to be happy," Jeanette said.

"When we were kids, I was always getting Brett into trouble," Charles said, giving a mischievous grin. "We had a lot of great adventures." He went on to tell her of a few and soon he had Jeanette laughing. "Brett was a good kid, he wouldn't have had any fun at all if it wasn't for me." He gave Jeanette a wink.

The waiter brought their food and they were quiet for a while before Charles broke the silence again.

"So, you are recently divorced and have two beautiful children. What do you do for a living?" he asked.

"Well, right now, I am taking the opportunity to finish my education and hope to open a photography studio at some point in my near future. What about you?" Jeanette asked, hoping to keep him the focus of the conversation and herself out of the spotlight.

He took a bite of food and chased it down with the wine. "I'm in real estate. I'm opening an office in town and hoping to attract some city people to the charm of a more rural setting. I'm hoping that Brett will do some partnering with me to sell some of his beautiful houses."

"Is that why you were away for the last couple of years?" Jeanette asked.

"That and I was helping a buddy get his business off the ground. In the meantime, I've started an advertising campaign highlighting the southern charm and peaceful living." He laughed. "I'll probably go broke within a couple of years, but it's worth a try. I really love this area and would like to see it develop."

Jeanette nodded. It seemed a worthwhile endeavor and it might really help Brett.

After dinner, the drive home was much more relaxed. They talked about the kids, photography, and real estate and Jeanette was surprised a little when Charles slipped his hand around hers and held it most of the way home.

When they got to her house, he walked her to the door. She knew that this was her cue to invite him in or say goodnight. She liked Charles and the date had been really fun, but she wasn't ready for anything more.

"You know, my Friday nights have been pretty bleak up to this point," Charles said, with a cocky grin. "I sure wouldn't mind if a certain blond would drag me out to the bowling alley or a movie next week."

Jeanette had to laugh at the look on his face. Her smile faded when he pulled her closer to his body. She certainly wasn't expecting his kiss. His lips melded with hers and before she knew it, she was welcoming his passion in her new liberated life. He slowly withdrew leaving her wanting. She was stunned when he whispered, "Good night, Lydia."

He turned and left before she could respond.

Lydia? Why did he call me that? she wondered before walking inside.

*****

210

In the house next door, Josh heard the car pull up and watched as a man walked Jeanette to her door. His heart plummeted watching him kiss her under the dim porch light. Josh punched the door frame as the man walked away. What did he expect, really? She was a beautiful woman and he couldn't say two words to her without stuttering.

'Well, Joshua Truitt,' he said to himself, 'it's time to grow a backbone and fight for the woman you want.'

He walked to the bathroom and looked into the mirror, trying to see himself through her eyes. The shaggy hair framed his plain face and the glasses looked ghastly. He took off the glasses and pulled his hair back. It was time to change his style, throw off the shroud of timidity and start living his life.

Chapter Eleven

It was inevitable that Jeanette would dream of Lydia that night after laying in bed for hours, reflecting on why Charles would have called her by that name.

In this dream, Belinda and Lydia were visiting Lydia's family. It was Saturday and Lydia's only day off. As always, Lydia's mother was waiting to receive the hard-earned wages that her daughter brought home. Things looked much better in the small house, though, and the little ones weren't crying from hunger.

They spent the day playing with the children and Lydia noticed that Belinda seemed to take up with Sophia, the baby. Sophia was two years old by that time and had Lydia's fair hair and blue eyes. She also had the cutest short curls that covered her little head. Lydia's own hair was as straight as a board and her mother had reminded her of it constantly when she was small.

It was a happy day until they went back to the plantation and Edgar Mallory was waiting for them. He looked angry and Lydia was sent directly to her room. She wasn't normally disobedient, but she hid on the basement stairs so she could hear him speak to Belinda. Had she done something to get her friend in trouble?

"I heard you've been in town today," Edgar said, his words had an underlying malice to them.

"Yes. Mother said I could go. We were just visiting Lydia's family," Belinda said.

"You don't need to be associating with people like that. I gave Lydia this position because her father is a worthless lout.

He works at the mill and then drinks up every penny until there is nothing for his family to live on. I know for a fact that Lydia gives her wages to her family to support them. They are not good people, Belinda. They are trash. I don't want you going to their home again."

"Lydia is not trash! And neither are those little babies. If you could see them, you would know that," Belinda shouted and started walking away.

"No, she isn't. Lydia is a good girl in a bad situation which is why I hired her, but we can't save them all, Belinda. Not all of those kids are going to turn out like Lydia."

Lydia could hear the hesitation before Belinda answered. "I don't get it, Dad. Why did you hire Lydia? What brought her to your attention? You don't give most people in this town the time of day." The anger had went out of her voice. "You told me that you had found someone that I could spend time with. To be my friend. But why choose Lydia?"

"This discussion is over. You are not to go to that house again. You can spend time with Lydia on the plantation."

Lydia could hear his heavy boots walk away. She wandered to her room, feeling hurt and bewildered.

*****

Jeanette spent the morning doing her homework as was her new routine. When she finished, she made herself a glass of iced tea and went to sit on the patio. The huge boxes with the play equipment were still sitting there.

It's not going to put itself together, she thought with a sigh.

She went in the house to get some tools and found a screw driver and an adjustable wrench.

She began pulling the pieces out of the boxes and laid them out in the yard. She came across the bag of hardware and the instructions. It didn't look that hard.

Thirty minutes later, she looked at the structure and realized that she had definitely messed up somewhere. The only two wooden beams left were supposed to be the same length and didn't even come close. Sighing, she sat down at her new patio table. She heard a door shut nearby and saw a large black dog bounding across the neighbor's yard. The man came out behind him. Josh something, wasn't it? He looked over and saw Jeanette sitting there and waved. She waved back and then watched him play Frisbee with the dog for a while. He seemed strangely more athletic than his clothing implied. Even on a sunny, hot afternoon, he was wearing slacks and a button up shirt.

Jeanette was taking a sip of her iced tea as the Frisbee drifted over the fence and landed in her yard. The great black beast followed, jumping the four foot fence as if it were nothing. It picked up the Frisbee and then turned its big brown eyes toward Jeanette. Without a qualm, it walked over to her and dropped the Frisbee in front of her.

Stunned, she just sat there not knowing what to do. Jeanette had never been around animals and certainly not a dog of this size. The dog looked her in the eye and nudged the Frisbee toward her with his nose.

"Just toss the Frisbee back over the fence." Josh whatshisname called out. "He won't bite. He's nothing but a big puppy."

Jeanette had visions of reaching down to grab the Frisbee and her hand being bitten off at the wrist. She bolstered her courage and slowly reached toward the Frisbee. The dog gave a happy grin and his whole body wriggled in anticipation.

She couldn't help giving a low chuckle as she grabbed the Frisbee and threw it toward the fence. The dog caught it in midair just as it sailed over the fence and landed gracefully on all four feet.

"Looks like you could use some help," Josh yelled over, gesturing to the half constructed swing set.

"I messed it up somewhere," Jeanette answered as she walked toward the fence to talk to him. She noticed that he'd gotten a haircut. It looked much better, actually. "I think I mixed up the wooden beams and now what is left won't work."

"Hold on. I'll come take a look." He was already walking toward the gate before she could object.

He came through the gate in her yard a moment later. She shrugged. What would it hurt to let him help her? She handed him the instruction paper.

He looked it over and then looked at the jumbled mess of her attempt.

"Let's start over," he said. "You take that end and I'll take this one." He pointed toward the long center beam. It took them about ten minutes to undo her work.

Together, Jeanette and Josh got the play equipment put together and Jeanette had to admit they had fun doing it. Josh wasn't as creepy as she had thought. Just incredibly shy and really fashion-challenged. The dog had sat and watched them patiently and Jeanette reached down to pat him.

"Thanks for the help. Hold on a minute and I'll get us some iced tea," she told Josh and went to the kitchen. It had been so kind of him to help. She would never have gotten that done by herself. It was simply a two-person job.

She went back out with the iced tea, handed him a glass and gestured for him to take a seat at the table.

215

"It looks great! The kids will be so excited when they see it." She smiled at him.

Embarrassed, he blushed lightly as he pushed his glasses up the bridge of his nose. "How many kids do you have?" he asked.

"Two. A boy and a girl. They are spending the summer with their dad," she told him.

"Must be hard for you to be away from them." He lifted his eyes to meet hers.

"It is. This is the first time I've ever been away from them. Do you have kids?" she asked.

"No. I've never been married." He took a drink of the tea.

Jeanette wondered if he'd ever even dated. It wasn't often that she met someone more timid than she was. He wasn't bad-looking now that his hair wasn't in his eyes. She found herself wondering what he would look like without his glasses.

While she was thinking about it, he had drained his glass.

"Well, I had better be going. Franklin hasn't had his dinner yet." Josh said and stood. The dog stood at attention, ready to follow his master.

"Thanks again," Jeanette said and watched him walk away. She wondered how he could see where he was going when he stared at his feet while walking. He sure was an interesting character.

Chapter Twelve

The next day was Jeanette's day to work at the museum. She was hoping that Maria would have something to report about the books they had found in the chapel. She took her laptop along in case she had time to study. She was on her way to the car when Gracie called.

"Hello," Jeanette answered.

"Hello! You haven't called me to tell me about your date with Charles," Gracie said, sounding a little hurt.

"Sorry. I've been a little distracted." Jeanette tossed her things in the passenger seat and got behind the wheel. "It went pretty well, actually. He asked me to go out again this Friday."

"Really? That's good news. You said you've been distracted. Are you okay, Sis? It's not that chapel cemetery thing, is it?" Gracie sounded concerned.

"No," Jeanette said, wondering if she should tell Gracie about her dreams. It was getting so close to her wedding; she didn't need anything to upset her. "I'm okay. Just a little overwhelmed with school work."

"Well, if you need anything, I'm here for you."

"I know. Thanks. I have to get the museum before Maria thinks I'm not coming. Love you," Jeanette said and hung up.

At the museum, Maria was in the office with two books laid out in front of her.

"Are those the books from the chapel?" Jeanette asked.

"Yes, actually. I'm trying to decipher the writing. Not easy with the weather damage. This is a record of deaths and burials of the family, which is pretty long. There are family members here that we didn't even know existed. The other book is the same only for the deaths of slaves. It is fascinating, really."

"I have a question for you. A little off the subject," Jeanette said.

"Sure. What is it?" Maria looked up, curiously.

"Lydia was hired as a maid at the plantation when she was thirteen years old. Belinda had thought that he might have some kind of ulterior motive, but I'm wondering if Edgar had some ill dealings with Lydia's family. Maybe he was indebted to them for something or they were blackmailing him. Is there any way to get such information?"

"Well, we can look into financial records, maybe, but as for actual details, probably not. Is there a reason why you are asking?"

"I don't know. Edgar wanted Belinda to believe that he was being charitable to a child from a poor family, but I just don't buy it."

"I don't either," Maria said, resolutely. "From the word of the townsfolk at that time, Edgar thought he owned the town as well as the plantation and wasn't kind to anyone. You could always ask someone that was here at the time. Art might know or even one of the bridge club."

"I'll do that,"Jeanette agreed. With that, Maria packed her things in her bag and got ready to leave.

"Are you okay, Jeanette? You look a little pale," Maria said, looking at her closely. "If you don't feel up to this today, I can stay."

"No, no. I'm fine, really." Jeanette dredged up a smile and Maria left looking assured.

"I'm really fine," Jeanette said aloud after Maria left. "I'm having delusions and strange dreams, but I am fine." She sat down at the desk and opened her laptop. As she did, she heard the faint ring of wind chimes from the other room. Ignoring it, she turned her mind to her homework.

*****

Belinda was cursing those damn chimes. This was the second time she'd set them off. Her intention wasn't to frighten Jeanette further. She looked around. He was here. She could feel him and he was getting stronger. Moving toward the center room, she saw the black mist floating in and around the exhibits. Even if she had to battle him, he wasn't getting near her girl.

*****

Jeanette finished her work and realized that there was only about twenty minutes before lock-up time. She put her books and laptop back into her bag, stood up and walked through, quickly looking over the place before leaving. It looked normal until she got to the front entrance. Then she stopped in her tracks as a cold feeling came over her. Goosebumps formed on her arms. Between her and the door a black form hung in the air. It was between a fog and a mist, but she was sure that she wasn't imagining it.

She wondered what would happen if she simply walked through it. If she didn't have to take the time to set the alarm, she would have been tempted. The mist was stationary but moving constantly within itself as if it was trying to take another form.

Jeanette stood there transfixed by the shifting shape and had no idea how to get past it when the door suddenly opened and the mist dissipated in the bright sunlight.

"What the hell?" Josh said as he looked toward the space where it had been.

Chapter Thirteen

She hadn't realized that she'd been holding her breath and took a deep gulp of fresh air.

"Please stay right here," she begged him as she was setting the alarm and then followed him out the door. She locked it and practically ran to the safety of her car. She slid in the driver's seat and sat there with her head in her hands. She looked over when Josh tapped on the passenger window.

She unlocked the door and he got in the car.

Still looking stunned, he asked, "What was that?"

"I don't know. It was just there when I was getting ready to leave. It was blocking my way out." The stress of the last weeks on top of this was just too much and she couldn't control the sobs that started racking her body.

"Hey, hey." Josh reached out awkwardly and patted her shoulder. "Why don't I drive and you can tell me about it?" He saw that they were already getting some looks from people walking by.

Jeanette nodded and got out to trade places with him.

Half-way home, she turned to him. "What about your car?"

"I walk most everywhere. I didn't have my car. Are you okay?" he glanced over at her.

"I'm better," she said, swiping her face with her hand. "You saw that thing, didn't you? I wasn't imagining it."

"I did. The whole thing was weird. I had no intentions of going into the museum. I just had a feeling and felt drawn to it."

"I'm glad you did. I think you stopped it," Jeanette said, trembling.

Josh instinctively took her hand to comfort her. "Well, it's over now."

"Is it? I don't think it is," Jeanette said, as they pulled up in her driveway.

Josh turned to her and handed her the keys. "What do you mean?"

"I don't know what I mean. I thought maybe I was just going crazy. But you saw that, too."

"Why don't we go inside and I'll make you some tea," Josh said, looking at her so kindly that she just wanted to burst into tears again.

Inside, Jeanette sat at the kitchen island and watched him as he put water in the teapot and set it on the stove.

"You are wearing blue jeans and a t-shirt," she said, without thinking. She was just surprised.

He smiled slightly.

"Sorry. I'm just used to seeing you in slacks."

"I'm just flattered that you noticed," he said and looked down toward his feet again. "There's this girl I'm interested in and my brother gave me a few tips."

Jeanette flashed him a smile. "That's nice. Let me know if I can help." Amazing how a little romance can change someone's outlook on life.

"Thanks," he said, still not meeting her eyes. "So, that thing in the museum, you've seen it before?"

"No. That was new. This has something to do with the plantation." She had to tell someone and he'd already seen that black cloud. "There were some things that happened at the plantation last year and we had thought it was over."

There was something about Josh. He was so easy to talk to and before she knew it, Jeanette had told him the entire story. She couldn't tell how much he actually believed.

"That's one heck of a story," he said, looking her in the eye for once.

"It is. I wouldn't believe it if I hadn't been there."

"So, how is this tied to the black mass at the museum?" he asked.

"I don't know, but a few weeks ago, I saw Gladys McCarthy in my bathroom. She'd been dead for three months." Jeanette wondered if he would believe her.

"Really?"

"Look, I know this all sounds crazy. But now, for the last couple of weeks, I've been dreaming randomly about Lydia, Belinda's maid."

"If all of this story started at the plantation, why aren't you talking to your family about this?"

"Their wedding is in just a couple of weeks. I don't want to spoil it for them and it seems that whatever is going on has to do with me. I just don't know how or why."

"What about your boyfriend? You haven't told him?" Josh was looking down at the countertop again.

"Charles? He isn't exactly my boyfriend. Friday was our first date. He would think I was totally loony and probably tell my brother which is what I was trying to avoid." She looked up at Josh. "And you know what he said after he kissed me Friday night? He said, good night, Lydia." Jeanette said, stressing the word Lydia.

"That's creepy," Josh said. "Are you going out with him again?"

"This Friday. I really like him. The thing is that I don't think he realized what he'd said," Jeanette said, frowning.

Just then, Jeanette's phone rang.

She was surprised to hear Aubrey crying into the phone.

"Mommy, I want to come home. Me and Jasper want to come home now."

"Honey, I can't get you until August. Can you tell me what is wrong?" Jeanette asked, wondering where Sandy and Jim were.

"They yell at Jasper, Mommy. All the time. They make him cry. Daddy took his Bobo, too," Aubrey told her. Jasper's Bobo was his favorite blanket. Why would Jim take it from him?

"Aubrey, is Daddy there?"

"No. He and Sandy went outside. They are yelling. I think they are mad at us," Aubrey said and began crying harder.

"Don't worry, Baby. I'll call and see what is going on, okay? Give Jasper a hug from me."

"Okay," Aubrey said and hung up.

224

Jim had better do some explaining, Jeanette thought as she dialed his cell phone. It rang several times before he answered.

"Hello."

"Jim, what is going on? I just got a call from Aubrey. She was crying her heart out. And why would you take Jasper's blanket?"

"Well, really, I don't think it is any of your business what we do here. I'll have to have a talk with Aubrey about using the phone without permission. Remember, Jeanette, I don't have to let you have any contact with them at all on my time," he said, snidely.

"Perhaps not, but I can call the authorities and have them do a welfare check," Jeanette said, angrily.

"Don't threaten me, Jeanette! I could easily file for full custody."

"You could file, but I can guarantee you won't get it." Jeanette hung up phone down. How dare he talk to her that way!

"Family trouble?"

Jeanette had forgotten that he was still there. "Yeah. My ex-husband. He makes me so mad. He doesn't want the kids. He just doesn't want me to have them."

"I'm sorry," Josh said, with a sad look.

"You are such a sweet guy." Jeanette patted him on the arm. "I hope that girl appreciates you."

"I-I'd better go," he said, looking embarrassed. "Franklin will need to go out by now."

225

Jeanette walked him to the door.

"Thanks again for listening," she said as he stepped out the door.

Chapter Fourteen

For the next few days, Jeanette saw little of Josh and wondered if she had offended him somehow or if he'd just decided that she was really nuts. Either way, she kept herself busy with schoolwork and discussing wedding plans with Gracie.

Friday night, Jeanette and Charles went bowling. They had a nice time, but Jeanette knew she was distracted. Charles just didn't seem to be the dream date she'd thought. She did agree to a third date, but it was reluctant. It wasn't that he'd done anything wrong. She just didn't find him as attractive, somehow.

She had made the decision to talk to Art about Lydia, but thought she would be most likely to catch him at home on the weekend. It wasn't something she wanted to discuss at the café.

Friday night was the first night in days that she dreamed of Lydia.

"I think that Billy really likes you." Lydia and Belinda were sitting on Lydia's bed. They were a couple of years older than the last dream.

"Of course, he does. We've been friends forever," Belinda said, missing the point.

"No. I mean he really likes you. He keeps looking at you when you aren't watching."

"We aren't down here to discuss Billy," Belinda said, defensively. "We need to talk about the ghosts and what we are going to do about the curse. If you haven't noticed, we

*can't even walk through the house without seeing them. I feel
like we're being watched all the time."*

*"I try not to think about it." Lydia shivered. "If your
father even knew we'd been down in the tunnels, he'd tan our
hides, for sure. I don't think he likes me, anyway. He gives
me bad looks. I wonder if he is going to send me away."*

"I won't let him sack you, Lydie."

*"He's changed. He isn't the same. I know you love him,
Belinda, but he-he's different." Lydia didn't want to offend
her only friend in the world, but Belinda always had blinders
on when it came to her father. As the property seemed to be
awakening with ghosts and evil seemed to be seeping into the
mansion, Edgar Mallory was becoming dark and brooding.
For some reason, Belinda couldn't see it or she just didn't
want to. Lydia saw it and she was afraid. She was very
afraid.*

*"It's not my father. It's the curse, Lydie, can't you see?
It's what the curse has done to us all. We have to end it.
Mama is taking me shopping in Atlanta next week. I'm going
to find some help." Belinda jumped off the bed.*

*After Belinda left, Lydia got ready for bed. Before she
went to sleep, she took a box of salt from the top drawer of her
dresser and sprinkled a line in front of the door to her room.*

*****

The house was quiet as Art entered. Even after Meredith
had been gone so long, he still wasn't used to the silence. He
still expected to hear her clattering around in the kitchen. He
missed the cool glass of lemonade that she always brought
him when he got home, but most of all he just missed
Meredith.

He'd tried to keep himself busy by helping out over at the
plantation, but the truth was that he was just too old to be of

228

any real use. Just today, he had come to a decision. He was going to sell the house and apply for a room at the plantation. He just couldn't stand living alone any longer. There he could at least have a little company.

It wasn't an easy decision to make. He had built this old house when he'd bought the property from Edgar Mallory years ago. He and Meredith had dreamt it all into existence and they had been happy here. It had been a good life. Well, until Billy had died. He was the light of their lives. Nothing was quite the same after that. They knew in their hearts that there was no farm accident. He had been murdered, pure and simple. There was nothing worse than losing a child except knowing that someone had purposely took that young life away.

Edgar had lied to them all—to the whole town. He told everyone that Belinda died, not Lydia. Art supposed that Edgar got the surprise of his life when he learned that Belinda had taken on Lydia's identity, lending credibility to his story. All those years, they had believed that Belinda was dead along with their grandchild. If only they had known.

Art sat on the tattered couch and didn't bother to turn on the television. That wasn't any fun anymore, either. Not without his wife's amusing comments as they watched together.

Instead of bringing home dinner and sharing it with Meredith, this last year, he had just stayed at the diner and ate at the bar. At least, he had the waitress to chat with for a few minutes. Now, there was nothing to keep him from going to bed early. He went into the bedroom. He hadn't bothered to clean out her things. He had figured that he wouldn't be far behind, anyway, and it could wait for someone else to do it.

He went to bed while it was still light outside. He was asleep for only a short time when he startled awake. He knew the pain in his arm surely meant one thing. He would be joining Meredith tonight. He grabbed his arm as the pain in his chest exploded. Above him glowed a face that he had not forgotten. The red eyes, ready to devour him.

"Get away from me. I'll not be going with you!" he yelled out. At that moment, Meredith appeared and pulled Art away. Away from his body and away from the demon. He had eluded Alfred's grasp. His last conscious thought was the realization that Alfred was on the loose. He prayed a last prayer for the souls of his friends.

Chapter Fifteen

Early Saturday morning, Jeanette got a call. It was Gracie and she sobbed out that Brett had just found Art dead. It was their habit to take Art breakfast from the plantation on Saturday mornings. Brett was still with the emergency crew.

Jeanette dressed quickly and went to be with Gracie. She had gotten pretty attached to the old man over the last year. He was her only living relative.

She saw Josh walking up the road as she rushed to her car.

"Good morning," he called out.

Jeanette waved as she got in the car and sped off. She walked into the retirement home to find Mary Joe behind the front desk. She gestured to the office and Jeanette went in to find a weeping Gracie curled up on the wide couch. She sat down and put her arms around her.

"I'm so sorry, Sis," Jeanette said, rubbing Gracie's back.

"He had a heart attack, they think." Gracie straightened and wiped her nose with a tissue. "Charles was here this morning, too. He and Brett had some words. Brett was already feeling badly before he found Art."

"Did it have to do with me?" Jeanette couldn't help asking. She didn't want to be the cause of Brett's rift with his friend.

"No. I don't think so. I think it was business," Gracie said. "I wouldn't worry about it." She reached out and touched Jeanette's arm.

"How did your date go, this week?"

"Okay, I guess. I agreed to another date."

"Oh. It sounds like things have cooled off. Any particular reason?"

Jeanette didn't really want to discuss it, but could see that Gracie needed to get her mind off Art. "Not really. I just have had too much on my plate, I guess. It's more like bad timing. Jim is giving me trouble and things are just—well, stressful."

"I'm sorry, Sis. I guess I've been so obsessed with the wedding and all that we haven't had much time to talk."

"You're supposed to be obsessed. Don't worry about me, Gracie. I'm the big sister, remember?" Jeanette gave her a hug. "Have you guys decided what to do with the chapel?" she said, changing the subject.

"Brett is going to tear it down and build a new one with memorials to my ancestors. He knows how much the family connection means to me." That set Gracie into another bout of sobbing.

"Grace, you have family that loves you right here. Me and Brett, Mary Joe, and Maria. I know it seems like family just slipped through our fingers, but you and I know that blood isn't everything," Jeanette said.

Gracie nodded. "I know. We are lucky, aren't we?"

"Yes, we are."

*****

On the other side of town, there was a young boy that wasn't as lucky as Art. Jake Brisby had been sick with the flu for a week and his temperature spiked that night. The twelve-

232

year-old had been delirious for the last several hours, crying out in his sleep about evil snakes with red eyes. The child died in the early hours of the morning, greeted by several familiar, yet dreadful spirits who whisked him away.

Bobby Brazel, the town drunk, declared himself sober when the vision of his mother appeared to him in the alley behind Drew's Bar. She had been dead for ten years and certainly looked it.

Mayor Stiles was greeted by a huge black snake with glowing red eyes when he got up in the night to use the bathroom. It's safe to say that he didn't need to go after that.

Happenings of the supernatural took place all over town, but, so far, everyone kept it to themselves and everything appeared to be normal. Over the next few days, though, there were seven deaths. It was a lot in a week for a town of only a few thousand people.

*****

There must have been at least five hundred people at Art Grandy's funeral. Gracie and Brett stood in the front row. Gracie was the only family member left. She was crying softly through the service.

Jeanette knew that Gracie had been counting on Art to give her away at her wedding. Now she really had no family left at all. Jeanette stood by her side, trying to comfort her the best she could.

Art had been a beloved patriarch of the town and many came to the graveside as well. Jeanette was shocked to find out that the man had actually been a hundred and ten years old. That had to be some kind of record and no one had realized that he was that old.

What remained of the bridge club stood together as the casket was lowered. It hadn't been very long since their last

233

visit to the cemetery and Gladys' grave was only a few feet away. The dirt hadn't even had time to settle. The grim group were quiet—not their usual magpie selves at all, even after it was over. They left quietly together.

Chapter Sixteen

By the time Thursday rolled around, Jeanette was emotionally exhausted. She dreaded having to be alone at the museum, but she'd never been one to shirk her responsibilities.

Though she was nervous all afternoon and kept looking over her shoulder and listening for the sound of wind-chimes, all was quiet and she got home that evening without incident.

When she got out of the car, she saw Josh heading into his house with Franklin. He didn't even turn to look at her or wave. She was positive now that he hadn't believed a word of what she'd told him last week. He probably thought she was a freak.

After eating a microwave dinner, Jeanette decided to make an early night of it.

The dream of Lydia was different that night. It was the first dream that included Billy. By this time, Belinda and Billy were definitely a couple and Lydia was feeling like the third wheel. Lydia had begun to cover for her friend when Belinda would slip out at night to meet Billy. She tried not to think too much about what they were doing.

It was late one night during one of Belinda's rendezvous that Lydia was pacing her room, worriedly. Edgar was supposed to be gone, but she heard the ruckus upstairs when he came home early.

By this time, she was used to lurking in the basement stairway, eavesdropping and went to do just that.

There was crashing around and loud cursing. It wasn't uncommon lately for Edgar to come home drunk and raving, but it sounded worse than usual.

Lydia knew that she had to get to Belinda to warn her, but had no idea how she was going to get out of the house without Edgar seeing her. She had to cross the wide hallway to get to the kitchen and the back door. If she hadn't been so nervous, she might have made it.

"Lydia!" she heard the roar behind her and her heart nearly jumped from her chest.

"Yes, sir." She turned to him and tried to seem natural.

"Why are you out of your room at this time?" he had stomped toward her and stopped only a couple of feet away.

She looked up into the angry face. "I-I I was a bit hungry." It wasn't the best excuse, but the best she could think of.

"You get two meals a day. Is it not enough? Are you that greedy?" he was shouting.

"I-I'm sorry," Lydia said, fearing the worst. At that moment, she saw Belinda slip into the kitchen. Thankfully, she was quiet.

"From now on, you will have a curfew of 9:00. You will stay in your room until morning. Do you understand?" He brought his face close to her own. She thought her heart was going to stop as she saw a strange red glint in his eye.

"Yes, sir," Lydia said and watched Edgar walk away, cursing as he walked into the banister on his way up the stairs. Lydia sighed in relief and without looking at Belinda, who she knew had heard the last part, she ran back down to her room.

Jeanette woke up. She looked at the clock and realized that it wasn't time to get up yet. She lay there for a while thinking about the dream. It wasn't exactly a newsflash that Alfred had possessed Edgar. Why was she having these dreams?

*****

That night was her third date with Charles. She dressed nicely, determined to have a nice time and give their relationship a chance. The resolution was short-lived.

That evening after they had ordered, the conversation naturally took a turn to the upcoming wedding.

"Are they planning to have the wedding at the plantation?" Charles asked, curiously.

"No. The park in the town square. The reception will be at the plantation," Jeanette explained.

"I think it's a marvelous thing they are doing with the plantation," Charles said, changing the subject. "If it had been mine, I would have set myself up as king of the manor."

"It's awfully big for one family. I can't imagine living there," Jeanette said.

"Stepping into it for the first time, I felt like I was stepping back in time. I could have easily took on the role of owner of the plantation and hiring people to serve me hand and foot. It must have been awesome back in the day." He grinned, dreamily.

Jeanette was far too practical to understand his way of thinking. "I suppose." All she could think of was no indoor plumbing or electricity.

"It must have been quite a rush to see all those slaves working in the fields and a house full of servants all at their master's command." He went on.

Jeanette suddenly didn't like the glint in his eye. No one man should have power over others' lives. Not that way, anyhow. Was he saying that he condoned slavery? Perhaps she was taking his words too seriously.

"To be the master of all of it. It would have been something," he finished.

"Sounds like a god complex to me," Jeanette said, glad that their meal arrived at that time, providing the distraction.

Jeanette had ordered chicken fetticini. He had ordered some kind of shrimp pasta.

"Well, how is the schooling coming along?" he asked.

"Fine, thank you. I should have a nice head start on my required courses."

"It will take up a lot of your time, won't it? With two small children, I wonder how you will do it." He looked at her with a frown.

"You don't approve?" Jeanette asked. She was feeling more and more annoyed as the date progressed.

"Well, I should think at your age, it might be difficult. I had thought you were more the stay at home mom type," he said, and smiled as if he hadn't just insulted her.

"I don't think anyone is too old to go back to school and I find your insinuation that a woman with children can only be a mother completely ridiculous," she told him, angrily.

"I'm sorry if I offended you. I didn't mean it that way, really," he said, and dropped the line of conversation.

Jeanette ate the rest of her meal in silence. Somehow, she had picked her first date as a man that had the same outlook as her ex-husband. She certainly didn't need that. This was their last date, for sure.

Chapter Seventeen

Jeanette was just glad to get away from Charles by the time the date was over. What an egotistical jerk! How had Brett stood him all those years as a best friend? She got out of his car, went into her house and slammed the door. Well, now she knew why she didn't date.

She locked the front door and dropped the contents of her purse in the tray on the stand beside the entry. Then she went upstairs. There was only one cure for the night she'd had. She went into the bathroom and started a bubble bath. In her room, she began to strip her clothes off when she heard a loud crash downstairs.

She looked around the room for something she could use for a weapon. There wasn't much to choose from. She grabbed the flashlight from the table. It would do some damage if she hit someone in the head with it.

With her bathrobe wrapped around her, she quietly walked to the top of the stairs. She could hear someone walking through the kitchen down there. She figured her best chance was to stay at the top of the stairs where she had a little advantage if someone came up.

It was then that she saw Charles walk out of the kitchen and stand at the bottom of the stairs. He hadn't looked up yet, but she saw the glint of a knife in his hand. She froze for a second, knowing that she would have no chance against him. She ran to the bathroom. It was the only room with a lock on the inside.

She had left her cell phone on the stand downstairs. Why would Charles be coming after her like this? Was he completely psychotic?

Locked inside, she sat with her back up against the bathroom door. The small window would be no help at all. Even if she could fit through it, it was a straight drop to the ground. Tears started squeezing out the corners of her eyes. She hadn't even thought about installing an alarm system. Suddenly she heard a loud ruckus downstairs and shockingly a barking, growling dog. Then silence.

Cautiously, she opened the door. Her curiosity drove her to the stairs where she was attacked by Franklin. She let out a scream until she realized that it was the dog licking her to death. At the bottom of the stairs, a voice called out.

"Down, Franklin." The dog moved off of Jeanette and ran back down the stairs to his master. "Sorry about that. He tends to get overly friendly."

It was Josh. "Where is he? Where is Charles?"

"He took off. Franklin got a good piece of him first, though. The cops will be here soon. I called them as soon as I saw that guy snooping behind your house."

"Thanks!" Jeanette said, coming down the steps and burst into tears, to her mortification.

"Oh, hey." He put an arm around her shoulders. "It's okay. You're safe now." She clung to him for a moment, still scared out of her wits. She finally recovered enough to pull away a little. He pushed his hair out of his eyes and pushed his glasses up the bridge of his nose at the same time.

"Thank goodness you own a grizzly bear," she said, finally, chuckling. She bent down to pet the dog. "You are both my heroes tonight."

Josh stayed with her while Jeanette spoke with the police and then he gave his own statement. They took pictures of the broken glass in the back door and commended Josh and his dog for their bravery.

241

How am I supposed to tell Brett about all this? Jeanette thought. She decided that she couldn't sleep here tonight and called Gracie to see if she could stay there. She wouldn't sleep at all until she knew that Charles was caught.

The more she thought about it, the more it felt like the whole town had gone crazy.

Josh offered to drive her over to Gracie's and Jeanette decided to let him. She wasn't in any condition to drive and she didn't want to run into Charles again, alone.

"I thought you were mad at me," Jeanette told him in the car. "Or that you just thought I was crazy."

He glanced over at her, his shyness taking over again. "I'm not mad at you and I don't think you're crazy," he mumbled.

They pulled into Gracie's driveway.

"Brett isn't here," Jeanette said, disturbed. What if Charles came here after her?

"Would you like me to come in and stay until he gets here?" Josh suggested.

"You don't mind? It shouldn't be long. Surely, Gracie has called him by now."

Gracie met them at the door and enveloped Jeanette in a hug, looking curiously over Jeanette's shoulder at Josh.

"Come in. Come in." She double locked the door after they got in.

"Where is Brett?" Jeanette asked.

"He went out looking for Charles, of course. He was raving mad. Who is your friend?"

242

"Oh, sorry. Gracie, this is my neighbor and savior of the night, Josh Truit. Josh, this is my sister, Gracie."

"Thank you so much for saving Jeanette. You have no idea how precious she is," Gracie said, emotionally, and then noticed how the man didn't take his eyes off of Jeanette. "Or maybe you do." She finished, with a sly grin. "You two go sit. I made a pot of coffee."

After Gracie returned with the coffee, Jeanette told her the entire story.

"I don't get it," Gracie said, shocked at Jeanette's story. "According to Brett, he is the greatest guy ever. I'm so sorry that happened to you."

"I don't get it, either. The date wasn't great, but it wasn't that bad. I don't know if he was intent on rape or murder. The question is, why?"

"Brett hadn't seen him for nearly two years before he came back a month ago," Gracie told her. "He sure didn't seem the psycho type."

"It was almost like he was a different person tonight," Jeanette said and told her about the conversation about the plantation.

"Wow. I can see why he wasn't your dream date."

"He looked thrilled at the idea of owning slaves and being lord of the manor, I think he called it. Being a bigot doesn't necessarily make him psychotic, though. That came as a shock," Jeanette added.

"He'll be lucky if Brett doesn't rip his head off. I hope the police find Charles before he does."

On cue, the doorbell rang and Jeanette followed Gracie to the door.

"It's me," Brett said from the other side as Gracie opened the door.

"What happened?" Gracie asked as Brett hugged both women, one with each arm.

"He's been arrested. I spoke to him and he acted like he had no idea what was going on." Brett walked through and the trio followed him back to the living-room.

"Brett, this is Josh Truitt. Jeanette's neighbor."

"Yes, we've met before." Brett shook Josh's hand. "When I was working on the house. Good to see you, Josh, and thanks for watching out for my sister."

"No problem. I guess, I'll be going now."

"Good night, Josh. Thank you," Jeanette said, as she followed him to the front door.

"I'll see you tomorrow," he said and left.

Gracie stood in the hallway looking at Jeanette, curiously. Jeanette caught her look.

"So? Josh Truitt. Seems like a really nice guy," Gracie said.

Jeanette walked by her and back into the living-room. "It's not what you think. He's just a friend."

"He is awfully into you for a friend," Gracie said.

"Don't be ridiculous. Besides, he is interested in someone. He told me so."

"Oh, he is interested in someone, alright. Jeanette, the man couldn't take his eyes off of you. He is smitten."

"I'm not interested in Josh. He is a nice guy and a friend. That is all," Jeanette said, glaring at Gracie. "I'm really tired. I'm going to bed."

Jeanette went upstairs to her old room and lay back on the bed. She wasn't interested in Josh, was she? He was just a friend. A friend that was in the habit of rescuing her at odd times. Twice in a week, as a matter of fact. And he was attractive...if she discounted the glasses and khaki pants.

Her second date with Charles hadn't gone as well as the first. Could it have been that she'd already spent enough time with Josh that she just didn't see Charles the same way? She had to admit that she was rather fascinated by the blue eyes behind the thick glasses and even found it endearing how he had the habit of pushing the glasses up when he was nervous. Now that she thought about it, she was far more attracted to Josh than she'd ever been to Charles.

Rolling over in the bed, restlessly, she realized that it didn't matter one iota how attractive she found Josh if Gracie was wrong and he was only being a good friend and neighbor.

Chapter Eighteen

Jeanette went out the next morning and found the biggest dog bone she could find and bought the makings of a nice meal. She decided to have Josh over for dinner as a thank you.

She realized now that she did really like Josh and her feelings for him kind of sneaked up on her when she wasn't paying attention. She wasn't totally convinced of Gracie's opinion that he was 'smitten', but she thought this might give him the chance to speak his mind if he was. Lord, he was so shy, if she left it up to him, he may never admit it.

When she got home, he was outside collecting the mail and came over to help her carry the groceries inside.

"Thanks," she told him, as she set her handful on the counter.

"Anytime. How are you feeling?" he asked, setting down his load.

"Not bad, actually. I'm sorry for Brett. He is feeling hurt, I think. Charles was supposed to be his best man at their wedding."

"That's tough."

"It is. He'll be okay, though. They've been through much worse." She began putting the groceries away. "I was thinking that maybe you and Franklin could come over for dinner tonight. Kind of as a thank you." She turned and smiled at him. She waited nervously for him to tell her he had a date or something else to do.

"That would be nice. Thanks," he said, smiling at his feet.

"How about a glass of iced tea?" she offered.

"Sure," he said.

She poured them each a tall glass. "Gracie really liked you. She could talk of nothing else after you left last night," Jeanette told him.

"They seem like nice people." He pushed his glasses up, nervously.

"They are. Gracie, for some reason, had the idea that you are attracted to me. I assured her that you were interested in someone else," Jeanette said, primly and holding her breath.

He looked at her in dismay and set his glass down. "Jeanette, I-I…"

"Yes?" she prodded.

He broke eye contact and looked down. "The only woman I'm interested in is you. I know I'm not exactly a catch or anything."

"Really? What's wrong with you?" Jeanette asked, releasing her breath in relief. Her eyes swept up and down his tall frame. "Well, other than you are obviously fashion-challenged."

"I don't have a lot of money, no flashy car."

"Well, the money thing isn't important. I'll buy you a flashy car if you want. I'll take you shopping for some matching clothes. But I'm not sure I can deal with you looking at your feet all the time. What is it with them, anyway? Those shoes absolutely do not warrant that kind of worship." She looked at him seriously as he met her eyes.

247

"Josh, I don't care about any of that. You are the sweetest man I know. Not to mention that you have the sexiest eyes and geez, all I want right now is for you to…" She was cut off as his mouth came down on hers.

All shyness fell away as longing took over. Jeanette had never known what could be conveyed in one kiss as she responded and matched his desire with her own. They were both breathless as he released her.

"I think we are compatible enough." She gave a low chuckle, still feeling her skin tingling from his kiss.

"I've got to go let Franklin out before I have a lake on my kitchen floor." Josh ran a hand through his hair.

"Why don't you bring him over when you're finished? I got him a present," she suggested.

"Should I change into my jeans?" he asked, joking.

"Don't you own a pair of shorts? In case you haven't noticed, it's sweltering outside. We can barbecue tonight on my new grill. I got steaks."

"Be right back," he said, and escaped through the door.

Jeanette didn't remember ever feeling as happy as she did in that moment. Somehow everything felt right with Josh and natural as if it was meant to be. Why hadn't she realized it weeks ago?

She ran upstairs to find something nice to wear. Searching through the closet, she chose a tangerine sundress. She slipped it on and slid her feet into a pair of sandals. Looking in the mirror, she refreshed her make-up and picked out her hair.

She got back downstairs just in time to let Josh and Franklin in.

248

"You look beautiful," he said, and Jeanette felt herself blush as she bent down to pet the dog.

*****

"Have you had any more dreams?" Josh asked, as they cuddled on the couch late that evening, Franklin laying at their feet.

"Night before last. I don't know what to think about them," Jeanette told him.

"Any more black clouds?" he asked.

"No. That sure was creepy."

"Don't I know it. I saw it again in my house a couple of days after the museum incident."

Jeanette leaned up to look him in the eye. "Really? Did it do anything? Are you okay?"

"It didn't do anything but float around my house for a few minutes and disappear. It's pretty weird. Franklin went bananas. I've heard around town that other people are seeing things, too."

"What kind of things?"

"I'm not real sure. People aren't being very specific. The lady at the supermarket called it 'strange happenings'."

"I can't help but think this is all connected to the plantation. Otherwise, why would I be dreaming about Lydia?" Jeanette wondered.

"If you need me, I'm just a few feet away. I'd better be going, but don't be afraid to wake me up." He picked up her cell phone and saved his number in the contacts. He kissed her and stood. "Goodnight, Honey."

She walked him to the door as the dog followed. "Goodnight."

She locked her door behind him and wandered upstairs in a lovesick daze.

Chapter Nineteen

Charles sat in the town jail, still wondering what had happened. He had been angry when he had come back to town and realized that a legitimate heir had taken over the plantation. The family was supposed to be dead and he was about to play his card. He was going to purchase the property and make his home there. Now, he didn't have a chance at it. *I shouldn't have stayed away so long,* he thought.

Still, he didn't know what had happened last week. He had just asked that homely little woman out to please Brett. It was no big deal, really. Then he suddenly wanted to kill her. It wasn't the first time he had had that feeling, but he had never carried it through. He remembered breaking into her house and intending to slice her throat. He just didn't remember why. He didn't care enough about her enough to want to kill her. If he was going to do something that drastic, he would have planned it without the risk of getting caught. Instead, he had blatantly broke into her house, not caring if the entire neighborhood was watching.

How was he going to get out of this one? At least, they couldn't prove attempted murder. Breaking and entering with a weapon was the most they could get.

*****

Mary Joe, Gracie, and Jeanette were at Gracie's house making flower rosettes and decorations for the wedding.

Mary Joe was chattering away, giving them all the local news as she had heard it at the café. It seemed that nearly everyone in town was seeing something strange. Jeanette had kept it to herself all this time about seeing Gladys in her bathroom. She wasn't sure now that she hadn't imagined it at all. Also, she couldn't help but think that the strange dreams she was having somehow tied into it all. She didn't want to say anything in front of Mary Joe, but she thought it might be a good idea to talk to Gracie about it.

The problem is that Gracie was kind of ignoring the situation. She was caught up in her wedding plans and Jeanette certainly didn't want to take that excitement from her. After the wedding, Gracie and Brett were planning a month vacation in Bermuda. It would be too late by that time. Something serious was going on and it had to be connected to the plantation, somehow.

Then Mary Joe began asking questions about Jeanette's ordeal with Charles.

"Oh, well, it is over now. Charles is in jail," Gracie told her, getting Jeanette off the hook.

Jeanette twirled her ribbon around the base of the flower and tied it off. Snipping the flower off, she was ready to attach it to the vase when a thought occurred to her. What if Charles was just Charlie, Brett's pal, normally, but he was different because of the things going on in town? Could something be influencing him? Like Alfred had influenced Edgar and Gram? She looked up and her mouth made a small 'o' as her line of thought came together. Then just as suddenly, she had to dismiss it. Alfred not only had been banished, but he could only possess someone in the bloodline. At least, wasn't that what Art had said last year?

*****

Back at Marilyn's house, the three sat around the table with a monopoly board in the center.

"We started something," Lucy said. "We started something and now our friends are dying."

"Don't be silly, honey. None of this was our fault. Art was living on borrowed time as it was. Gladys had a heart attack. Sometimes things just happen," Veronica said, shaking her head.

"No. Lucy's right," Marilyn said. "We all saw something come out of the board that day. Something evil. Can't you feel it all over town? Something bad has come to Swanson and we are to blame."

"I saw snakes in my bedroom last night," Lucy said. "They were there one minute and gone the next. I think they were there to get me. I'm not scared to die, but I am scared of the snakes."

"Do you think it is really Alfred Mallory?" Veronica asked, a shiver going through her small frame.

"I don't know what it was," Marilyn said, "I do know that there have been five deaths in just the last week. That is a lot for this town."

"I heard Jimmy Belmer tell Mary Joe that he had seen snakes, too. In his kitchen. Snakes with red eyes."

"The snakes I saw had red eyes," Lucy said in a whine.

"Do you think we should tell someone?" Veronica asked, looking the two women in the eye.

"Who? No one would believe us, anyway," Marilyn said.

"Too bad that we can't get Alfred into this board game," Lucy said. "We could just send him to jail, do not pass go…"

Chapter Twenty

The next couple of weeks were full of wedding plans, dress fittings and then last minute preparations. Jeanette was caught up in the excitement. She intended everything to be perfect and was in charge of the decorations and the seating at both the park and at the plantation ball-room. Josh was more than glad to help and by the day before the wedding, everything was set up and ready.

That night, Jeanette was surprised that Jim let the kids call her and they had a good visit even though she could tell that they weren't happy. She got the impression that Aubrey had been coached as to what to tell her and what not to. She was worried, but helpless to do anything. They still had another month before coming home.

She took a long bath and went to bed early, knowing that tomorrow was going to be a long, busy day. The dream began in the field by the pond.

Belinda had planned a picnic and Billy was there. Lydia could tell that something was going on that she didn't know about. By now, she was used to the furtive glances between her two friends, but there was something different about it this afternoon.

Finally, Belinda decided to tell her. She pulled out a box and opened it to reveal some feathers and stones. "We are going to going to break the curse tonight," she told Lydia.

"How?" Lydia asked, more than a little frightened.

"In the tunnels. We can trap the demon. The voodoo lady in Atlanta showed me. Are you going to come?"

254

Lydia didn't want to. She was afraid of the tunnels. They were dark and creepy. She knew that she couldn't say no, though. "Okay."

"I knew you would help!" Belinda grinned.

"How can you trap a demon?" Lydia asked.

"We have to get him to leave my dad. You can't trap a demon that has a body. We have to lure Alfred out of him first. Then we break the curse using these. It will work."

"I still don't understand. How will you lure Alfred out?" Lydia asked.

"Billy can do it. He has the blood of Dahlia. He can call Alfred out. We break the curse and then trap Alfred. My father won't even know a thing."

"You still haven't told me how you are going to trap Alfred," Lydia said.

"The trap is drawn on the ground. I have a picture of it in the tunnel. He can't move out of the circle and we just have to have a vessel to collect him. The lady gave me a chant that will draw him into the vessel. That is all. We can do it," Belinda said, positively.

It all seemed a little too complicated and far-fetched to actually work.

The dream skipped and the next thing Jeanette knew, Belinda was slipping a cross around her neck. "I have the ruby necklace. The cross will protect you, Lydie."

They were already down in the tunnels and they had lit a dozen candles that cast an eerie glow on everything.

Billy didn't look quite as sure of himself as he had that afternoon and let Belinda do most of the preparation. They

255

drew the demon trap in the dirt near the tunnel entrance. When everything was set, they held hands and Billy started reading the chant that would bring Alfred. Before he was finished, Belinda began her chant to break the curse. Lydia stood a few feet from them chewing her finger nails.

After ten minutes nothing happened.

"Did it work?" Lydia asked.

"Only one way to find out," Belinda said and grabbed the uncorked bottle that was supposed to contain a demon. Billy and Lydia followed. Outside, everything was abnormally quiet and not a breath of wind stirred. There was nothing in the demon trap that could be seen. The three walked slowly toward the house.

"Look." Billy pointed the tree line surrounding the pond. Several white forms flitted through the trees.

"We didn't change a thing," Belinda said, disheartened. "I don't understand. Why didn't it work?"

Lydia put her arm around her friend. "Maybe we can try again."

"Maybe, they are too strong. Alfred is too strong," Billy said. "I have to get home." He walked away through the field.

"Come on, Belinda. We'd better get to our rooms before your father finds us out after dark." Lydia shivered with the thought of being caught.

"I just don't understand," Belinda said again, near tears.

*****

Jeanette woke up early with the dream still fresh in her mind. Today was the big day and she tried to shrug off the melancholy mood that the dream had left her with. Today was a day for celebration.

Chapter Twenty-one

Jeanette spent the morning at the park, making sure that everything was right. When they were convinced it looked perfect, Jeanette and Mary Joe went to Gracie's to dress. The wedding was at 1:00 and they would have dinner at the reception at the plantation.

When they arrived, Maria was already there and Gracie had just been zipped into the dress.

"Wow! You look beautiful," Jeanette said, stunned at the vision Gracie made. Gracie gave her a gorgeous smile.

"You girls better get dressed!" Maria said, shoving them out of the room. "Hurry. We still have to do your hair and make-up."

The next hour was focused on the bridesmaids. They were all ready by the time they were due to leave for the park.

They were all laughing and giggling on the way. Gracie had to stay inside until the wedding started, unseen through the tinted windows.

Jeanette went to speak to the minister. Brett and Josh were already in their places. Jeanette was shocked to see how dazzling Josh looked in the best man's tuxedo. Without his glasses, he seemed nothing like the man she had met a few weeks ago. He must have felt her staring at him because he raised his eyes to hers as she approached.

"You look beautiful," he told her, as she took her place at the top of the gazebo.

"So do you," she said, unable to take her eyes off of him. Finally, she turned her eyes to the crowd.

258

The bridge club ladies looked charming, though it was always sad to see only three of them, now. They sat in the front row. The chairs weren't nearly enough and there were people standing everywhere. Many hadn't received an invitation, but wanted to get a glimpse of the young couple from the plantation.

At 1:00, they got the music started and they were ready to begin. Jeanette stood in the gazebo watching Gracie walk up the carpeted walkway. She looked lovely. Jeanette couldn't help shedding a few happy tears. A couple of little girls from the church were in front of her tossing flower petals randomly, looking adorable. She was saddened a little that Aubrey and Jasper couldn't be there.

Josh held out a hand to Gracie to help her up the stairs in her long dress. Dozens of people were snapping pictures along with the professional photographers as they all stood together. The plan was that the minister would stand with his back to the crowd, while Gracie and Brett stood on the second step for the benefit of the photographers. The bridesmaids and groomsmen stayed at the top, but moved toward the edge of the top step. Jeanette had marked their spots earlier that day so that there would be no confusion.

Gracie and Brett stepped down to their markers as soon as the music stopped. The minister began the ceremony.

"Dearly beloved, we are gathered here today to join this man and this woman in holy matrimony."

Jeanette looked over the crowd as the wedding proceeded, only looking back down as her brother was sliding a ring on Gracie's slim finger. She glanced over at Josh, and their eyes locked for a moment. They shared a smile just as the minister said, 'You may kiss the bride'.

Then a shrill scream came out of the crowd and Lucy Cowan collapsed in a faint. Everyone ran toward her, including Brett and Gracie. Jeanette and the others stepped down from the gazebo.

A loud clap of thunder and a bright flash of light was the last thing she remembered before everything went dark.

*****

Jeanette woke up in the emergency room with Gracie, Brett, and Josh leaning over her, all frowning in concern. Gracie was still in her wedding dress and looked very out of place in the examining room.

"What happened?" Jeanette started to sit up and felt her head throbbing.

"You have a goose egg. You'd better stay down until the doctor sees you," Brett said, pushing her gently back down.

"The roof of the gazebo fell," Gracie said, crying. "Josh saved you. He pushed you out of the way. Everyone else is okay."

"Lucy. Something happened to her, didn't it?" Jeanette asked.

"She is okay—a little hysterical. She said something about 'raising the dead'. I don't know," Josh said, shaking his head.

"Oh, aren't you guys supposed to be at your dinner and reception?" Jeanette realized.

"We need to be with you," Gracie said.

"I'm okay," Jeanette told her. "Really. Josh can stay with me. You can, can't you?" she gave him an imploring look.

"Yeah, honey. Of course, I can. She is right, you know." Josh turned to Brett. "You should be with your guests. I'll call you if anything happens. We can come out after the doctor sees her."

"I'm fine, Gracie. You go and have fun. I'll be out there with you before you know it," Jeanette told her. No matter how she felt, she wasn't going to miss seeing them off on their honeymoon.

"Jeanette, I don't think we should leave you," Gracie objected.

"Listen, Grace. I'm really okay. I might have a headache. That's all. I want you to go," Jeanette said, determined.

Brett was finally able to pull Gracie away and Josh and Jeanette were left alone in the room when the doctor entered.

"Well, young lady, it seems that you have quite a bump on the head." The doctor took a close look. "Actually, the swelling is a good sign though it will hurt like the dickens. Your x-rays look okay. The bump will go away in a day or two. If you become nauseous or have blurred vision or the headache persists, see a doctor immediately. I'm going to give you a prescription for a pain reliever. You should go home and take it easy for a few days."

"I can go, now?" Jeanette asked.

"You can go home." The doctor agreed and handed her a sheet of instructions along with the prescription.

Josh helped her up and her head throbbed painfully.

"Let's get you home," Josh said and walked her out.

"I'm not going home, Josh. We have to get to the plantation."

261

"Babe, you are in no condition for a party." He tried to reason with her.

"I'm not going to do the lambada. I just have to be there for Gracie and Brett," Jeanette told him. "They'll be leaving tonight."

Chapter Twenty-Two

An hour later, Jeanette found out that they weren't leaving.

Gracie made her stay in the lounge and rest with an ice pack on her forehead. She'd brought her a plate of food. Josh sat with her and munched on a green salad as Brett filled them in on what had happened.

"Lucy saw an apparition of a woman and then there was a flash of lightning, out of a blue sky that hit the gazebo. Then the roof collapsed, barely missing all of us. Lucy and the other two bridge club members want to speak to us after the reception. I'll bring them in here so we can hear what they have to say, but they seem to think that all of this is their fault."

"Their fault? How could that be?" Jeanette asked.

"I guess we'll find out," Gracie added. "We are almost finished out there. We'll open the gifts and after the initial toast, we can slip away with the ladies. The orchestra was paid to play until 5:00. The dancing and food should keep the guests happy."

Jeanette stood after they left. "I don't want to miss this," she told Josh, and walked into the ballroom, Josh trailing behind. They sat down at a table near the door and watched as the happy couple toasted and ate cake from each other's hand. The photographer snapped pictures of everything. Jeanette wished that she had her camera as well.

When the gifts were opened and they had had the first waltz, Gracie and Brett made their escape.

Back in the lounge, they all listened to Lucy's confession while the other ladies nodded in agreement that all she told was true.

"Then Gladys was dead," Lucy said, hysterically as Jeanette tried to comfort her.

"None of this is your fault," Jeanette told her. "You couldn't have known something like that would happen."

Gracie hadn't said a word until now. "You called on Alfred?" The ladies all nodded in unison. Gracie turned to Brett, "If this is Alfred, what are we going to do?" She had gone pale.

"There is more," Brett said, showing Gracie some pictures. "One of the guests took these right before the gazebo fell. I took them off the memory card and printed them a little while ago." Gracie passed them to Jeanette after looking at them.

The first one depicted a perfect picture of a female apparition standing close to Lucy. The second one showed the lightning strike, but in the bright blue sky above the Gazebo were two glowing red eyes.

"The guy didn't see the ghost or the eyes when he snapped the pictures. He didn't notice until he was looking back at them a little later," Brett said, as Jeanette passed the pictures to the bridge club. Gasps and exclamations followed.

"What are we going to do?" Gracie asked, looking at Brett for an answer.

"I think we should call it a night and talk about this tomorrow. Jeanette looks like she is about to collapse and it's already been a long day," Brett said and looked at Josh. "Why don't you and Jeanette come to our house in the morning? We'll talk about this more rationally and see if we can figure out what's going on."

264

*****

Josh drove Jeanette home and then went to his house to collect Franklin and change his clothes. Jeanette changed out of her clothes, too, and was in a pair of pajamas and a robe when Josh returned.

She was in the kitchen getting ready to make coffee when he came in and took the can from her.

"Sit down, honey, before you fall down."

Jeanette didn't argue. She felt too miserable to do anything else. She picked up the bottle of pain pills from the table and took two. She started to get up to fetch a glass of water when Josh gently pushed her back in the chair.

"I'll get it," he said, quietly.

After she'd drunk half of the water, she folded her arms and rested her head on the table.

Josh said nothing until the coffee was done and took the cups to the living-room. He came back promptly and helped Jeanette to the couch.

He settled himself at the end of the couch with her head in his lap.

"Does it look awful?" Jeanette finally asked and reached up to touch her lump.

"It looks sore. I'm so sorry that you got hurt." The pain in his voice made her open her eyes and look up at him.

"It wasn't your fault. Gracie said that you saved my life today. That makes three times, already. Maybe, you're my guardian angel." She kissed his hand.

"It has occurred to me that something is after you. The thing at the museum, Charles, and now this," Josh said.

"Any or all of us could have been killed today," Jeanette said.

"Then why are you the only one hurt?" Josh asked. "Babe, Brett and Gracie weren't under the gazebo and Mary Joe and Maria were on the second step. It was you and me directly under it. If that woman hadn't called out at that moment, the two of us would be dead. The others may have been injured, but not dead. I think I was collateral damage and it was intended for you. I'm not trying to scare you, but I've been thinking this through all day."

"Why? Even if it is Alfred, why would I be the target?"

"I don't know. But what if Charles was being controlled by the evil force that has been doing things in town?"

"I thought about that. The thing is, Alfred only possessed people in his own bloodline," Jeanette said.

"Could Charles somehow be in the bloodline?" Josh asked, pointedly.

"I suppose anything is possible. Sweetheart, I just can't think anymore tonight. My head is killing me."

"It's okay. You rest. I'm not leaving you here alone tonight."

"Josh?" Jeanette asked weakly.

"What is it, Babe?"

"Where are your glasses?"

He chuckled softly. "I bought contacts," he said, caressing her hair. He leaned in and tenderly kissed the top of her head.

"Oh," she said and finally fell asleep.

Chapter Twenty-Three

Back at Gracie's, they all sat around the table, silent at first. Then Jeanette began to speak. She told Brett and Gracie about everything; from seeing Gladys in her bathroom to her being a target as she and Josh had talked about last night.

"Alfred is back. There is no doubt. He used the bridge club to get here. He is no longer tied to the plantation, so there is no containing the damage. Any ideas?" Gracie said.

"Josh and I think maybe he has taken over Charles. If you think about it, it makes sense. He's never showed any signs of being psychotic before all this happened. People don't just suddenly change their personality. Brett has already stated that he isn't acting like himself at all," Jeanette said.

"Charles wasn't the same after he first came back, though." Brett admitted. "Maybe not psychotic, but he acted like he was majorly put out about something. When I confronted him about it, he just laughed it off."

"When we banished Alfred from the plantation, we gave him the world on a platter, didn't we?" Gracie asked, weakly. "He was no longer trapped on the plantation."

"No, Grace, we didn't. We couldn't know that he would find a way back. We have to find a way to banish him for good. I just don't understand why he is so focused on me. I had so little to do with it all," Jeanette said, shaking her head. "If Josh hadn't shown up, I think Charles would have killed me."

"Tell them about the dreams." Josh nudged Jeanette.

"Dreams? What dreams, Jeanette?" Brett asked, looking her in the eye.

268

"Well, I keep having these dreams. They are about Belinda, Billy, and Lydia. In the dreams, I see everything from Lydia's point of view. They are all on the plantation. I don't know if they are coming from an outside force or my imagination. It's just that they are so detailed."

"We never found out what really happened to Lydia," Gracie said. "We only know that she died on the plantation. You know, she is one spirit that never came to us. If she was trapped at the plantation like the rest, she left quietly with the others."

"This is all rather confusing," Josh said.

"Not really," Jeanette told him. "It is really pretty simple. Anyone that died on the plantation after Dahlia's curse was trapped on the plantation until the day that Gracie released them. We assumed they all went to where they were supposed to go that night, but what if some of them stuck around waiting for Alfred to find a way back? Not all of those spirits were good. He had his own following that terrorized the living. The good spirits primarily stayed below in the tunnels unless they were helping Gracie."

"So, now he is using a few that stayed behind along with the dozen or so he has collected in town since his return to strengthen himself to terrorize again. Only with a bigger playground this time," Brett said. "If he could gain enough strength to possess Charlie, then the rules have changed. Before he could only possess those that were blood descendants, right? Isn't that what the voodoo queen told us?"

"Perhaps it's time to give her a call," Gracie said. "I think Jeanette is right. For some reason, Alfred considers her a threat. I can't think why I wouldn't be his first choice for an adversary."

"Because he knows that you can defeat him, perhaps," Jeanette thought.

269

"I don't think so. The blood thing was just to break the curse," Brett said. "There has to be a reason that he is going after Jeanette. Maybe, it is just revenge against Gracie. He knows that you two are close."

"Maybe. I just can't figure out these dreams. I feel like they are trying to tell me something. Something that I just don't quite get," Jeanette said, dismally.

*****

During the next few days, things in town were escalating. Someone else had leaked photos of the wedding to the newspaper that were just as detailed as the ones that Brett had found. People were starting to panic as more of the ghoulish specters were seen. No longer were people embarrassed or afraid to discuss it and it was all that was heard everywhere.

Josh and Jeanette stayed primarily at the house and most of the businesses in town shut down for the duration. Nearly everyone was afraid to go out after dark.

It was the night before Gracie and Jeanette's trip to Atlanta that Jeanette had a dream of Lydia.

Edgar came to Lydia's room. He didn't bother to knock, but burst in and cornered her in the tiny space.

"You knew it, didn't you? You knew that Belinda was sneaking around with that boy."

Lydia cowered in the corner by her bed, not knowing what to do or say.

"Answer me!" he shouted, making her jump.

"They are only friends," Lydia tried.

"Only friends?" Edgar, in his rage, reached out and slapped Lydia off her feet. "Tell me the truth."

270

"They're in love. They're gonna get married," Lydia said, bravely.

"Gonna get married? Is there a reason they need to get married, Lydia?"

Lydia could see the red in his eyes, and saw the blow coming but was helpless to avoid it. She fell to the ground at the punch to the side of her head.

"Answer me, now. Is there a reason that they need to get married?"

Lydia could only nod, feeling nothing but pain and shame as she betrayed her only friend. She sensed more than saw Edgar leave before blacking out.

Then suddenly the dream changed. She instinctively knew that she was on the plantation. She was in the field, but it was dark. Behind her, she heard someone coming up on her, but she was out of breath as if she'd been running. She turned and looked behind her. It was Belinda. She was screaming as a man stepped toward her swinging a scythe, missing her by inches.

Lydia ran toward Edgar, building up enough momentum to knock him over.

"Run! Get out of here!" she shouted at Belinda.

"I can't leave you, Lydie," Belinda yelled back as Edgar got to his feet. Lydia looked around for a weapon, but they were in the middle of the open field. There was nothing. Belinda had gotten to her feet and put some space between her and Edgar.

Edgar had lost his blade in the fall and was looking for it in the high grass.

271

"Belinda, you have to save the baby! Run now! I'll be behind you, I promise!" she cried out.

Belinda nodded and ran, Edgar at her heels. Lydia ran, too, chasing them. She jumped on Edgar's back as she caught up and her weight brought him down. Lydia looked up to see Belinda running on toward the light of the Grandys' house.

Smiling in the knowledge that she'd saved her friend, she didn't even notice that Edgar had her by the throat until the pain overwhelmed her.

"I will kill you now and I will torment you every day until eternity." Edgar moved his mouth, but it was Alfred's unholy voice that came out.

"No, you won't," Lydia said and found the strength to kick him off of her. She rolled to the side as he brought the scythe down burying it in the ground beside her. She let out a scream as she rolled again. She knew that she had to pass the border of the property. If she died on the plantation, she would be trapped forever. Just as the scythe went through her middle, she rolled off across the boundary line.

Alfred didn't even notice as he finished the job. The last thing Lydia saw was the metal blade and the red eyes above it.

Chapter Twenty-Four

Gracie and Jeanette went to Atlanta to see Almira Hayes.

Almira looked up when she saw them come into her shop. "Ah! There you are." She locked the front door behind them and motioned for them to come into the back room. "I could feel you coming. Would you like lemon in your tea?"

"Yes, please," Jeanette answered automatically. Gracie nodded.

"Have a seat, ladies and we will talk." She brought a tray over and set it on the table in front of the old divan.

Jeanette and Gracie sat down.

"Now, tell me," Almira said, as she slowly stirred her tea.

Jeanette started and told her most of the story and let Gracie finish.

Almira nodded. "I should have foreseen something like this. Alfred is a strong entity. You weakened him greatly, but as he builds his army, his strength will return and he will be a difficult adversary."

"What can we do?" Gracie asked.

"Well, the first thing you have to do is protect your town. You can keep the demon out, for a while. It will give us time to form a plan. You are the one that he wants." She turned to Jeanette. "I can sense it, but I don't know why. You need to keep yourself protected. I can make you a talisman. Keep salt on the threshold of your doors and windows."

"How do we protect the town?" Jeanette asked.

"You must create a sanctuary. I will help you." Almira stood and went to her desk where she searched through a thick book. It took a few minutes for her to find what she wanted. Finally, she wrote out a list of words and brought them back to them. "You must use these symbols. In five places around the outskirts of town, creating a circle. Try to place them as evenly as possible to create your sanctuary. This will separate the demon from his army. They won't be able to cross into the circle into town and he will lose some of his strength."

"We can't keep Alfred out of town?" Gracie asked, apprehensively.

"No. But he won't be able to terrorize, either," Almira said. "This will give us time to plan before the full moon. I will be in contact with you."

*****

In the car on the way home, Jeanette looked over at Gracie who seemed tense.

"Do you think this will work?" she held up the sheet of symbols.

"I see no reason why not," Gracie said. "I just don't like you being the target of Alfred's wrath and him free to walk about town. Maybe you should go stay at the plantation. He can't go there."

"I'm not going to let him run me out of my home," Jeanette said, adamantly. "Besides, Almira said that he wouldn't be as strong." Still, she couldn't help reaching up and touching her bruised temple.

That evening, Jeanette and Josh went to each of the five places that they had mapped out, placing a sign with what looked like some kind of hieroglyph writing on them, forming an as close to perfect as possible circle around the town .

274

Josh insisted on sleeping on Jeanette's couch since she refused to stay at the plantation. It was nice to have him close and she knew that she was falling for him a little too quickly. She still kept up the boundaries that she felt was appropriate between them, considering that they had only been dating for a couple of weeks. Funnily enough, Franklin began sleeping upstairs beside her bed.

She complied with the salt just to be safe and then there was nothing to do but wait.

They did see a difference in town. People began to feel safe as the ghosts had disappeared and businesses opened again.

Jeanette knew that it wasn't over. Not by a long shot.

*****

It was a few nights later that Josh came upstairs and tapped on her bedroom door.

Jeanette had just gotten to sleep and looked at the clock. It was 11:00 pm. She opened the door, still dazed.

"Hi," she said.

"Hi," he said and pulled her against him. "Go get dressed, honey. I've got something to show you." He kissed the top of her head and let her go.

Jeanette did as he asked, but wondered what could have him so rattled.

She pulled on the clothes she had worn earlier and went downstairs to meet him.

They got in his car and drove to the outskirts of town. He turned off the headlights.

275

"Come on." He got out and she opened her door. He stood leaning against the hood of the car. "Look," he said, pointing out at the field.

At first, she didn't see anything. Then, her eyes adjusted to the dark and she saw them. There were dozens of apparitions standing in the field. None of them approached, they seemed unanimated. They were watching, though. She could feel their eyes on her.

"What are they doing?" she whispered, sliding her hand into his.

"What do they want?"

"I don't know. It's like they are waiting. They have been out there for the last few nights. Garret Chapman, the mechanic? He told me about it last night. I thought you should see it," Josh told her.

"I just can't figure it out. This all seems so personal to me. Why does Alfred want to torment me?"

"Your dreams," Josh said. "There is something that I thought of earlier. I was just sitting right here in the car, watching them." He gestured toward the ghosts in the field. "What if you are more than just Lydia's great niece? What if you are Lydia?"

"I don't understand," Jeanette said, confused.

"What if you are the reincarnation of Lydia? Perhaps, you did something in your past life that he is avenging now?"

"What? Let's just pretend for a moment that is true. Wouldn't killing me once be enough?" she asked, unbelievingly.

"Not if you escaped. I've been thinking about what Brett said the other day. If Lydia was killed off of the plantation, she would have escaped Alfred's grasp."

"Why would she have been so important?" Jeanette said, uncomprehending.

"Because. She saved the child. The child that could destroy him. In your dream, you see yourself distracting Edgar so that Belinda could get away. I could see that he could blame you for it all. If Belinda hadn't escaped, he would still reign at that plantation. Now, to top it all off, he has been banished from his home." Josh squeezed her hand.

Jeanette let all that sink in. It was all true, she realized. It just took a fresh set of eyes to see it all clearly. Her dreams weren't just watching a scene from a distance. She could feel the fear and emotion as if it was really happening to her, because it did happen to her.

"Oh, God." Jeanette leaned back against the car. "I think you're right. That is what the dreams are for. Alfred warned me that he would torment me until eternity."

Suddenly, she was getting light-headed and she went limp as Josh caught her. He picked her up and put her in the back seat of the car.

"Jeanette! Honey, are you okay?" Josh was leaning over her.

Jeanette looked up at him, not knowing what had happened.

He could see her eyes open and breathed a sigh of relief. "You just scared the heck out of me."

"Sorry." She sat up. "What happened?"

"I think you fainted," he said.

277

"I fainted?" She had never fainted before.

"Come on. Let's get you home. I think you've had enough shocks for one night."

Chapter Twenty-Five

It was a week later that Almira called Gracie with a plan. Alfred could be trapped if his army of specters were dispelled. The problem was that they would need a lot of help from the town. She suggested calling a town meeting a couple of days before they put the plan into motion. If they could get some people from Swanson to help, the plan would work.

When Gracie told Jeanette, her heart dropped.

"Grace, no one is going to help when they think that it is over and done with. How are we going to convince them it isn't?"

"I don't know. We have to try, though. I know the bridge club will believe us and Mary Joe and Maria. Maybe a few will influence the rest."

Jeanette remained doubtful. Even if people didn't think that the danger was over, they would think twice about risking themselves in any way to help get rid of Alfred.

*****

The day before the meeting, Lowell Harper was repairing his fence, cursing the bulls that had gotten loose that morning. He saw that the post was ripped in half where the animals had broken through. About fifty feet away, a post was stuck in the ground not far from the road.

He ignored the weird writing on the post and shrugged as he pulled it up. It would work to replace his fence post, temporarily, at least.

*****

It didn't take long for chaos to ensue when the apparitions were back in town that night.

Jeanette and Josh were relaxing on the couch after dinner when Franklin started barking and going berserk. He was in the kitchen and when Jeanette walked in, there were snakes all over the area by the back door. They hissed as Josh took the broom swiping at them. Their ruby red eyes glowed.

Jeanette ran out the front of the house and opened the back door just in time for Josh to sweep the serpents out. Before Jeanette slammed the door shut behind her, one struck at her ankle barely missing her. She stepped into Josh's arms, terrified. He caressed her back trying to calm her shaking form.

"What happened? The posts aren't working, anymore?" Jeanette asked, her breath returning to normal.

"We had better find out," Josh said.

They drove to every spot until they found the missing post.

"Someone moved it," Jeanette said, shaking her head in bewilderment. "Do we have another post?"

"We'll have to get one. Come on."

*****

Charles was pacing back and forth in his cell. It was time, he knew. Time for Alfred to get him out. It wouldn't be long. He could feel the energy building. It was terrifying at first to feel Alfred thinking and taking over his movements. Now it became exciting and with the demon inside, he felt invincible. He knew and understood now why Alfred wanted Jeanette dead. It served his purpose as well. Killing Jeanette would punish Gracie and Brett for taking the plantation from him.

What he didn't understand was why Alfred didn't get him out of this cell. Why did they have to wait?

*****

Jeanette and Josh got the post replaced, but not before there were many disturbances in town. It was enough to get people riled and Jeanette felt that it could only be a good thing. This would be the push they needed to motivate the townspeople.

Late that afternoon, Jeanette got a call from Maria. She sounded excited, and asked Gracie and Jeanette to come to the museum.

At 2:00, Gracie, Brett, Josh, and Jeanette sat in the office at the museum with Maria.

"You won't believe what I found in the church records. It is a journal entry of a sort. There is no telling who wrote it, but it gives a detailed account of what happened on the first day of the storm that ran for ten days and flooded most of the area.

Services were held that day for Elizabeth Mallory. She would have been Alfred's granddaughter. During the service, a phantom wind rushed through the building and the body of the dead child rose up out of the coffin. The actual form of Alfred stood inside the door. He was attempting to take the girl's soul, according to the person who wrote this. Suddenly, Alfred let out a horrifying shriek and the child fell the three feet back into the coffin. The demon left in a puff of black smoke. All the people, family and servants left the chapel, in terror. Only the child's mother stayed behind to finish burying her daughter. Before she buried her, she removed Dahlia's cross from around the girl's neck.

It was believed that the necklace had originally belonged to Dahlia who cursed the plantation and it was a natural

281

talisman against Alfred. It's my opinion that this was written a while after the chapel incident.

Actually, I have seen reference to Dahlia's cross several times before, but I had no idea what it was. I just thought that you would all be interested in hearing what happened at the chapel," Maria finished.

"I wonder what happened to it," Gracie said. "The cross, I mean."

Jeanette thought for a moment, but shook her head. It couldn't be. Surely, Lydia's necklace wasn't Dahlia's cross, was it? But then, maybe that was what had saved her. It was miraculous how she had rolled over the boundary-line of the plantation a moment before she died.

"We could certainly use it now," Brett said. "We didn't find anything like that at the plantation house."

"I think I know where it is," Jeanette said. "I think Lydia was wearing it when she died. If she was buried in Belinda's grave, she might still be wearing it."

Belinda stood listening to the group and gave an audible sigh of relief that Jeanette finally understood. Luckily no one noticed as they filed out of the room.

Chapter Twenty-Six

That night, the four of them were at the city cemetery.

"You don't think anyone will notice us out here? Isn't it illegal to dig up a grave?" Jeanette asked, setting down the lantern at the end of the grave plot.

"Well, it is in my family plot. I don't think anyone will even notice with everything else going on," Gracie said.

Brett and Josh each started at a different end of the plot.

"This would have been a lot easier with a back hoe," Brett complained.

Jeanette picked up a shovel and started to help. The ground was packed pretty hard and she barely made a dent in the ground. Two hours later they finally hit the coffin. Josh and Brett brushed off the dirt with their hands.

"What do you think a body looks like after being buried for fifty years?" Jeanette asked, wrinkling her nose.

"No getting cold feet now," Brett said, cracking open the side with a nail bar.

He and Josh lifted the lid on the top half of the coffin. Jeanette looked down and saw a skull surrounded by straw colored hair. The cross was there but it had fallen into the rib cage. There were scraps of rotten material still attached to part of the mummified remains. Thankfully, there was no smell at all.

Gracie put her arm around Jeanette's waist and pulled her back away from the casket. Josh grabbed the cross and they pulled the lid back down. He handed it to Jeanette and they climbed back out of the hole. She put it in her pocket and helped fill in the hole.

She was quiet as the others joked about grave robbing.

*****

While they were retrieving the cross, Charles was awakened in his cell. The voice inside his head told him that it was time. Excitedly, he jumped up from the bunk. He wasn't certain just how he was getting out of his cell.

The officer on shift was sleeping soundly when he heard the loud clanging. He woke with a start and sighed when he realized that it was the prisoner. He walked back, intending to tell him to knock it off. What he saw, made him rush to open the cell.

Charles stood on the cot in his underwear. The jumpsuit he'd been wearing hung over a water pipe in the ceiling. The other end was tied around his neck.

The young, stupid cop unlocked the cell door and Charles laughed aloud as he pulled his head out of the knot and wrapped it around the neck of the guard so fast that the cop had no time to think. Charles was cackling as he tightened the makeshift noose around the man's neck and pushed the cot out from under him. He took the officer's weapon and walked out the door.

He didn't understand why he couldn't just go to the woman's house and shoot her in the head. The demon inside his putrid mind insisted that it still wasn't time. Instead, he headed out of town to the old Grandy house. That was where he was to hide and wait for time.

Lucy Cowan was sitting by the front window in her living-room, knitting a scarf and watching television when she caught movement out of the corner of her eye. She gasped and a hand flew to her heart as she watched Charles walking

284

down the street in nothing but his underwear. Everyone knew that he was supposed to be in jail, she thought as she picked up the receiver on her rotary phone.

*****

Jeanette spent half an hour washing away the dirt from the cemetery. She scrubbed it out from under her fingernails. She was certain that she could still taste it when she was finished and took a whole ten minutes brushing her teeth.

When she was finished, she washed the cross that she had pulled out of her pocket before her shower and laid on the bathroom counter. It wasn't very large, but it was beautiful. If it really belonged to Dahlia, how had a poor slave afforded it? Perhaps it was a gift.

Dressed, she went downstairs to let Josh and Franklin in. They had sat down on the couch to watch the evening news when a knock came at the door.

It was the sheriff. He looked relieved to see Jeanette.

"Ms. Galeman, I came to inform you that Charles Maxwell has broken out of jail. He killed the guard on duty. He took his gun and is armed and dangerous. I thought you needed to know. I'm stationing a patrol car on your block. To be safe, please keep your phone on you and lock the house up tight." He looked toward Josh.

"Why don't we just spend the night at my house?" Josh looked questioningly at Jeanette.

"That's a good idea," Jeanette agreed. "He wouldn't look for me there, surely."

The officer nodded, "I'll relate that to the men."

He left and Jeanette went upstairs to collect her things.

Chapter Twenty-Seven

The meeting at the town hall was just beginning when Jeanette and Josh stepped in and took a seat at the back of the room. It was full of people and some were standing along the walls and along the back or the room. The Mayor was standing at the podium. Almira Hayes sat behind him next to Gracie.

"Calling this meeting to order," Mayor Stiles said and clanged the mallet. The loud rumble of voices quietened immediately and all eyes turned to the front. "This emergency meeting was called due to the unexplained happenings that have been plaguing our town for the last few weeks.

As many of you know, there have been odd manifestations and more deaths than usual. We have several members of the community here that might shed some light on what is going on and hopefully have a timely resolution to our problem. They have asked for this opportunity, please give them your attention.

Gracie stepped up to the podium.

"Some of you don't know me. My name is Gracie Lawson. I inherited the Mallory plantation that is just outside of town. My husband, Brett Galeman and I decided that the plantation house would be a beautiful place for a retirement home and that the historical value of the place would be an added attraction.

Soon after we began our renovation, we found out the place was haunted, just as the legend said. There was a voodoo curse and this curse had trapped a lot of souls on the property, including the most evil of them all, Alfred Mallory."

It had gotten so quiet while Gracie was speaking that you could hear a pin drop. Those that normally would object and claim it was all gibberish had already experienced enough for themselves to make them believe.

"We came up with a plan and we were able to banish Alfred and release those spirits. The problem was that, though Alfred was banished from the plantation, we didn't even consider that our town could be in jeopardy. A few months ago, Alfred was released when a few members of the town were innocently playing with a Ouija board. It was something that was bound to happen. He would have found some way, eventually. Now we have Alfred and his acquired army of lost souls to battle. We have to banish him for good."

"You brought all this down on us!" One man stood in the front row. "This is your fault!" Several others stood in agreement.

Brett stood up and looked pointedly at the leader. "Back off, Lee. This isn't Gracie's fault. We can't control the evil in the world. All we can do is fight it and Gracie has done that. Now we are going to need help. This is bigger than all of us. We have to fight him as a town this time. All of us together. That's why we have brought you all here."

The men sat down and gave Gracie their attention once more.

"When I first moved here, I was struck by the sense of unity and neighborly love. It was a place that I immediately wanted to be part of. That is the key to ridding ourselves of this evil. Good and evil cannot take up the same space. My good friend and voodoo queen, Almira Hayes is here to help us. I'll let her explain," Gracie said, stepping down.

"Basically, what Gracie just said is the plan. We need everyone that is willing to participate to meet at the plantation tomorrow night. Whatever Alfred is planning, he will put into effect on the night of the full moon and it won't be pretty. We
287

will protect the town and draw them away outside of town. The plantation is a perfect place. Alfred can't cross the border of the purified ground. Everyone bring all your friends and neighbors that you can, but leave your children here protected in town. At 11:00 p.m. We have to be ready by the time the moon is high."

"You really think this will work?" Lee Montgomery asked.

"I do. We have a plan that I cannot explain here. He can hear us and is likely watching what we do. Just for safety, everyone stick together until tomorrow night. Stay in twos, at least. It should be safe in town, but be on watch, in case. I will see you all tomorrow."

Chapter Twenty-Eight

Charles was more of a spectator in his own body now as Alfred kicked the door of the Grandys' house open. With super strength, Alfred ransacked the place in anger. Charles watched, stunned and terrified at the demon's rage. Meredith's prized china cabinet went down in a pile of wood and ceramic splinters. After demolishing most of the interior, Alfred went to the bedroom and found a set of clothes. He'd been nude since he left the jail. Now, his fingers were awkwardly trying to button one of Art's shirts as he was getting dressed for the upcoming battle. Finally, he let Charles take over and he obediently finished dressing himself in the plaid shirt and blue jeans. Art had been a little smaller and the jeans were tight, but he managed. He could hear Alfred's ravings in his mind. As soon as he finished lacing the boots on his feet, Alfred took over his body once more.

It seemed as though they waited forever with Alfred's insane ramblings filling Charles' mind. He slept after a while and was startled awake hours later by Alfred's call.

At Alfred's command, Charles took two knives out of Art's hunting cabinet and hid both in his clothing. Alfred's weapon of choice was a sharp axe he'd found by the woodpile outside. Grasping the axe, he took Charles' body completely once more and started across the field. The ghosts of the spirits he'd collected glowed like white lights all over the field. As Alfred approached the plantation border, they fell in with him.

Charles lost his fear and the excitement began to build inside him. This was it. This was the moment when Alfred would be the victor and would reign over Swanson and Charles was his chosen vessel. He felt an instant of great gratuity to his master. The plantation had been taken from him, but Alfred had given him the world in its place.

289

Marching in the midst of the grotesque specters, he felt a pride that he'd never sensed before.

Just as they began to make out the long line of townspeople at the edge of the plantation, a great rippling light was released into the air and the blue electric line made its way toward them. Fear gripped Charles as the streak neared leaving an empty field where the spirit army had been only seconds before.

The ire Alfred had shown in the Grandy house was nothing compared to the shriek of fury that exploded in Charles' brain at that moment.

*****

Almira headed the meeting at the plantation. There must have been five hundred people congregated in the ballroom. *All that is missing are the pitchforks and torches*, Jeanette thought, amused.

"All you are required to do is to make a long line at the edge of the property. Brett has marked the property line with a rope. As long as you remain on this side of the rope, you will be safe on the sanctified ground. You will link hands and you will lend me the power to dispel the hold that Alfred has on the souls of your friends and neighbors. Once that is accomplished, Alfred will be caught in the trap that we have created.

"The plan is simple. This will only work if all of you keep in mind that we are here for one purpose and that is to get rid of the evil in this town. Let's not add to it by having any negative thoughts or persuasions. We are all a family here. A large family that has been invaded by something horrid and rancid. Ridding ourselves of this bleeding ulcer is the only way we can move on.

All of you in one mind. Your unity and love for your community, your neighbors and those you've lost. That is

290

what counts. You are making a stand against this evil. Are you ready?"

Deafening cheers went through the crowd and everyone filed out of the room.

Outside, Josh kept a hold of Jeanette's hand and somehow she ended up in almost the exact center of the line. Josh was on her left and Gracie was on her right. Almira had really told her nothing. What was it that she was supposed to do? What if she failed? They were all counting on her.

It wasn't until Almira began her chanting that something happened to Jeanette. She saw the vision of Belinda standing before her, waveringly. Jeanette turned to Josh and Gracie wondering if they could see anything. Neither were looking toward the image and it only grew more solid as she watched.

"It's time for you to remember," Belinda said, and reached out to touch Jeanette. She placed her hand lightly on Jeanette's upper arm.

Suddenly, everyone around her was gone. It was a strange sensation, but it was if all the dreams flashed through her mind all over again as if on fast forward, but stopped suddenly and paused on one sentence. "We have to get him to leave my dad. You can't trap a demon that has a body. We have to lure Alfred out of him first."

Jeanette snapped back to herself just in time for her arms to be jerked over her head as everyone in line raised their arms. Then, miraculously, a brilliant blue streak of electricity came off of them in a wave. It rippled through the field like a shock wave, dispelling apparitions as it went. Finally, the only one left was Charles Maxwell standing in the center of the field, only about a hundred feet from Jeanette.

Jeanette didn't even hesitate. She knew what Almira did not. Alfred could not be trapped as long as he resided in another body. There was only one way to fix that problem.

291

She stepped over the rope and into the field. It was Alfred that could be heard shrieking and enraged. If Charles was still in there, he wasn't showing himself.

"Jeanette! What are you doing?" Gracie screamed, terrified for sister.

"Let her go," Almira said, now standing directly behind Gracie. "This is her fight."

"Charles!" Jeanette shouted. "Charles, you are still in there. I know it. You have to fight him!"

"You stupid, girl. You are finally coming to me. Haha! You cheated me. I will have your bloody soul!" Alfred howled.

"No. You won't. I won't let you keep Charles, either," Jeanette said, coming close to him.

Alfred had stepped directly into the trap while she distracted him. Trying to walk out of the circle, he fell back, sending a visible electrical current through the air.

"There is no way out. We have you. Now, let Charles go," Jeanette said, calmly.

"You little fool. Don't you see? He wants me within him. He is rejoicing that I will have my revenge, for it is his revenge as well. He must take after my side of the family," he said with another evil laugh.

As long as Alfred had a body, they couldn't trap him permanently and he knew it. Jeanette stood, almost mesmerized by the axe in his hands as flashbacks of the scythe ran through her mind. His power was gone along with his army, she realized. All he had now was the weapon he held.

She reached up and touched the necklace around her neck, Dahlia's cross. Alfred saw her movement and the cross and

292

his rage returned full strength as he threw the axe. Jeanette leapt to the left and the blade missed, but the handle grazed her shoulder knocking her back.

Brett and Josh were standing behind Jeanette now, but neither were expecting what came next.

"Come on! You want Charles, come and get him," Alfred taunted.

Jeanette didn't hesitate for a second, not seeing the hunting knife in his hand. She ran at Charles, ramming him in the stomach and he flew out of the circle. She looked down as she heard Alfred laugh. The knife went in her abdomen clear to the hilt.

Chapter Twenty-Nine

Jeanette woke up two days later in the hospital.   Gracie was in a chair, sleeping by her bed. There was a horrible ache in her stomach.

"Grace…Gracie," Jeanette said, waking her up.

Gracie sat up. "Jeanette? You're awake?" She gave a short laugh. "Thank God! Oh, I'd better get a doctor." She ran into the hall and practically dragged a nurse back through the doorway.

"Hi, there," the chubby brunette said and walked toward the bed. "Jeanette, right?"

Jeanette nodded.

"It's good to see you awake. I'll call the doctor and let him know. Are you having any pain?"

"A little. In my stomach," Jeanette said.

"I'll ask the doctor for something to put in your I.V. Some discomfort will be typical after the surgery you've had." With that the nurse left the room.

Jeanette turned to Gracie, who was texting on her phone. "Surgery?"

"Honey, when they brought you in here, we all thought for sure you were dead. They had to take out the knife and repair some damage inside."

"It will scar, huh?" Jeanette asked, dismally.

Gracie laughed. "If it does, it will be a badge of honor! I've never seen anyone as brave as you. You are a hero, sis." She leaned down and kissed her on the forehead and Jeanette saw her wipe a few tears off her face. "I thought I lost you. I love you so much!"

"I love you, too, Grace. Is everyone else okay? What about Charles?"

"Charles is fine. I wouldn't waste a moment of thought on that jerk. At least, he is back in jail and it sounds like he may spend some time in a mental institution."

"Well, he isn't possessed anymore," Jeanette said.

"Everyone else is fine—just worried about you. Brett and Josh are on their way up," Gracie said, looking up from her phone.

"Josh?" Jeanette said, a little flustered. "I must look horrible."

"Trust me. You, alive, is the most beautiful thing any of us will see for a long time," Gracie assured her.

"Gracie, come on. You have to at least have a comb in your purse," Jeanette whined.

Gracie pulled out a comb, but wouldn't let Jeanette have it. "It will be a while before you are going to be able to lift your arms up enough to comb your hair. The doctor warned us about that, already." She combed Jeanette's hair for her, finishing as Brett and Josh came into the room.

"Hey, Sis." Brett came directly over and gave her a light hug.

"Hi," Jeanette said trying to hug him back, but realizing that Gracie was right. It hurt a lot to raise her arms. She looked over at Josh, who was shyly looking at his feet. "Josh, come here. I need to see you."

Josh walked over to the bed and Brett backed away so he could get close. He took her hand. "I'm so happy you are okay," he said, looking down at her hand. A tear fell from his nose and landed on her arm. She squeezed his hand.

"Well, anyway, Brett and I need to go downstairs and make some calls. There are loads of people to give the good news to," Gracie said, and tactfully dragged Brett out of the room.

Once alone, Josh pulled a chair up next to the bed.

"Josh, what happened afterwards? After Alfred stabbed me. Did Almira get him?" Jeanette asked.

"She got him. I didn't see any of that, but I know she did and Brett did bury the box in the tunnels. They are being filled as we speak."

"Good. It's over. I'm so glad," Jeanette said, smiling weakly at him. "Kiss me, Josh."

He reached out and cupped her cheek. The shyness dropped away as he kissed her gently on the mouth, her eyes, cheeks, and hands. "I love you so much. If you ever go near a madman with a knife ever again, I'm going to spank you, so help me God."

"I love you, too," Jeanette said, smiling and leaned back against her pillow. She was asleep again in seconds.

*****

A few weeks later, Jeanette was sitting on her couch while Josh was clattering around her kitchen. He had stayed with her since she got out of the hospital. Brett and Gracie had finally gone on their honeymoon and life had gotten quiet and back to normal.

She was still a little stiff but feeling much better. When the phone rang, she figured it was Gracie again, checking up on her. It wasn't. It was Jim.

"Hi, Jeanette. Here's the thing. Sandy really wants to go see her parents in Vermont. I'm working and just can't take off to babysit. If it's okay with you, I'm just going to bring them home early. I know they are my kids and I love 'em, but I think it would be a better arrangement for you to keep them full time. I could take them for a weekend now and then if you like."

Jeanette smiled into the phone and had to keep herself from sounding too happy. "That would be fine, I guess, if that's really what you want."

"It is. Oh, and we'll be at the airport at 8:00 tomorrow morning to drop them off and go on to Vermont."

Typical of him to make those plans without consulting her first, but in this case she was just too happy to complain.

"The flight number is 206, gate 13," he said and hung up.

Jeanette jumped off the couch and her stomach reminded her painfully that she wasn't quite ready to run a marathon. "Josh!" she yelled and went into the kitchen. She flew into his arms with a huge grin on her lips. Life couldn't get any better. She was safe and finally with a man she loved. He pecked her cheek and her happiness only grew. "The kids are coming home."

25534185R00169

Made in the USA
Charleston, SC
06 January 2014